BAD LATITUDES

BAD LATITUDES

A Novel by Al Pope

TURNSTONE PRESS

Bad Latitudes
copyright © Al Pope 2004

Turnstone Press
Artspace Building
607-100 Arthur Street
Winnipeg, MB
R3B 1H3 Canada
www.TurnstonePress.com

All rights reserved. No part of this book may be reproduced or transmitted in any form or by any means—graphic, electronic or mechanical—without the prior written permission of the publisher. Any request to photocopy any part of this book shall be directed in writing to Access Copyright (formerly Cancopy, the Canadian Copyright Licensing Agency), Toronto.

Turnstone Press gratefully acknowledges the assistance of The Canada Council for the Arts, the Manitoba Arts Council, the Government of Canada through the Book Publishing Industry Development Program and the Government of Manitoba through the Department of Culture, Heritage and Tourism, Arts Branch, for our publishing activities.

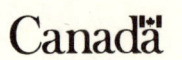

Cover design: Tétro Design
Interior design: Sharon Caseburg
Printed and bound in Canada by Friesens for Turnstone Press.

National Library of Canada Cataloguing in Publication Data

Pope, Al, 1954-

  Bad latitudes : a novel / by Al Pope.

ISBN 0-88801-293-4

      I. Title.

PS8631.O64 B32 2004   C813'.6   C2004-900948-6

For Lois.

BAD LATITUDES

Whitehorse, Summer, 1978

Drum

A slow, steady bass thrum disturbs the chill air of a May morning. At the bottom of Sixth Avenue, the floors of the grey apartments vibrate; a summer student stirs in her sleep when the cotton sheets reverberate against the peach-downed skin of her back. An old woman curled in her clothes on the riverbank dreams of a long-ago drummer, muscles like tree burls on his naked shoulders. The first carpenter of the morning stretches his back and remembers a girl, ponytail flapping to the beat of the jitterbug, chubby hands sweating in his. In a crooked bedroom at the bottom of the clay cliffs, Abe turns over and rests his hand on Sky's waist. She sighs and moves back against him, and her skin is warm where it touches his. He kisses the shadow behind the curve of her chin and whispers.

"You're awake."

The grass at Rotary Park shines with dew that's all but frost. On Second Avenue, commuters squeeze their brakes and peer out through fogged-up windows at the apparition in front of the bandstand. Perched on its tripod of pine poles, the drum must reach nearly eight feet tall. The skin looks like the whole hide of a good-sized moose. In front of it stands the drummer, a lank, ragged, white kid in Indian buckskins and beads. He winds up like a baseball player, swings like he's going to drive that poplar stick right through the centre of the drum, but then, at the last instant, he hesitates. Although two pedestrians on the sidewalk sixty feet away would swear the stick never touches the skin, it sounds.

A mile farther, two hairs in the mole on Sky's shoulder resonate. Abe is certain she's feigning sleep. She lies on her side with her back to him, head down into her shoulders, a slightly less than foetal curve to her skinny back. He lifts aside the sheet and rises to his hands and knees, and then, bending, kisses her waist. He moves down the line of her hip, down her thigh, blowing a thin, tickling draught of breath on her skin, and pauses to kiss the outside of her knee. Drawing a tiny circle with the tip of his tongue on this known sweet spot, he watches for a reaction. Her body tenses; she's fighting the urge to shiver. He laughs. "Now I *know* you're awake."

Sky doesn't answer. She moans and mumbles, as if in sleep, and rolls over onto her belly. As Abe repositions himself to tickle the hollow of her spine with his wisp of beard, the rhythm of the drum begins, very gradually, to pick up. From one beat in ten seconds, to one in eight, six, three.

A green '67 Chev pickup, step-side, pulls up to the pumps at Whitehorse Esso. A balding man in workboots swings out and slams the door, scowling toward the park. The gas jockey is a smooth-faced kid; he follows the man's look and laughs.

"What's goin' on down there?"

"Fuck," says the man in workboots. "Fuckin' hippies."

It's been going on all summer. He'll drum for hours, the beat growing gradually faster and then slower again, the simple rhythm never varying. He keeps it up each day until the

Mounties come and make him stop because it's late and people are complaining. No one knows why they don't shut him down for good. No one knows why his drum hasn't been vandalized by some sleep-deprived, night-shift janitor, or why he hasn't been beaten up by one of the construction workers on the new YTG building site. At first, when the drum stops, the whole town sighs with relief, but then after a while there's a sense of something missing. People stop what they're doing and wonder what's wrong, as if they'd been wearing a hair shirt all their lives and can't get used to not itching. When it starts again, there's a moment of relief before everybody stops what they're doing and raises their eyebrows.

"Oh shit," someone will say. "It's the goddamn drummer again."

In the blue war-built shack along the edge of the clay cliffs, Abe kicks off his shoes and feels the vibration in the floor: *bu-ung*, says the drum a mile away, and *u-ung* the worn-out oak flooring replies. Deep in the earth the sound resonates, growing weaker as it radiates, but never quite dying. *Yukon*, it says to an SFU English major, waitressing in a truck stop outside Prince George. *Why the hell did I come home this summer? There's eight men to every woman in Dawson. Think of the tips.*

Yukon, it says to a sleeping biker on a broken couch in a Calgary basement hideout. He wakes to an idea: a job in the mines, a new identity. The Yukon, he thinks, nobody'll find me there. *Yukon*, it says to a scattered world of leftover hippies, new-wave drifters, long-haired hoboes, back-to-the-landers, fugitives, and misfits, come to the Yukon.

Yes, Abe's feet say, come to the Yukon, kick the doors open, bust the windows, let the winds howl through the place, we're due for an invasion. It's over eighty years since the gold rush, thirty-five since the highway; the place is ready for a change of character. Whitehorse still looks like a gold-rush town with an army camp plastered over it, and it feels like nothing new's happened in—well, in at least twenty-two years, since the day Abe was born. Or at least, it felt like that, before he met Sky. And then started to meet some of her friends. Before Sky, before the accident, Abe felt about the same way as everyone else—to him, hippies were guys like Rocky and Mac, long-haired, loudmouth construction workers on an endless high-school party. If it hadn't been for the accident, he'd probably never have met Sky. He used to see women like her on the street, women in head scarves and beads, their bellies bare, their long skirts swishing the sidewalk, but he never spoke to them. He thought of hippies, guys and women both, as impostors: putting on airs like they'd invented the idea of living in a log cabin or a plywood shack down in Sleepy Hollow, or driving around in a pickup truck with a half-husky dog in the back. As if nobody before them had ever picked berries or snared a rabbit or used pack dogs or made smoked fish. Later, he discovered he likes being around them. He likes the women's crazy, sexy clothes and the weird way they talk. *Far out*, they all say, and *if that's what you're into, man*. It sounds stupid, but there's something, what?—innocent maybe—about it that he can't help but like. Best of all he likes the fact that they all speak the same way. They don't have one language for just men, and another for when the women are around. He even kind of likes the crazy way they all want to charge off into the bush without knowing at least the basics, like how to hunt and fix your chainsaw and put up a wall-tent or build a cabin. Every old-timer he knows has a story about rescuing a couple of them, frozen stiff or half drowned or lost and starving.

Hanging out with Sky's friends, Abe even tried smoking pot. It terrified him. He can't imagine how some of them do it. They smoke it every time they get together and every time they part, as they set out on any kind of expedition and as soon as they return, after every meal, before commencing work of any sort, and as soon as the work is done. Often they smoke it while they work. Up on scaffolds, running machinery: Abe would have panic attacks if he tried it.

Red wine, now that's another thing. He was drinking too much when he met Sky, mostly Jack Daniels whisky with beer chasers. He didn't drink when he was with her, but it didn't take long for her to figure out that he drank almost all the rest of the time. She didn't lay down the law. Without his knowing at first that it was happening, she eased him off the whisky and on to red wine.

"*It's the lovers' drink,*" she said, dabbing a little on his nipple.

"*I thought that was gin.*"

"Good*ess, you have a lot to learn.*"

Abe would swear the surface of the wine in his glass vibrates visibly to the beat of the drum. Or maybe not. When he looks at it straight on, the ripples disappear. He picks up the glass, puts his feet up on the wire-spool coffee table and leans back. They've been living in this house for a month, and this is the first time Sky's been gone. She's in Dawson for two weeks, supposedly making a pile of money selling trade-bead jewellery and giving massages. Although he's lonely without her, there's a certain relief at being alone, too. He's used to solitude. He's used to plenty of musing time.

It's an odd train of events that brought him here, although here is only three blocks from his mom's house, where he spent the last half of his childhood, whenever he wasn't in the bush with the old man. But to come to the point of living in this house with Sky, to come even to the point of meeting Sky, took an event of catastrophic proportions. It took the accident. And the accident would never have happened if lead-zinc prices weren't sky-high, or if the stubblehumpers hadn't come to build those miners' houses, or Rock and Tunnel hadn't decided to accept Abe's substandard first aid ticket and send him to Faro, or Rocky hadn't been hungover, or God knows what other random factors hadn't been at work. If those things hadn't happened, he'd never have met Sky in the first place.

It's funny how the drum fades out after a while, and then all of a sudden you notice it again. Boom, boom, boom. It's begun to spread, too. All over town the gravel back roads echo to the sound of basement drummers: hip young French Canadians with congas they brought from Africa, heroin addicts drumming their way back from the edge of disaster on drums their grannies helped them make, skinny white high-school kids with lank hair and Sears drum kits, loose-breasted hippie girls on drums they made themselves out of hollow spruce logs. Car salesmen with pens on desktops. Some of them riff along, improvising to the beat; others are content just to follow the steady bung, bung, bung. Some of them chant or sing or moan. A few people have begun to pick up the beat on dusty guitars, on pianos out of tune after a hard winter by a wood stove, and clarinets gone slack-valved from lack of use. An old man stands outside the door of his cabin near Ear Lake and scratches a tune on a fiddle he thought he'd given up on thirty years ago.

Each day the hypnotic rhythm seeps deeper into the soul of the town. Pedestrians walk in time to it, a slow, swinging, long-legged stride. Bank clerks count out money to it, cabbies tap it on their steering wheels. The cops who come periodically to shut the drummer down find themselves speaking in time with the drum. Yesterday, an impromptu band gathered in front of the post office. Everything they played, no matter what its metre, rhythm, or tempo, they fit in around the beat of the drum. Their open instrument cases filled up with money so fast it was spilling out onto the street. Hippies opened the gate on the post office lawn and danced barefoot around the mountain ash tree; postal workers inside tapped their feet and wiggled their hips while they sorted the mail.

More and more every day, the town vibrates to the beat of one drum.

When the clay cliff comes through the wall of Abe's house, he's busy trying to tune his guitar. Spatulate fingers as fat and swollen as if all the evening's wine had pooled in the tips grapple with the extreme proximity of the A-string to the D, of D to G. Ears like bags of wet cotton wool struggle with tiny pulses in the ringing harmonics—is that flat, or sharp? He has achieved satisfaction in all but the matter of the ever-awkward B when he's shaken into consciousness of external things by a sound very much like the City of Whitehorse dump truck turning around in the driveway, except louder, a deep rumble that shakes the house and is followed almost immediately by a thundering boom, the complete collapse of the back wall, and the entry by force of approximately one third of a houseful of grey-white clay.

"Holy," he says. Sitting in the middle of the couch, the only place in the house where a drunk can play a guitar without bashing into things, he now finds himself in the position of an audience member—say, third row, three seats from centre-aisle—with the ruined back wall of his house as the stage.

The wall is broken near the middle and the two halves have been pushed well into the room. Both the adjoining walls lean in at the top corners. The house, an ancient squatter's shack, seemed when it was whole to be made of some flimsy cardboard-like stuff, but he now observes that the innards consist of quite substantial-looking chunks of wood. Those, that is, that aren't in splinters.

Almost at once Abe recognizes the seriousness of the situation. Clearly, the wall is beyond repair. The house is not going to be so comfortable without it, nor with the presence of all that clay. Maybe they could put a big tarp across, and have a smaller house, easier to heat. Might even get the old woman to give them a deal on the rent, too. He wonders whether Sky's going to like it this way.

It crosses his mind that there might be some danger inherent in the circumstances, but then, gauging the distance from the wall to where he sits, and the size of the biggest, most out-thrust shard of wood, he doubts it could reach him. And there's just that one string left to tune. He looks around on the floor, and discovers that his wine glass has escaped again. This is no time to stand on ceremony; he picks up the bottle, and drains it. Now what's going on with this guitar?

When each string is tuned to perfection, Abe strums a chord, and finds the sound worse than when he started. He's in the process of inspecting the fingers of his left hand to be certain that they are obediently configuring a G major in the first position, when suddenly it strikes him: the drumming has stopped. He is just trying to grasp this fact, it being too early in the evening for the drummer to stop, when several vehicles arrive, very fast. Most of them seem to have flashing lights.

Klondike Highway

Connie's back is killing her as she sags and bounces into the cracked vinyl seat. Whoever rode the passenger side in this truck for the first fifteen years of its life must have weighed about three hundred pounds. Every time she surreptitiously checks the speedometer, it says fifty miles an hour, but it looks a lot faster watching the gravel and the endless fir trees fly toward her in the pocked windshield.

Or maybe it's pine trees; she's not about to ask Gary and get a lecture on Yukon conifers. Honest to God, who do these people think they are? Ever since she got to Whitehorse, it seems like everybody she's met has been treating her like the original virgin-tourist from Ontario, which is where all these new-wave hillbillies or whatever they're supposed to be seem to have forgotten they came from themselves. That is, unless they're from Calgary like Gary here.

She can hardly wait to see Natalie again, in September. They will scream together over this place, especially over Gary. Gary thinks he's cute, which maybe he would be if he weren't so damn condescending. There's a bunch of black curls sticking out from under his stupid, floppy, farmer-Jones hat, and he has a nice, lean body under the bellbottom overalls—but really, what year is this? And just because she doesn't wear army boots and have her butt sticking out of her cut-offs doesn't mean she's his maiden aunt.

"So what's a nice lady like you doing in the wild North?" he actually said to her when they were coming out of Whitehorse, swaying around a curve in the gravel road that definitely should have had a guardrail.

So far, meeting my best friend's weird sister's weird friends, is what she thought, but she kept it to herself.

The women are the ones Connie really can't figure: it's either the Sadie-Mae look, in halter tops and cut-off blue jeans, or it's Earth Mother, like Dawn—it is just about impossible to believe is Natalie's sister—peasant blouses without bras, so they hang straight down from her nipples, and those long cotton skirts that you just know there's nothing underneath. Connie'll have to talk Nat into a Summer of Love party when she gets home.

The thing she really doesn't get is why they all chase after these deadbeat guys who seem to be on pogey all the time, and live in those pathetic little hovels they're all so proud of. Dawn's place is a school bus, yet, with no heat except a great big wood stove made out of a goddamn oil barrel that you can't use in June because it gets about a hundred degrees in there, so you freeze instead when it goes down to around zero or something at night. It has no wheels, and it sits on blocks in what looks to Connie like a hobo-jungle that was allowed to take root along a dried-up riverbed. The locals call it Squatters' Row, and seem to think that living there confers some kind of status.

An old station wagon lies gutted across the trail to the creek behind Squatters', and like water itself the path has split up and gone both ways around the wreck. Connie's hands turned numb in the icy creek water, holding the blue jerry can under the surface.

"Here, you hold it like this," Dawn said, with her sweetest

beam, taking the bucket from Connie and showing her how to immerse it without getting her hands wet.

Connie tried to look suitably grateful, but, judging from the way poor Dawn recoiled, she suspects she must have given her one of what Nat calls her fuck-off-and-die smiles.

She tries to picture Natalie and her sister together, but it's beyond her imagination. Nat is the city.

Natalie in Kensington, going over the Persian rugs on the sidewalk rack like Sherlock Holmes, and then shaking a fist of triumph when she found a flaw in her favourite plum and leaf-green floral.

"Your ass is mine, Giorgio. Half price, or my name isn't Zsa Zsa Gabor."

"Wait a minute, Nat, you can't take a twelve-foot rug home on the subway."

"Zen ve'll order a cab, dahlink, says Nat, tossing an imaginary feather boa over her shoulder before turning to confront the store-owner, who is just coming out the door."

Gary reaches in the case for what must be his fourth beer since Whitehorse, and offers it to Connie with a shucks-ma'am grin before opening it with his belt buckle and taking a drink. If she'd known the guy was going to be drinking, she'd have taken the bus to Dawson, but it's kind of hard to bale out now.

"Wow. Look at that," he says as the truck crests a hill, and they see a wider expanse of bush. He says this just about every time the horizon broadens to include more than the immediately neighbouring trees. Whenever the view is really spectacular, he gets out and takes a pee. "Incredible, eh?" he'll say from the far side of the truck, to the accompanying sound of his urine hitting the gravel. Jason was very fastidious; Connie has never actually held a conversation with a pissing man before. Without thinking about it, she had somehow expected the first time to occur under more interesting circumstances.

"Where are we?" she asks.

"Just past Pelly. Better'n halfway. One place we could stop for coffee if you're into it."

"I don't mind. Just so long as I don't miss Rita."

"I wouldn't sweat about Rita. She'll hang cool in the Eldo till we get there."

That's easy for Gary to say. Rita is about the only reasonable human being Connie has met in the two weeks she's been in the Yukon. Besides, she has a place in Dawson, with a spare room, and she knows where to find work. If Connie misses Rita, she'll be alone in Dawson City, where hotel rooms are a hundred bucks a night, she hears, if you can find one. She doesn't want to end up wherever Gary is tonight. They pull into a huge gravel parking lot. Around the perimeter there are gas pumps, a big steel building that must be a garage, and a restaurant with a sign in the window that reads *Temporaly closed do to lack of water*. There's a sprinkle of rain in the air as they turn back onto the highway.

"I'm gettin' burnt," says Gary. "I was thinkin' of maybe cruisin' to these friends of mine's up the road a bit, hittin' them up for a coffee. You into that?"

"Sure," she says. What the hell? It'll be a cultural experience. Likely they'll sit around on tree stumps in some dingy cabin, drinking coffee that tastes like the sole of a shoe and bitching about the government.

"Dale and Andra are good people," Gary declares. Connie has heard several Yukon couples described in this way. It seems to mean that he has facial hair and she says *fuck* a lot.

The road into Dale and Andra's house is a couple of wheel-ruts through the bush. Trees brush the side of the truck and there's one hill where the track is half washed away, so Connie is pleasantly surprised, not to say amazed, when they come to a clearing and at the end of it she sees not some typical Yukon bush hovel but a modern-looking house. The walls are made of logs the colour of honey and there are two gables along the front. The rest of the roof is covered in dark glass boxes, which she knows must be solar panels. Behind the house a smallish mountain stands alone; the lower face of it is loose gravel. The whole thing is a postcard; it seems hard to believe it belongs to a friend of Gary's.

"Great, eh?" Gary says. "Don't see that in Ontario, eh?"

"Beautiful. No." She realizes for the first time how desperately Gary needs confirmation that this is the greatest place on earth. As they approach the house, she's wondering why; does he have doubts? Maybe it's like a religion with him: Yukon Worship, or North Worship, or something. And maybe he does actually see through the postcards and wish he was back in Calgary, where surely there must be some kind of culture beyond the endless celebration of moose and mediocrity. But he can't just turn his sacred pickup south and go home, because you don't leave a church that easy. Christ, he'd have to learn to talk all over again. Or maybe not, for Calgary.

There's even a lawn, she can't believe it, and a path from the parking area to the house. There's a hell of a noise coming from inside. It sounds like a fight. There's a man's voice, and a woman's, and plenty of crashing about. Gary looks concerned.

"I don't know," he says. "Might have picked a bad time."

"But, hadn't we better make sure everything's all right?" Connie asks.

"I guess, I don't know."

"I think we'd better."

Gary knocks on the door, but not loudly enough to be heard over the man's yelling. The woman isn't exactly screaming, she's kind of shrieking back at him, but something is crashing in there, and the guy sounds violent.

"Open it," Connie says, but Gary is doubtful. "Come on, open it."

He does, timidly sticking his head inside. "Hello?" he says, still too quietly.

"Hello?" Connie calls, louder. They step into an entrance hall that looks out onto a wide living room, the front wall all windows. The sound of the fight comes from down a hallway, the man's voice tight, the woman's rising in pitch.

"They must be in the kitchen," Gary says, and clumps down the hall, making lots of noise with his boots and calling out loudly. "Hello? Dale? Andra?" And ridiculously, "Anybody home?"

The kitchen is a shock: broken dishes all over the room, chairs are knocked over. A woman about Connie's age stands backed into a corner. Her lip is split, and her face is puffy red on one side. She's a big, strong-looking woman, even a little bigger than the man who confronts her in a fighter's stance, but it is instantly clear he has the upper hand. Both of them are breathing hard, as if they'd just finished a fast run.

The man turns to face them. He's thin and wiry and tough-looking, crewcut salt-and-pepper hair. Although Gary is bigger, Connie can see he feels threatened. "Er, is everything okay here?" he says. "Looks like we kind of walked in on somethin'."

"Yeah, well, maybe you'd better just walk right back out again, hadn't you?"

Gary hesitates and then looks at the woman. "Andra, you okay?"

"Andra is just fuckin' fine, Gary, so why don't you just butt the fuck out."

Gary looks over at Andra, and the guy starts to move toward him. He holds his ground until she speaks.

"Go, Gary. Just go. We'll catch you next time. It's okay, this is all over."

"Okay," Gary says, doubtful, but obviously glad to end the confrontation with Dale, "that's cool." And then, to Connie, "Better cruise, I guess."

Connie looks to see if he's serious. Just go, and that's it? She looks over at Andra, and their eyes meet. For a minute the battered face is cold, hard, but then the eyes waver, and the mouth softens, and then it's written there, plainly, that she's terrified to be left, and terrified to say so.

"Look," Connie says. "Why don't you let us give you a ride somewhere?"

"Who the fuck are you?" Dale yells, moving on Connie, threatening not so much to hit her as simply to drive her out of the house by the sheer force of his person. "Why don't you mind your own fuckin' business?"

Gary and Andra both speak at once.

"Hey, take it easy, man," says Gary. "We're outahere, we're outahere."

Andra is moving toward the door. "You going in to Dawson?" she says. "Maybe I will take a ride."

"You're not fuckin' goin' anywhere. You're stayin' right here and clean up these fuckin' dishes you broke." Dale turns to Connie again and sticks his finger in her face. "You don't have to worry about sweet fuckin' innocent little Andra here, sweetheart, she can take care of herself. Ask her who tore this fuckin' place up. Ask her. Ask her how I got this." He turns his neck to show a deep scratch, almost bleeding, from the jawbone back to the hairline.

"Just for tonight, hey babe?" Andra says. "Let things cool off a bit, eh? I'll come back and clean up in the morning, okay? Okay, Dale?" All the time she's saying this, she's making a wide path around Dale to get to the door. He's looking from one face to the other, all around him, like a cornered dog trying to decide who to bite, and she's almost at the door when he pounces.

All four of them shout at once. Dale grabs Andra by the hair and pulls her round. "Cunt," he yells, and goes for her throat with the other hand.

Gary yells "Hey," and tries to throw his arms around Dale's shoulders, but Dale turns on him, hits him in the stomach, hard, so he crumples a bit, and then on the jaw, up from underneath, and his head flies back and leaves blood on the white Arborite counter as he falls. Dale swings around and grabs Andra again and starts slapping her.

"Cunt," he screams. "Fuckin' cunt."

That's when Connie finds the blade in her hand.

"Here. You're going to need this."

"Get real, Nat, it's not the gold rush anymore."

"Are you kidding? That's exactly what it is. It's crazy up there."

"Anyway, women who carry weapons just end up having them used against them."

"Not if they use them first," says John Wayne. *"Listen, sister. Ya gotta cut him, and cut him good. Then maybe ya can parlay."*

Connie holds the switchblade, screaming she doesn't know what at Dale's back while he tries to bash Andra's head against the doorway. Andra's strong enough to resist that, so he punches her hard in the face, and is winding up for another when Connie sticks the knife in his butt, up to the hilt. It takes a second push to get it all the way in. She pulls it out, and holds it in front of herself defensively, but there's no need. Blood comes oozing out of Dale's jeans like water draining from a hose, and he sinks to the floor, clutching his ass.

FARO

Union of Rock and Tunnel Workers, local 2044, Whitehorse. A little wooden shack on a dusty street.
"*Ever work construction?*"
"*No. But I, er, helped my dad build a couple of cab—er, houses.*"
"*Got a sponsor in the union?*"
"*Uh, no, I ... no.*"
"*Got a first aid ticket?*"
"*Yeah, I do.*"
"*Current, industrial?*"
"*It's current.*"
"*Basic, eh? Naw, that's no good. Get your industrial, I'll send you to Faro. Twelve-eighty an hour for a labe, two bucks extra for a band-aid. Full camp, kitchen, rec-hall, the works. Five-minute walk from the bar.*"
"*I'd need two weeks.*"
"*Yeah. Shit. That's no good, either, is it? They're cryin' out for guys up there. I hear they're bringin' in carps from Winnipeg. Tell you what,*

let me make a couple calls, see what I can do. You got a number I can contact you?"

"*I'm a hard workin' man / And I can't seem to stop.*"

Rocky is crowing, strutting down the wooden path from the job-bus to the camp. He's such a little prick, Abe thinks, but you've got to admire him for sheer gall. He's really rubbing their noses in it. Bruce and Joe are walking right behind him, and he knows it. Mac puts up his hand, and Rocky high-fives with him, and they both cackle. Mac says, Fuckin' stubblehumpers.

That's another lunatic, that one. The two of them probably won't even show up for dinner. They'll be down to the hotel till two in the morning, and up in time to catch the job-bus at seven-thirty tomorrow. They're especially cranked-up today, because they won the wobble. Three of the labourers were caught loading some plywood into the back of one guy's pickup truck, and the company was going to fire them. You could tell all morning something was going on. Men striding back and forth across the muddy jobsite from one partly built house to another: Bruce, the foreman, going in to see Joe, the superintendent; Joe going over to talk to the three labes, who were standing around over by the tool crib; one of the guys calling Pete, the Rock and Tunnel job steward, down off a roof, a hurried conference around the radial-arm saw, where Payday Dave, the carpenters' job steward, had scored the jammiest job on the site. Rocky came around and spoke to Abe, who was caulking the seams on pwf basement walls.

"We're gonna wobble 'er."

"You what?"

"We're wobblin' the job. They're tryna fire three of our guys. Fuck that shit. Put your tools down."

The picket lines were up for about two hours, and then the company caved in. They had come all the way from Lloydminster, Saskatchewan, to build forty houses in forty days, brought all their own lead hands, and they all, including the super, were due for big *bonuses at the end if they finished on time. Everybody went back to the cookshack for lunch, as usual, but then the carpenters wouldn't get back on the bus. They had no sympathy for the labourers, but they couldn't cross the picket line. After that, the company decided it wasn't worth it. Abe doesn't know what to make of it all; he's been trying to keep his head low all day. If they can't fire you for stealing their plywood, what can they fire you for?*

Rocky and Mac must have found a party to go to. Abe wakes up to the sound of them bellowing; their voices ring in the empty hallway of the trailer. He looks at his watch on the bedside table. Quarter past four. These guys are out of their minds. Three hours till work starts.

Rocky barely makes the bus that day. He comes stumbling on, still dressing himself, obviously badly hungover. Mac, already aboard, laughs at him.

"Can't fuckin' take 'er, eh?"

There's a push on to get some walls stood. There's four houses closed to the weather, and another six with the walls framed and sheathed and lying piled up on the floors, and the drywallers are just about caught up. Bruce calls in the labourers to help. You can see that a few of the carpenters are pissed off about the jurisdiction, but they're not saying too much. Most of them flew here from Winnipeg; the Manitoba carpenters are on strike, and these guys are working seven tens, making the best money they've ever made, instead of sitting home going broke. They don't want any trouble in Faro.

Bruce is driving the crane, in too big a hurry. They're standing basement walls. There's a carpenter's apprentice there, barely out of high school, drilling holes through the top plates, and setting eyebolts in them. Then Abe hooks the chain into the eyes, and holds it up. Rocky, perched on top of a wall corner, uses hand signals to guide Bruce, who is working more or less blind.

Later, some will say that there should have been a carpenter signalling for the crane, or at least a labourer who was properly trained, and not still half drunk from the night before. Others will say the crane operator could have seen what he was doing if he had taken the time to move the crane. Some will claim that Abe himself was at fault, that the chain let go at one end. Others will blame the apprentice, saying it was the eyebolt that failed, or they will say it was Bruce's fault, whose idea the eyebolts were in the first place. The coroner will call it accidental death. The investigation will not settle the matter to anyone's satisfaction.

Rocky wasn't even hurt. When the hoisted wall broke away, it swung clear for at least ten feet before it hit the standing wall, the wall he was standing on. Somehow Rocky managed to fall clear. Abe and the young apprentice were under both walls when they came down. The kid died in intensive care in Whitehorse, head injuries. Abe spent six weeks in hospital with a broken back. They didn't know at first if he would walk. He went on permanent disability at twenty-one.

The winter Abe spent at the town place with his mom so he could go to high school, there was a show he liked to watch on TV. It was about an army field hospital, in Vietnam or something. Every week, there'd be a scene that began with the sound of helicopters. Someone would call out Incoming! and the whole place would spring into action.
    "*Plasma!*"
    "*I need a nurse over here!*"
    "*Doctor, this one's lost a lot of blood.*"
    "*This man's dead, get him out of the way!*"
    "*Plasma, plasma, I need plasma over here!*"
    "*Next!*"
    From his vinyl seat in the waiting room, the physiotherapy unit at Whitehorse General looks a lot like that MASH tent. Understaffed, under-equipped, and small, they whip people through there so fast, it seems like the best therapy they get is running through the motions.

"*Next.*"

He gets a five-minute examination, a sheet of Back Strengthening Exercises, and another of Back Stretching Exercises, and some time booked on the exercise machines. The harried-looking physiotherapist suggests he spend some time at the Lions Pool. As he leaves, she hands him a business card. He turns the card over. SKY BLUE, REGISTERED MASSAGE THERAPIST, *it says. There's a sun and moon symbol in one corner, and of those yin-yang things in the opposite one. He supposes it's worth a try.*

The door opens on the sound of soft music and the smell of incense. The tiny waiting room has a hippie kind of look to it, East Indian scarves draped over the window ledge, oriental brass ornaments, a couple of easy chairs that might have come from the dump. Through the wall, music tinkles. There's a murmur of voices. He's exactly on time. He'll never get down into one of those chairs. Beside the door into the parlour, or studio, or whatever it's called, there's a stool. He perches on the stool, and just at that moment, the door opens in his face. Two women come through, talking, and don't see him at first, although he's only a couple of feet away. They are relaxed, intimate. He feels like an eavesdropper.

"... started using that oil. It's got a lovely scent, doesn't it?"

"Oh, yes, I love it. It's thirty dollars, isn't it? I've only got two twenties, I hope that's all right?"

"Sure, I'll just get some change. It's in my purse here ... oh. Hi."

The masseuse, or whatever, is thrown off balance for a second, finding him behind the door. This makes Abe all the more embarrassed.

"Hi, I'm, er..."

"Abel. Hi. I'm Sky. Excuse me a sec."

She fetches the woman's change. "Okay, I'll see you next week, same time?"

The massage room is just like the waiting room, only bigger, with a table in the middle of the floor, and one straight-backed chair. The table looks a lot like a hospital gurney, and has a hole near the end, obviously to put your face down into. The lights in the room are very soft. It's almost dark.

"Have a seat, Abel. So you've got a sore back?"

He tells her the whole story. She is all compassion and professional interest.

"Okay, let's see what we can do about that. Just strip down to your underpants, and climb up on the table. I'll leave you alone for a minute."

"Oh."

"Something the matter?"

"It's just my, er, back."

She smiles. "It's all connected. Back, legs, neck."

"Um. I just, er, haven't"

"Not wearing any? That's okay. Just get your things off and get in under the sheet."

It's not the kind of massage he expected. There's none of that slapping or kneading or any of that stuff. It's more a kind of laying on of hands, as if she had some holy hippie power to heal. The weird thing is, it seems to work. He lies on his belly, feeling better than he's felt since Faro; his discomfort at being nude in front of a strange woman begins to fade. She shows neither embarrassment nor interest, other than a general air of clinical Earth Motherliness.

She places one hand on the back of his head, the other at the base of his spine, and pushes, steadily but gently. He feels a line between the two points, like something flowing through him. Something else is flowing, too. At the first stirrings of a hard-on, he feels himself blush. All his life he's been a victim of beet-red, full-body blushes. They were a torture to him in school; making Abe blush was a favourite sport during the half-year he spent in Grade 10. "Hey, man," Schwartz said to him in the shower one day when the guys had been ragging Abe about something, "Even your ass blushes."

At least she won't see the hard-on, which for some reason gets worse at the humiliation of having her see his ass blush, although it's only half out of the sheet, and presumably she's not actually staring at it.

For sure she'll leave the room when he gets dressed. All he has to do is lie there and look totally relaxed until she goes out, like the massage was so great he needs time before he can move.

"Okay," she says, in that soft, commanding voice, like a hypnotist, "why don't you roll over now, and I'll work on the front of you."

"You were so cute," she said one night in the bed with no legs, at four AM, with daylight coming in the window, "blushing from head to toe, and this big...." Overcome with giggles, she had to indicate his erection in mime, a flattened hand, bobbing stiffly at the wrist. She bent down to touch her head to the mattress, her shoulders shaking, and then sat back up. "And those blushes."

There was something he should be able to do, something besides wrapping his arms around her, something besides pulling her back down on the bed again: he should yell, maybe. He yelled. Throwing back his head and letting out a great, long, Tarzan yodel, he enfolded her, wrapped her up in himself like a gift, and squeezed.

"Hey, gently, eh?" she said, laughing. "You're a riot, Abe. You know that? You're just too much."

DAWSON

"I don't know, mining or something."
"Ha, that'll be the day," Stanley Kowalski says. "Mining".
"Cooking or something, in mines. And just shut your mouth."
"I never said nothin'."
"Anyway, I can find something. Just till September. Maybe I'm going back to school."
"Excuse me?"
"Seriously."
"Back to 'waste of my time and theirs' school? Back to 'full of posturing assholes' school?"
"Maybe. I don't know yet."
"I can see you now. 'Good-bye, zity lights.'"
"Don't they have city lights in the Yukon?"
"Dahling, zey have nussing in ze Yoo-kon."
"Then that's where I'm going."

Rita and Connie must have been sitting on the floor laughing for hours by now. They're not even all that high anymore, but at three AM, what does it matter? The time is one of the things they're laughing at. Connie keeps asking, "What time is it?" and then saying, "It *can't* be."

That's all it takes for Rita to lose it, fall over sideways laughing, and say, "It's the land of the midnight fucking sun. Get that through your head, you crazy drug addict." The room upstairs where Andra's asleep is far enough to the back of the ramshackle old house that there's no fear of waking her. It turned out that Rita's was where Andra was planning to go when she said she would take a ride into town. Apparently Dawson is so small that this doesn't even qualify as a coincidence.

It was incredible what a little blood loss did for Dale's sense of proportion. By the time they got him to the nursing station, he and Andra had cooked up a story about an accident with a hunting knife; apparently they both have police records. Gary's head had a bad lump on it, as well as a small gash, but he wouldn't go to the hospital. It was a weird scene in the cab of the truck, Dale propped up sideways, moaning, blood oozing out of his bandage, holding onto Andra as she drove, Connie squashed in between him and Gary. Whenever she moved, usually to avoid getting blood on herself, Dale would cry out. Andra stopped along the road and made Connie throw the blade into the Klondike River. Outside the hospital, she pointed to the blood on her sleeve. "Better change before you go in the bar."

Rita was in the lounge at the Eldorado Hotel, true to her word. Hooking up with her was like releasing a big spring that's been tightening inside Connie's gut for two weeks, getting a couple of extra-hard twists at the end. They drank for an hour, and then went on a walking tour of town, hanging onto each other's arms, and laughing the whole way. Dawson has got to be the most bizarre place in the whole world. It's one half tourist trap, with faux gold-rush false fronts on the stores, painted in garish pinks and blues, and one half broken-down ghost town, the genuine old Klondike buildings rotting into the ground. You can be walking down a wooden sidewalk, past the hulk of some ancient warehouse—grey logs rotted and sinking, caved-in tin roof—and have to go out onto the dirt road to get around a broken section, and then the next thing you come to is a chi-chi little outdoor cafe, where white-clad tourists sit sipping umbrella drinks.

The locals seem to be caught in the same time warp as Dawn and Gary and the rest of the Whitehorse crowd, but they're not so self-conscious about it. You can be like them or not, and nobody seems to give a damn. The feel of the town, at least on a clear summer evening just turning sweater-cool as a breeze drifts up from the Yukon River, is very relaxed, the perfect antidote to all that's been ailing Connie.

Now, collapsing in another fit of laughter onto the worn-out carpet, she has a flash of dragging the Persian rug upstairs to Nat's apartment, and she thinks fleetingly of arriving home safely, and then she thinks of Dale, in the hospital, nursing a grudge.

"Hey," she says, "hey," holding up her hands to stop the laughter for an announcement.

"Hey, what?"

"It's too bad I've got to get out of here. I was just starting to like this place." For at least the hundredth time tonight, Rita pretends to slap her on the shoulder and shrieks out a laugh, even though there's no possible way she could really get the joke.

The canoe rides high in the bow, its curved end pointing into the blue sky. Rowan's gear doesn't contribute much as ballast: change of clothes, sleeping bag, towel. The full-stock .303 propped up beside her weighs more than her whole pack. From the end of the bay the lake looks small, placid, and she sits back at her ease in the stern seat, but she's left a life jacket lying further forward to kneel on when she gets around the point. The water's almost always rough out there. Behind her, on the shore, she can hear Pete pulling on the starter and cursing—though he's holding back, on account of the dudes, at least two of whom are some kind of holy rollers. With any luck the dumb shit'll yank on it for at least five minutes before he thinks to check the spark plug and finds it missing. By then, even if he does jump in the other canoe, he's never going to catch up. Once again Rowan blesses the instinct that told her to bring her own truck to the landing. The road is godawful, which is the main reason the lake isn't fished out, but she's not afraid of bad roads. They would have flown her in but then she would have been stuck here, the only woman in camp, with Pete and Larry and three guys from Hamilton or someplace who wanted to drink beer and talk dirty and catch some big ones. Every two weeks the plane takes away the three guys and brings them back, looking different, but acting just the same.

Camp life went about as predicted. Guides were supposed to share the cooking, but the guys thought they could get away with leaving it to Rowan. When she told them she wasn't their goddamn servant, Pete said, "Well, what are you good for?" and Larry chortled. One of the dudes laughed out loud, one laughed uncomfortably, and the third, who is definitely a holy roller, looked away. The next day, Pete made a menstruation joke and they all laughed. Later, when all six of them were eating, he spoke across the campfire to the for-sure Christian—the guy who bows his head and mumbles before he even takes a drink of his coffee—"Say, you know why it is that Muslims don't allow women to swim in the ocean?"

"No," the dude said, his curiosity obviously aroused.

"Because they make the fish taste funny." The dude didn't get it, but the rest of them all hooted, and then one of his buddies leaned over and spoke in his ear, and he blushed, but in the end, he laughed, too.

Larry was less vocal than Pete. He was more of an ogler, and occasionally a toucher. He'd find a reason, surrounded by open country, to squeeze between Rowan and the sawhorse and rub his ass up against her. Yesterday, when she went to take a piss, Larry followed her into the bush. When she stood to pull up her pants, he stepped out from behind a tree.

"Need a hand with anything?" It was, in a way, the moment she'd been waiting for. Guys like Larry never seem to notice till it's too late that she's just as strong as they are, and faster moving. Of course, when they do find out, the hard way, it's Rowan who takes the shit over it. *Dyke*, they call her, partly to cover their own humiliation, *ball-buster.*

They have no right to talk like that, even if it does happen to apply in this case. She smiled at her own joke, which must, she thinks, have looked pretty sadistic, since at that moment she was kicking Larry a good one, square in the nuts, with a full-shank hiking boot, ladies size ten.

Larry still couldn't walk properly this morning. Rowan knew she had to get out of camp before he got better. Without the element of surprise, she could have trouble handling him, and group male vengeance, though unlikely with the dudes around, was still not out of the question. Pete agreed when she told him she had to leave.

"After the plane goes on Thursday I'll run you out to your truck. We'll just have to get someone else. I fuckin' told him not to hire a woman."

"Actually, I'm gone right after this," she said, indicating her breakfast.

"Like flying fuck you are. I can't afford to waste half a day ferrying your fat ass outa here."

"I'll take the canoe."

"No fuckin' way. I need that canoe."

"You can pick it up when you go out."

"Dream on. You want outa here today, start walkin'."

Rowan didn't respond. Pete let it go; he must have thought he'd won the argument.

"I cooked," Rowan said, getting up after breakfast, and nodding toward the dishes. Pete rolled his eyes, and then shrugged. The kettle was steaming on a rock by the campfire; it wouldn't take him more than fifteen minutes to shift his carcass and five more to get the dishes done. The dudes were down at the creek-mouth, trying a few casts. That was when she pulled the spark plug.

Rowan's well out in the middle of the bay when Pete discovers the missing plug: far enough away to take an interest in the way he bellows. A howl of rage, she thinks: it's not just an expression.

"She's goin' down now. You can see it along the Klondike. 'Nuther day an' she's over."

"Another day my ass. Look at them fuckin' creeks."

"She'll be right up past here."

"Fuck off."

"Bet you ten bucks I'll paddle my canoe right up to that fuckin' door."

"Hey. Widen the door, you can paddle her right in."

It's possible that conversation around the Pit never does get any more enlightened than this; Connie wouldn't know. At the moment, it's fairly predictable that only a few minutes will pass anywhere in Dawson without talk turning to the level of the water in the Yukon River: who's in town because their shack is flooded, who's packing to leave town until it's over, what it was like in the last big flood, the quantity of ice in the creeks or snow on the hills or the amount of rain compared to last year, the number of moose, or wolves, or ravens, sighted close to town, far from town, in town, anything that might be an indication of how high the water will come. Here in the Pit, everybody's an expert. They all know to the minute when the water will turn, to the foot how high it will rise, and to the dollar how much damage it will do, and no two opinions are the same. She thinks of incantations, ancient Rome.

"Gimme four sticks a dynamite, I'll fix that fuckin' ice. Right fuckin' now."

Bars, according to Rita, are where you get jobs.

"I don't want to be a barmaid, Rit."

"Not a barmaid. Camp jobs. They don't advertise in the paper, you know. You find the guy in the bar. Or somebody in there knows somebody, or heard something. Come on."

"Rita, it's ten AM."

"Yeah. We'll start at the Pit."

It's possible to drink coffee at the Pit, and Rita and Connie both do, but the majority of the customers at ten o'clock this Thursday morning are drinking draught beer. It may be a wiser choice than the coffee, and on the second round, Connie orders a Coke, while Rita has a "half-and-half," which turns out to be beer and tomato juice.

"Only vinos drink before noon, dahlink, unless it's champa-gne."

"Was that supposed to be Zsa Zsa? Because you slipped into Eva."

"Like hell I did."

"Nat, listen, I've got to get out of here. Seriously."

"What here? My place?"

"Yeah. Everywhere. Toronto."

"What's exactly the matter with Toronto?"

"Nine hundred degrees in here in the summertime is the matter, Nat."

"I just keep my underwear in the freezer. It keeps me nice and cool."

Marilyn Monroe is one of Nat's best: she does the eyes and everything. Connie ignores her.

"I just have to get out of Toronto. Someplace cooler. Not so goddamn crowded."

"You sound like my sister. Back to the land, God help us."

"At least she went somewhere."

"Whitehorse is not somewhere."

"Whitehorse. Where is that, anyway?"

"It's novhere, dahlink. Or maybe it's Alaska. Vot does it matter?"

"Have you got an atlas?"

Connie doesn't know what a D8 is, but it seems to be something very important. The guy she's talking to operates one, and he thinks he could get her a job in the camp where he works. They need something called a bullcook. She's trying to get a translation out of him, but he just keeps saying, "a bullcook, you know? A fuckin' bullcook," as if eventually it's bound to sink in.

Rita explains. "It's like a chambermaid, except in camp. Swab out the bunkhouse, help out in the kitchen, whatever."

"It's good pay," the guy says. "Broad they had before was gettin' twelve-fifty. I'm goin' back up there right now."

"Today?"

"Right fuckin' now." He sees her glancing at his full glass. "Right after this one. Maybe one more." He laughs.

"Is there some way back to town if I don't get the job?"

"Oh fuck, don't worry about that. Nobody else bringin' any broads out there today."

"Er, what's the sleeping arrangements?"

"Up to you, I guess, eh? Last one slept in with the cook."

"Y'know, I think I might have to pass on this one. Thanks, though."

At this, the guy throws back his head and fills the room with his laughter. "Relax, eh, the cook's a broad. And there's two rooms."

"Woman, Dago," Rita shouts across the table.

"What?"

"The cook's a woman. Not a broad."

"She's a woman but she ain't a broad? What the fuck you talkin' about?"

"How long you been in the Yukon?"

Connie looks at her watch. Dago has taken slightly more than two hours to ask her this question, something approaching a record. Like dogs pissing on hydrants, everybody here seems to need to establish seniority, claim turf, right up front.

"Not long," says Connie, hoping to cut the conversation short. She would prefer for Dago to concentrate on keeping his wheels out of the two deep ruts in the narrow track. It's typical of people here that they would use the word "road" to describe a pair of treacherous trenches you have to avoid for twenty miles, at the risk of bending something serious-sounding Dago's been telling her about, called a tie rod. "Couple weeks," she says.

"Figured. I can always tell a Cheechako. You know what that is?"

Connie knows what that is. It is impossible to spend one day in the Yukon without learning that Cheechako is the local word for newcomer, or greenhorn. "Yeah," she says.

"It's the men, isn't it? You think they're all going to be Jimmy Stewart? 'Why shucks ma'am, Ah don't rightly see why a lady shouldn't expect flowers, m-multiple orgasms, and a phone call.'"

"Bitch. Do you use that in your act?"

"Not yet."

"Because if I find out you've been doing me in that sleazy club...."

"They're not going to be any better up there, you know."

"Sleazy clubs? Or orgasms?"

"Men."

"They can't get much worse."

"They can, you know. They can all have beards, and fur cowboy hats."

"Anyway, it's not the men. It's Toronto. I just need to be somewhere else right now."

"So, to translate, you're going to run off and die tragically in the wilderness because Jason broke your heart."

"Oh, will you drop the Jason bit? That was months ago. I don't even think about Jason anymore, unless you bring him up."

Jason, Jason, asshole of assholes, jerk of jerks. Coppertone Jason of the Speedo tanline, Jason of the sculpted hamstrings, the athlete's grace. I'll-always-love-you Jason, we-are-one-person Jason. No, she wasn't judging all Toronto men by Jason. She was judging them each individually. She was judging them in groups. She didn't like the effete artsies and she didn't like the arrogant young suits and she didn't like the wake-and-bake potheads or the meat-and-potatoes working classes and, right at the moment, she was off tanned, gorgeous gym-jocks. Yes, she was fantasizing about a different breed of men, out in the wild Northwest. All right, of course it was a stupid fantasy. So what? What's worse, chasing stupid fantasies, or putting up with stupid realities?

"Know what a sourdough is?" Dago says, with the air of someone about to say something very clever. Oh God, Connie thinks, stop me if you've heard this one three million times. "'Sa guy who's sour on the Yukon and doesn't have the dough to leave." He laughs hard enough at his own joke that he doesn't seem to notice he's laughing alone. That's fine by Connie, who has no desire to antagonize Dago. He's her ticket to this job, which now she needs more than ever. Less than twenty-four hours ago she was swearing she'd never take another ride from a strange man in a pickup truck, but the situation's changed since then, after what Rita told her about Dale this morning.

Rita's known Dale for years. She says he follows a known pattern. He gets mad and starts hitting, he settles down and is remorseful. One day later, he's right off the deep end: assaults, stalking, death threats. He's been charged, but by the time he gets to court, he's a changed man, every time. He wraps judges around his little finger. Whenever he blows up, Andra gets out of town for a few days. That's why Connie took the first camp job that came along, even though it meant going with Dago. Rita assured her Dago isn't as bad as he seems. It's just talk, she said, ignore it. Sure, Connie said, ignore it. Like ignoring a bull in your kitchen.

"*Jesus* fuck." Dago hauls frantically on the steering wheel as the truck lurches suddenly to the right, slams down into a wheel rut, and then bounces out again, airborne. Connie has a flash of blue sky before her head hits the roof. The action comes to a sudden halt with a loud bang. When she collects herself, Connie sees that Dago has swerved to miss an oncoming truck, and hit a tree. "*Fuckin'* hell. Fuckin' *fuckin'* hell," Dago says, and thumps on the dash with his fist, as a tall, broad-shouldered woman climbs out of the other truck. He throws open his door and strides over. The woman says something Connie doesn't hear, but whatever it is, it's obvious she's not intimidated by Dago. Connie tries to open her door, but finds it blocked by the trunk of a tree. She slides over and gets out on Dago's side, in time to hear the woman speak.

"You asshole," she says. "Still never learned to drive."

"First time I ever seen anybody on this road," Dago says. "Where ya been?"

"Up Partridge."

"Hah," Dago laughs. "With Pete and Larry?" The woman nods. He laughs again. "Three meals a day and half a bed, eh?"

"Guess I forgot to read the fine print."

"Guess so did they." They both laugh. "How long'd you last?"

"Three weeks. And still a virgin." She raises a clenched fist, and they laugh again.

"So you lookin' for work?"

"Looks like it."

"Tony needs a loader operator." It's at this moment that the woman realizes Connie is standing awkwardly behind Dago, listening to their conversation. She leans to see properly past him; he turns to look. "Oh, Rowan, this is . . . um."

"Connie," says Connie. "Hi."

"Hi."

"New bullcook," says Dago, who has taken the few steps back to his truck and is in the act of getting down on the ground to look up underneath it. "Fuck," he says.

"Tie rod?" Connie offers. He gives her a look of contempt.

"Oil pan. Fuckin' oil pan," he says. "One little fuckin' stump, lands right on my fuckin' cocksuckin' oil pan."

"Is it leaking?" Rowan asks.

"Fuckin' pissin' out." They contemplate the truck for a minute. Connie can't imagine what there is to gain by staring at a broken truck, but Rowan and Dago seem to achieve some kind of silent communication in the process.

"Well, what do you wanna do?" Rowan asks, as if they had already telepathically gone over the options, and it was merely a matter of choosing one.

"What do you wanna do? You wanna talk to Tony?"

"Sure," Rowan says, and shrugs. "What the hell, eh? Jump in, sister."

Camp

The roar of diesel engines announces camp. Some kind of yellow tractors crawl around on tank tracks and huge rubber wheels, apparently intent on turning the bush into one vast gravel pit. So far they've conquered an area about the size of a large mall parking lot. A creek runs down one side of the gravel pit, its far bank a vertical wall about the height of a house. Somebody has a firehose trained on it, for no obvious reason. On the opposite side of the clearing, close to the wall of scraggly-looking trees, three trailers stand, two of them long white metal boxes, the other a cute little blue travel-trailer, its tongue and back corners propped up on tree stumps.

"Bunkhouse, cookhouse, job shack," says Dago, pointing. "Tony's runnin' hoe." He looks at his watch. "He seen us comin' in. Why'n't you just go in an' grab a coffee? Ida's always got the pot on. He'll be along pretty quick."

"Ida?" Rowan says. "Great. Why didn't you tell me?"

Dago shrugs. "Needed a loader operator."

Ida doesn't say much. She's about sixty, painfully skinny, with the loose-skinned look of someone who used to be fat.

"Only two beds in here," she says.

"What's the bunkhouse like?" Rowan asks. "Single rooms?"

"Yeah," says Ida. "They got single. Common shower, though. If that matters." She turns away and lifts a steaming kettle off the propane stove. "Bullcook helps with the dishes," she growls over her shoulder. Connie looks a question at Rowan, who shakes her head. After a moment, Ida looks over her shoulder. "Ain't you the new bullcook?"

"Not yet," Connie says. "I'm just here to apply for the job."

"Oh, you'll get the job, all right." Ida turns and gives her such a theatrical once-over, Connie has a hard time not to laugh.

"I don't know," she says. "Maybe I won't take the job, if that's the way things are."

"That's the way things are, sweetie," says Ida, turning back to her dishes again. "Don't matter where you go. And it don't last forever. You get to be my age, you have to know something to get a job. Little cutie like you, all you gotta do is wiggle your ass. Might as well make the best of it while it lasts."

"What does that mean, anyway, bullcook?" Connie leans over her plate and looks along the table to see if anybody knows the answer.

"'Sa fuckin' bullcook," Dago says, and stuffs an enormous chunk of steak in his mouth.

"Yeah, you told me that before, Dago, but where does it come from?"

"Fuck should I know?"

"Cook's husband," Tony says, gesturing with his fork toward Ida.

Tony knows things nobody else does. He seems to be an ex-everything: biker, logger, fisherman, paratrooper. He's got a tattoo on his arm that shows a pair of wings and the words *Ride Free Or Die*. The first time Connie saw it, she asked if he was an ex-subway rebel. Tony didn't even smile. "Never been on a subway," was all he said. The only time he's ever been east of Calgary was when he was in the service, but mention a town on the west coast, from San Diego to Anchorage, and he'll give you the history of its fishery, ask if you know so-and-so who runs the bike shop, and tell you about a bar down by the docks where he got in a fight, back in '69.

"Old days, loggin' camps was way out in the bush, eh? Real fuckin' bush camps, none a this hot showers'n flush toilets shit. Some old logger couldn't cut 'er anymore'd get his old lady a cookin' job, and they'd hire him, too, chop the wood, haul the water and that, eh? Swab out the bunkhouse."

"What's that make you and Ida, Connie?" Chuck, the mechanic, has no talent for comedy. People look down at their plates, flash each other looks, avoiding Ida's eyes.

Ida snaps at Chuck. "I don't have to feed you, you know."

Chuck looks like he wants to answer back, but he doesn't have the status. Ida is high up the camp pecking order, partly because she's a good cook, but more because of age and a kind of domineering grouchiness. Rowan's not scared of her, though.

"What's the matter, Ida?" she teases. "Don't think she'd make a good husband?"

Ida bristles. "One of that kind is plenty around here. Plenty," she adds, shoving her chin out at Rowan to make sure the point is taken before she gets up, slams her knife and fork down on her plate, and storms out. Everybody sits quiet while she bangs around behind the stove, and then the screen door opens, and slams shut.

"Hoo," says Chuck, and laughs.

Tony shakes his head. "Jesus fuck, Rowan." There's a pause. A couple of guys are looking out the window, embarrassed. Chuck and Dago are making here-it-comes faces at each other.

"What?" Rowan says.

"What? Where you think I'm gonna get another cook this time of year?"

"Where you think you're gonna get another operator?"

"Don't fuckin' push me, Rowan. All right? Don't push me, and don't push my cook. I've got a fuckin' camp to run."

"Hey, fuck man, it ain't Rowan's fault. Fuckin' Ida should mind her own business."

"Dago, what the fuck do you know about it?" Tony's anger is spent.

"Come on, man, everybody knows Ida's got a burr up her ass about Alice. So what?"

"Who's Alice?" Connie asks. Tony, Dago, and Rowan exchange looks.

"Gal I used to share a place with," says Rowan. Connie waits for further explanation. Nobody says anything.

"Yeah?" she says.

"Married to Ida's nephew before that."

"Oh."

"Yeah," says Tony. "Oh."

The bushes give off a pungent smell when they brush against them.

"Labrador tea," Rowan explains.

"Can you make tea out of it?"

"If you're desperate."

The mine is a desolate gash of industrial wasteland. The land's stripped bare and there are enormous piles of gravel and rubble. Her first night at supper, Connie asked if this was an open-pit mine, and everybody laughed. It turns out to be something called a placer mine. They're after the loose gold in the creek bottom. No one would think they'd have to tear up the land all around, but apparently the creek has moved a few times over the last few thousand years, and there could be placer gold wherever it's been.

With all its rubble and machinery, the place reminds her of a building site in the middle of a city, except that fifteen minutes' walk from camp, at night when the equipment's shut down, no one would even know it was there. With daylight until ten o'clock, the crew usually works in the evenings. They knock off around nine, and then the guys all sit around the cookshack and have a couple of beers before they go to bed. Dago and Tony stand right outside the back door every night and smoke a joint. Rowan likes to go for a walk. "You gotta stretch your legs," she says. "Work the kinks outa your back." Connie wouldn't mind a toke; she gets plenty of stretching making beds and mopping floors, but she needs to talk to someone besides Ida, at least once a day, and Dago and Tony just aren't it. So, the second night they were in camp, when Rowan asked her, "Go for a walk?" she went along. She knows now the guys are talking about them, but who cares? If they think she's a lesbian, maybe they'll leave her alone.

They walk up the hill behind the camp. The pine forest gives way to trembling aspens, and then to waist-high bushes, which Connie is learning to name: willow, buck brush, cinquefoil. Further up, wild rose, lupines, and spears of purple fireweed. After that, ground cover: juniper, sage, kinikinick. Caribou moss that crunches under her feet like dried bones.

Things scurry in the undergrowth. Not snakes, Connie is pleased to note. Of the very little that Nat knew about the Yukon, this was the only thing she considered good: that there are no snakes.

"*What happened to them all, I wonder?*"

"*Shnake rush,*" says Bogey.

"*Say what?*"

"*Big Shnake Rush of '98. Shome men made fortunes, shome men got bit.*"

"*Well, whatever the reason, I'm glad.*"

"*Ever sheen a shnake, shishter?*"

"*In science class. At the zoo, maybe.*"

"*Sho why get on that plane?*"

"*I dunno, Nat. I'll tell you when I get back.*"

Ten minutes' walk brings them to a worn footpath, just below the brow of the hill. One night Rowan stopped to show Connie a couple of hair-filled turds. "Wolf shit," she explained.

Connie stays close by Rowan on these walks.

Downstream from the mine the creek loops around the hill, obscured from view by the spruce forest that follows the banks. The path drops back down the hillside and meets up with the creek. Three stepping stones lead to a broad, flat rock where two people can sit comfortably and listen to the water go by. You have to sit for a few minutes before your ears begin to pick out the hundreds of different sounds, the constantly changing harmonies and discords that make up the water's roar. Rowan, it's obvious, would be content to sit quietly, letting her ears recover from the constant growl of the loader, but Connie's head is full of talk. All day while she works she thinks of things she wants to ask. How do they get the gold out of all that gravel, what happens to the fish when they tear up the stream like that, how did Rowan ever get started driving loader? How did she come to be a trapper?

What's it like, she wants to ask, but doesn't, spending all your life in this world of men, doing jobs the guys think are reserved for them, dealing with the hostility of people like Ida, the sniggers of idiots like Chuck? What's it like to be queer in a place like this? Connie never expected to meet anybody openly gay in the Yukon. Somehow she'd always imagined that being out was an urban phenomenon, that if you came from the country, like the guys down the hall from Nat, you moved to the city, broke the news to your parents on the phone, and then never went back. And then, in Connie's experience, there's always been something, she doesn't know what—unhealthy?—that's not it, but maybe something not robust about the gays and lesbians she sees around TO. Even the ones who dress tough, all swagger and leather, strike Connie as so vulnerable, she wants to reach out and pat their stubbled heads.

Connie's connected to the planet: Vibram soles, size five,

hooked into a ridge in the rock, she squats, her face turned to the failing warmth of the evening sun. Her eyes are closed. The sound of the creek flows over her, washes around inside her ears, and pours out. She's never really stopped to listen to a creek before; it's not what she thought: the water doesn't swoosh or roar or gurgle. If she listens long enough, it's not one thing making one sound at all. It's just millions of drops of water hitting the rocks and washing the banks and pinging off each other; it swirls into eddies and splashes over trees that have given up trying to hold onto the sandy banks and collapsed into the creek. Every drop is different, like snowflakes, and they all make different sounds. It has a rhythm, she's certain, but she can't find it, because there's no beat. Next person asks her what she's doing in the Yukon, she's going to tell them she's here to sit on a rock in the middle of a stream and try, without hope, to find the rhythm of the water.

Long before she came to the Yukon, Connie's been asking herself what she was doing wherever she was: in university, out of university, in Jason's arms (read: bed), out of Jason's arms/bed, sleeping in her old room at home, at the mall, in her skin. She hasn't had an answer since she was in Grade 13, and working part-time at Mac's Milk. What she was doing then was getting good marks and saving her money for college, which was what you did. Connie was saving her virginity for college, too, which was optional, and caused no end of bother with the two guys she was sort of going with, in a weird, high-school kind of way. Both of them were accidents, really, things she'd just kind of fallen into. Mark asked her to a school dance in Grade 11, and then just acted like they were going steady after that, without ever asking her. He started saying it, and she didn't know how to contradict him, and after a while, saying it made it real. He kept nagging her about "going farther"—*Shawna did it with Greg, all the girls are doing it once they're going steady*—he kept his hands to himself, more or less, but he sulked about it. Curtis, the skinny acidhead she met at a drama club she was in for a while, and saw in secret when Mark was working at the grocery store, never talked about it. They'd just smoke up and start to neck, and he'd see how far he could get before she put the brakes on. When she'd finally fish his hand out of her bra or her pants or wherever she'd allowed it to wander, he'd laugh, and go make tea. The two guys had each asked her, in their own way, why she was holding back. Mark was a jerk about it—*What are you saving it for?*—so she told him to fuck off, but Curtis sounded genuinely curious.

"I'm waiting for it to be nobody's business."

"Explain?"

"Like my parents. Like the whole goddamn school. 'Connie's lost her viriginity'."

"I don't get it. Who's going to tell your parents? Who's going to tell anybody? And who gives a shit about the whole goddamn school?"

"But that's just it. I don't want to do it with you just to prove something to them."

"So don't. Do it because you want. Or don't do it because you don't want. Not because of what people think."

"It's not like that. I just want it to be right, you know?"

"Hey, I'm into that. If it feels good, do it, right?"

"Yeah, but, I don't know. It feels good—shit, you know it feels good—it just, I don't know. It doesn't feel right, right now. I want to get out of here first. I want to feel—I don't know—"

She can fill in the word now: independent. She wanted to be independent, to have sex as an independent choice, not an act of rebellion, and not something all the girls were doing. Living at home, it would just all feel too teenage.

She'd been looking forward to university since Grade 9, planning it through all those years of guidance classes, all those nights in her room, the long evenings at the store. Where will I go? What will I take? What will I wear? Will I be popular? It wasn't until Grade 12 that she started to think, Will I fall in love? Will I have incredible, romantic, *adult* sex? By the time she was writing her entrance exams, her image of university had matured: it would be, she knew, very hard work. Probably there would be long hours of exhausting consultation with handsome young-ish lecturers, occasional visits to seriously hip student pubs with men in black turtlenecks. There would be the constant need to reject unwanted sexual overtures, to accept wanted ones, and to choose between the two. But mostly there would be a lot of hard work.

For some of Connie's friends, high school ended in a flood of tears. Connie tried to play along, she didn't want to hurt their feelings, but it was hard to conceal the way she felt about leaving the whole scene behind. There wasn't anyone in Markham she was going to miss very much. She dumped Mark, who fussed and railed—*I thought you loved me*—and left her options open with Curtis, who shrugged. On the day she left for Peterborough, to arrive for orientation week, she insisted on taking the bus. Her father seemed relieved to be spared the drive, but her mother had been both hurt and suspicious.

"I don't see what harm there can be in us driving you up there."

"It's just something I want to do myself, Mom."

"But how are you going to get all your things all the way from the bus station to the college?"

"Mom, they have college buses. I'll work it out. That's the whole point; I just want to work it out for myself, not for it to be something you do for me."

Her room in residence was very postmodern and Spartan, with its textured concrete walls and built-in plywood furniture. Formerly a women's college, Lady Eaton had now been co-ed for two years. There were two wings, really two separate buildings, one mixed, the other, known as the Nunnery, for girls only. Connie had battled with her parents, who were still paying most of her bills, for a room in the co-ed wing, but with no success. *But what for, dear?* her mother wanted to know. *You can see the boys in the cafeteria, or at class. You don't need to be in the same dorm.* At least Peterborough was far enough from Markham that her family wouldn't be showing up every weekend. That's why she chose Trent in the first place, even though she was accepted at University of Toronto first. As her father was fond of pointing out, she could have gone to U of T and still lived at home. *What could be better?* he said, at least three times that she remembered.

It took about a week for the bloom to wear off the Nunnery. The girl in the room next door had brought a TV, and several of the girls on her cellblock, as she soon dubbed the cold, lightless little cluster of rooms, would meet every afternoon to watch the soaps. Two brought their knitting. Three, including both knitters, wore bathrobes and fuzzy slippers. One pair of fuzzy slippers had floppy ears. Connie would meet them in the hall and look away in embarrassment; it was like being in high school and having to live with the nerds. At her desk in the evenings she could see the North Wing across the courtyard, lit up and inviting. Nobody, she was certain, was watching the soaps over there. There would be no fuzzy slippers in the North Wing. Over there people were drinking wine, discussing important women named Margaret, hanging artsy posters on the wall. Posters without kittens. She saw them in the cafeteria, guys with tie-dyed shirts and hangovers, girls with patched jeans and confident smiles they didn't learn from a teen magazine. These were the people she'd come to university to meet, the crowd she should be travelling with, but how to get to know them? There were a couple of guys in her English tutorial who lived in the North Wing, but they were so uninteresting: one was Japanese and cute, but he seemed so incredibly suburban and middle class in his golf shirts and variable tint glasses, she wanted to ask him if he came from Markham, too. The other was okay, sort of, but kind of scruffy and spaced-out; she didn't come to university to meet another Curtis.

It seemed like ages, but it probably wasn't more than two or three weeks before she saw the inside of the North Wing. It turned out to be as simple as arriving late enough for lunch one day that she didn't have to sit with Tina and Debbie, her neighbours from the Nunnery. As soon as she sat down, a big dopey-looking guy came over with his tray and asked did she mind—? His name was Ron, and pretty soon they were joined by his friends Dave and Annie, Gerry, and another Dave. By the time they'd finished eating, she was invited to a party that night at Dave and Annie's room. She had expressed surprise that the college had co-ed rooms, and everybody had laughed. It turned out that the two Daves had been roommates, until Dave started going with Annie about halfway through Initiation Week, after which it just made sense for the other Dave to take Annie's single room upstairs. There was nobody in the college administration who thought it was their business to pry into who slept in which room. Annie didn't blush or giggle or make any big deal about living with Dave; she treated it as a normal thing. The patches on her jeans, Connie noticed, were made of the same material as all the curtains and cushion covers in the residence rooms.

Only one room in each cluster was a double. As Connie crossed the covered walkway to the North Wing that evening, she could hear music blaring from the open windows of what must be Dave and Annie's room. It sounded like the Rolling Stones, but she didn't recognize the song. Two loud male voices joined in the chorus, but could they really have the words right?

Star fucker, star fucker, star fucker, star fucker, star, they bellowed. The record played without them for a few bars, where their knowledge of the words was obviously incomplete, and then one chimed in on *been givin' it to Steve McQueen,* and both rallied a few bars later for *I bet you keep your pussy clean.* Connie was at the door at this point, trying her South Wing key in the lock, discovering that it didn't fit, and wondering whether she really wanted to go ahead with this, when a deadly cute guy with black curly hair cut long and swept back off his face walked up, unlocked the door, and opened it for her.

"Hi," he said and smiled, and she could no more have turned and walked away from that smile than she could have evaporated into the air. "Forget your key?" he said, as they started up the stairs.

"Oh, no," Connie told him. "I live in South Wing. My key doesn't fit. I'm just going to a party."

"The one in the Zoo?" He sounded surprised, and looked her over as if checking to see if he'd misjudged her on first reading.

"Zoo?"

"Second floor? Right here," he pointed, as they turned the corner in the stairs and began to approach the door.

"Yeah. They call it the Zoo?"

"See for yourself," he said. Through the heavy door, two blaring stereos competed for supremacy, one still on the Stones, the other some kind of heavy metal. Over it all someone was yelling, "Party on!" On the plus side, there was a distinct odour of marijuana coming through the door. Hanging out with Curtis, Connie had developed a taste for weed, and she'd come upon no trace of it at the college until now.

"Are you going in?" she asked. The guy smiled—would that have been indulgently, or patronizingly?

"I think not," he said. "But have fun." He continued on up the stairs, turning to smile at her again, this time she would say knowing-and-mocking-ly. She watched him go before opening the door, which, she now noticed, bore a paper sign bearing the typed legend: Caution, Live Animals. Enter At Your Own Risk.

The door opened onto an empty hall, a cluster of rooms the mirror image of the one Connie lived in. By some twist of architectural logic, the washrooms at Lady Eaton were all part of the corridors, a swinging door at each end leading to another cluster of rooms. Connie had peed three times before she left for fear of having to use the unsegregated toilets in the North Wing. A male voice from the nearest open door shouted over the music, "He-ey. Come on in." She turned to look, and the room—the mirror image of her own, and slightly smaller than her mother's walk-in closet—was packed with at least a dozen people, mostly guys. Two girls sat together on the bed, and another perched on the desk with a guy. The music was too loud to talk, but nobody seemed to care. The guy who invited her in lit a fresh joint and passed it to her. As soon as she tasted it, she knew the weed was strong: it had that sweaty-armpits flavour that always meant she's going to end up tongue-tied. Thinking she might not get the joint back in such a crowd, she double-toked before passing it on. She scanned the room for any of the faces she'd met in the cafeteria, but none of them were present.

"Thanks for the toke," she yelled at the guy, "I'm going to go next door to Dave and Annie's." The guy nodded and gave her the thumbs-up, presumably going by body language, since he couldn't possibly have actually heard.

Dave and Annie's room was done up in contemporary revolutionary: posters of Che, Fidel, and John Lennon, Free Huey stickers, anti-war slogans, a Richard Nixon dartboard. There was barely room to squeeze in the door, and she stood outside, nodding hi to people she'd never met and feeling awkward. Two guys came down the hall, arms around each other and yelling.

"Screwed to the wall."

"Scrad to the wool."

"Totally fuckin' fucked, man."

They came alongside and one of them put his free arm around Connie. "Are you totally fuckin' fucked, man?" he breathed at her. "'Cause I sure as hell am."

Taking hold of his fingers, she pivoted out of his embrace, letting go of his hand before it would have begun to twist.

"No, I'm just right," she said. She could have hurt him, thought about it for less than a second, but it would have felt like a capitulation. Like, once you've had to use your self-defence moves on a guy at a party, what are you still doing there? Weird as this party was, she didn't want to give up on it just yet: it was the first excitement she'd seen at Trent. She pretended to treat the grab as good-natured fun, which the guy obviously thought it was, and he and his buddy went on down the hall, shouting.

"Right on, sister."

"Fucked to the wall."

"Could you believe that old witch today?" Rowan's voice brings

Connie back through a haze to consciousness of the river and the night air getting colder. She laughs. "What?" Rowan says.

"Nothing. It's just that I have this friend back in Toronto who says it's a compliment to call a woman a witch."

Rowan snorts. "No insult to Ida, anyhow."

"You didn't exactly go easy on her, though."

"Why should I? Friggin' old bag's on my case every time I turn around. You know the worst part about it? She knows it's all bullshit. Danny split up with Alice, I wasn't even in town. Middle of winter, I'm miles away. What does she think I did, make a voodoo doll of her? Little forked stick with her picture on it?" She puts two fingers up to her mouth and wiggles her tongue in between, and laughs. "Must think I'm one hell of a lady's gal." She looks at the water for a minute before she speaks again. "She's got this notion that Alice was totally straight, and I somehow turned her into a lesbian."

Connie laughs.

"It's like, one, I'm not interested in straight women, and two, they don't just convert, like Catholics and Protestants."

"Some do, though. Right?"

"Yeah but . . . it's like . . . there's this friggin' myth about lesbians, eh? They know the secret things a woman desires, right? It's this—I don't know, 1930s or something—this old-fashioned bullshit that lesbians can use some kind of magical friggin' power over women. You know, anyone believes that shit's got to be queer themselves to begin with." She shifts the weight of the gun. "Ida, now there's one for you, for sure."

Connie laughs at this, but Rowan holds up her hand.

"You know what they say: if you hate 'em that much, you are one."

Beer Strike

People blink and stare into the darkness when they come in the door of the Capital, shaking off the grip of a sun that hasn't set properly or gone behind a cloud in four weeks. There's a film of dust on the polished bar and the wooden tables, and an air of desperation in the narrow barroom. During the hottest part of the hottest summer in memory, the breweries are on strike. One new, blinking, customer, just in from camp with a pocket full of money, orders a round of hi-test for his buddies, calls for it across the room so everybody knows he's out for a celebration. A hollow laugh goes around the bar.

"What?" the guy says.

"Beer strike," a bunch of people yell, and hold up their bottles of Olympia.

"We got Oly," May, the bartender, tells him.

"Oly? Jesus." The guy sits down in disgust, nodding his head, presumably to accept the American beer that vile fate has thrown in his path.

The guy ceases to be a focus of interest, and Abe turns back to

Backhoe Mike. There's so many longhairs in town named Mike right now, they all have to have nicknames. Backhoe Mike is trying to explain to Abe what the problem is with the Indians, but he's so repetitive he can't seem to get all the way through a thought.

"They got their traditional ways, eh? Like their traditional fuckin' . . . traditions, you know? So, right. According to their—traditional, eh? Traditional, get it? It's like their fuckin'—er—tradition, right? Like their parents did, and their parents did it and their fuckin'—"

"Yeah," Abe says, "but listen a sec."

"What?" says Mike.

"I need my house fixed."

"What do you mean, fixed?"

"Scoop the mud out of there, stick the end back up."

"No fuckin' way, man. She's condemned. They ain't gonna let you do that."

"Listen," Abe says, "it's a squat anyway. If I'm living in it, they can't kick me off."

"They shut off the power, man."

"So what? I got a wood stove, I got a Coleman cooker, oil-lamps."

"How you gonna dig it out?"

"There's a hoe working down the road from me. They don't lock it up at night."

"Oh no, you don't."

"Fuckin' right, man," says Pigpen, another Mike, leaning across the table to get into the argument. "It's the fuckin' Yukon, ain't it? Where's your spirit of adventure?"

"What the fuck you mean, stick the end back up?" Big Jack doesn't lean forward to talk, he just sits back and hollers. "Fuckin' wall cave right in?"

"Yeah," says Abe, "but it's the gable wall. The roof's okay."

"Still gonna need to rebuild the wall."

"Well, sure," says Abe.

"You got the lumber?"

"I figured we'd tear down the shed and use that to build the wall. What do you think?"

Big Jack considers this for a moment. "I think you're fuckin' nuts." Then he breaks into a grin. "Let's fuckin' do 'er."

"That's the spirit," says Pigpen. "Let 'er buck."

A black and white dog throws himself at the end of his chain, snarling. On the other side of a wooden fence, a coyote knocks over a garbage can and spreads its contents across the alley. At a sudden tremendous roar, dog and coyote both turn and see a huge yellow machine trundling up the alley. The dog explodes in a frenzy of barking, while the coyote carefully judges the speed of the backhoe's approach and then finishes checking the garbage. As he grabs a chicken carcass and dashes off, an upstairs light comes on in the house.

"Shut up, Nanuk," a voice yells out the window, as the machine clanks and rumbles past in the half-dusk of a June night. "Assholes," the man says to someone inside. "I'm gettin' the mayor on the phone, right now. See if he likes it."

The doors of the Edge are open at nine AM. First customer to cross the threshold gets a free draught. Next five or six don't have any money most mornings, so if you're the first guy buying his own beer, you've always got friends. There's no draught because of the beer strike, so Abe's buying Oly. He's got his money out when Charlie Peter Bill shuffles over and mumbles at him. Charlie Peter's got no teeth and he's hard to understand but it's easy enough to figure out what he wants. Abe orders three extra Olympias for Charlie Peter and the two guys waiting at his table.

"Givin' liquor to Indians," says Backhoe, "they used to shoot you for that."

"No, they fuckin' didn't," says Big Jack.

"Threw you in jail, anyways."

"Yeah, well, that ain't the same thing as shootin'."

"Those guys'll just make a fuckin' mark outa you, man," says Pigpen. "When's it their turn to get a round?"

"Fuckin' bush-niggers," says Backhoe Mike. "Not long outa the fuckin' trees, eh?"

Abe leans forward, but he speaks quietly, so Backhoe has to lean forward, too, to hear him. "Did you know I was part Indian, Mike?"

Pigpen cackles. "Which part?"

Big Jack says, "So who isn't? Less they just got off the fuckin' boat. Never built the North on no white women."

"I could be status if I wanted," Abe says.

"Bullshit," says Backhoe.

"S'true. My mom's half Ojibwa. From up north Ontario someplace. Or quarter anyways, or something. But that ain't the thing. She's status 'cause she used to be married to a Native guy from Teslin."

"What happened to him?" Big Jack asks.

"Put his Ski-Doo through the ice."

"So when was this? I don't remember this," says Backhoe.

"Ah, neither do I, Mike," says Abe. "It was before she met my old man."

"Oh. Oh, I get it."

"Anyways," Abe says, his point made, "I want to thank you guys for the help tonight. Or last night. Or whenever it was. I owe you."

"We'll take your firstborn child."

"If it's a girl. But don't send her until she's sixteen."

"We'll settle for another round, cheap prick."

"No, seriously. I felt bad I couldn't do much."

"Hey, forget it," says Big Jack. "I break my back someday, you can do the same for me."

"Fuck," says Pigpen, "I thought that cop was gonna stop us for sure."

"We'd of been fucked if he had."

"Right after we smoked that rig, too."

"Fuckin' dumb farm boys," says Pigpen. "Probably thought it was a combine comin' down the road. Hey, Daphne, bring us another round of this piss, willya? And you better get three for Abe's red brothers over there while you're at it."

Exhaust fumes and road dust swirl around Sky's head. It makes a change from mosquitoes. Once in a while, a kid in the Airstream trailer convoy waves to her from the window of a big Chrysler, or a Suburban. She waves back, but doesn't bother trying to thumb. These people do not pick up hitchhikers; they could probably get kicked out of the wagon train for it, like selling liquor to Indians. It takes about twenty minutes for them all to pass. Sky doesn't hold the Airstreamers in contempt, as so many people here do. She was born in a school bus, in Brownsville, Texas, half a mile from the Matamoros border. Willow, her mother, had wanted her to be born in Mexico, for reasons obscurely connected with the writings of Carlos Castaneda and the position of the stars. They had travelled all her life, sometimes on their own, sometimes in convoys of school buses off to form a commune, protest a war, or discover America. As far as she can see, the only difference between those convoys and this one is style. That and the reaction they get.

One time in Saskatchewan, John, who was probably Sky's father (*It's hard to be sure,* Willow would smile, beatifically), pulled into a gas station on a dusty backroad and asked the man if he could do some work on the bus in his yard. The man took a greasy rag out of the back pocket of his coveralls and wiped his hands thoroughly before answering. Eventually he nodded to the side of the shop. "Long's you keep it out of sight."

John was under the bus, and Willow was nursing Moon inside when Sky, twelve years old, went into the gas station to ask if she could use the washroom. "Sure," the man said. "C'mon round here and I'll show you the key." Sky had lived all her life among skinny-dippers and hot-tubbers, and was not unfamiliar with the sight of a penis. Up until then she had quite liked them; the way they snuggled against their scrotums used to remind her of baby opossums clinging to their mothers in a book she had when she was four. But the gas station man's penis was so big and ugly and out of place that it shocked her: all angry and red, and shot through with purple veins, like his face, and sticking straight up out of a bush of black hair that was poking out of the fly of his blue, greasy coveralls. She backed away, frightened. The man advanced on her, the penis in his hand. Walking backwards, she missed the gap and bumped into the counter. Turning her head, she saw that she had narrowly missed banging into the two-pot coffee machine—*For Truckers Only*. The coffee pot was heavy in her hand. The coffee was thick and steaming and made a black splash across the man's crotch. Both Sky and the garage man were screaming when first John, then the mechanic, burst in.

The mechanic suggested it might be best if they left right away. John and Willow weren't the kind of people who call the cops; they put the wheel back on, threw the tools in the bus, and drove off. "It's okay, babe," Willow said, holding Sky against her breast. "He didn't mean any harm. People like that, they never get naked with anybody. Their little penises just have to get out and say hello once in a while." It was a couple of years later, in a different part of the prairies, that they heard the story of the guy who got a pot of coffee thrown on his cock by some hippie kid, and everybody called him Pink Dick after that. Sky wishes she'd looked at the name on his blue coveralls. She hopes it was Dick.

You never get a ride from anyone on a wagon train, but sometimes right after they're gone, somebody will be slowed down behind them and think, what the hell, might as well pick up this hitchhiker. Not this time, though. A family in a Pontiac passes without looking at her.

Sky told Abe she was going to Dawson to make some money. It's true there's money to be made; nobody's doing massage there right now, and she can always sell some of her jewellery. The Airstream people buy the cheap fake-Indian-looking stuff, and the hitchhikers go for the antique trade beads.

But she's not going to Dawson for the money. She can always make money in Whitehorse. Sky is giving herself some breathing space. Abe is a sweet guy, a kid really, but he drinks too much. She doesn't know if she'll go back to him or not. Probably she will, but she's going to get him on the phone first and make him promise to go easy. Again. She's laid it on the line before, once before they moved in together, and again a week or so ago, but he didn't seem to believe she'd go. "What have I done?" he said. It's true he hasn't done anything really stupid or outrageous yet, other than be shitfaced at supper a couple of times. What he doesn't understand is that Sky's not willing to wait for something bad to happen. She's been around drunks before. She knows that eventually things will get worse.

Walking, walking, walking. One foot in front of the other, the soft resistance of snow under moccasins.

"We're all right, laddie, as long as you come up to your name."

That was the kind of joker the old man was, give his kid a name like Abel Walker and expect him to live up to it: to walk fifteen miles on the shortest day of the year, at fifty below, from one line shack to the next, and then walk another twenty the next day, walking well into the night, to get out to the highway and hitchhike to town, because he'd run out of tobacco.

"She didn't get us this time, laddie," he said, as they arrived at the second cabin. Meaning the Hag, of course, his pet piece of Scottish bullshit. Abe is just about certain that he made it all up, that nobody in Scotland ever heard of the Hag, which is like his version of Wendigo, the mischief spirit. Trust the old man to turn it into a woman. Abe met a Scottish guy in the Capital one time, and asked him about it. He'd never heard of it. When Abe described it all, the guy said he thought it sounded Irish. The old

man's whole Scottish bit was just about bogus, too; he was born there, but he grew up in Alberta.

When Abe was five or six, he half heard a voice on the street say, *Hey, that's Grey Owl's kid.* It wasn't until years later that he understood. Grey Owl meant phoney, poser, white guy pretending to be an Indian. He remembers wondering if it was true. Did the old man want to be an Indian? He did move to the Yukon and get his first trapline as soon as he got out of school. He did wear buckskins and a long braid. Abe never knew that stuff was supposed to be Indian. All the Indians he knew wore jean jackets and ball caps. They were more likely to have hair like Elvis than like Crazy Horse. Is that why the old man married Mom, because of her Indian connection? But if he wanted to be an Indian so bad, why all the Scottish shit? Why, forty years away from any possibility of a genuine Scottish accent, did he insist on using expressions like *away wi' the fairies,* and harping on about the Hag and all that?

Abe knew people who resented the old man's trapline. It was supposed to be an Indian line, and they aren't supposed to change hands to white men. But it was really his mom's line, and she is an Indian, at least technically. Mom's first husband died on the trapline. She didn't like to go out there, but when she did, she always made them walk around the edges of that little pothole lake where he drowned. Even at forty below, when the lake must have been about three feet thick.

There's a bad current in that lake, she'd say. *You don't know where the weak spot's going to be unless you know ice, real good.* When she'd say things like that, she'd even have a slight Tlingit accent. It was one of his earliest and most puzzling questions about human nature. Why do people present themselves as things they aren't, even to people who know them intimately? Why does the old man bother to be Scottish when we all know he left Glasgow at the age of three? Why does Mom cling to that Native thing? She has an Ojibwa grandmother she hardly knew, no kids by her first husband. She has very little contact with his family, although when Abe was little, she insisted he call certain strange, aloof women and large, shy men Auntie and Uncle, even though they only ever met them at Food Fair, or in front of the post office.

It seems like everybody has to have a fantasy person they play at being once in a while, when they get sick of themselves. Abe wonders what his is. Who is he when he doesn't want to be Abel Walker? Drunk, the answer comes. When you don't want to be yourself, you get drunk.

Abe bought his guitar for fifty bucks out of the *Yukon News* want ads. The guy he bought it from got it at a flea market. Sometimes when he pulls it out of its case he likes to run his hand over the worn top and imagine all the different hands that have played it. Not this time, though. Today he's focussing on holding the damn thing without banging it on the concrete step.

"Jesus thing, sit still," he tells it, strumming the open strings. "He-ey. Not bad. Good enough for sidewalk music, anyway. Good enough for the Sally Fuckin Ann, eh? Eh?"

A small crowd has begun to accumulate at the steps of the Salvation Army. All are men, all but two are Indians, all are stone-sober except Abe, who strums a G chord and nods at the man nearest him.

"Hey, buddy, this the soup kitchen?"

"Yeah," the man smiles, pushing a shining hank of black hair out of his face. "But they ain't gonna give you no soup."

"Fuck that, man. Why the fuck not? I'll sing a fuckin' hymn, same as everybody else. Here, listen, listen, I'll sing you a hymn." Abe's fingers are drunk. His picking is clumsy, his voice wobbles on either side of the tune, squeaking, and roaring. "'You will eat, by and by, In that beautiful land in the sky. Work all day, live on hay, There'll be pie in the sky when you die (that's a lie.).' S'a fuckin lie, ain't it, buddy? How's that for pickin? That oughta be worth a bowla soup."

A burly man in uniform puts his hand on Abe's shoulder. "All right, move along. You can't play here, this is a doorway."

"I'm comin' in for some soup."

"Not today, friend. Why don't you come back tomorrow?"

"What am I supposed to do till then. Starve?"

"You're supposed to sober up."

"Ah, fuck you. Wasn't for us drunks, you guys'd have no fuckin' customers anyway. Let me in there."

"Can't eat here if you've been drinking. Just step aside, please. Come on, fellas."

"Hey, don't you touch my guitar. You saw that, did you see that? He pushed me. I'm within my rights. Get outa my way, sergeant. Don't you touch me, buddy, you're fuckin' with the wrong drunk. Where's the fuckin' soup? I'll sing a hymn, no problem. That's the deal, ain't it? Sing a fuckin' hymn, eat a bowl a soup. Here, listen... 'pie in the sky when you die THAT'S A FUCKIN' LIE.'"

The air in front of Abe swims like water and makes everything unreal and hard to control. That's why things get out of hand. He didn't mean for chairs to be flying around, people yelling. He didn't want the sergeant to go staggering backwards over a table and bleed, or the cops to come barging in, dragging him out. He just wanted to sing a hymn and eat some soup.

Hurricane

A sad little huddle of long coats and head scarves shuffles across the wooden railway bridge, crossing the river from the Indian village so slowly they look like they're waiting for the train to catch up. Some kind of rat dog tries to hustle the old women along, its white bob of a tail beckoning madly. The bright afternoon sun reflects off the river and the lake, slants through the open doors and glances between the shrunken clapboards on the train station, painting the dusty interior a mystery of shadows and shafts of light. Across the platform, across the tracks, across a vacant space, a pointless guardrail, and a dusty road, stand Watson's General Store and the Caribou Hotel, two gold-rush remnants, their tall false fronts in need of paint, stuck together downtown-style like they once expected to be the first two buildings of a thriving Main Street. Behind them, Carcross, population two hundred. Log cabins and pothole roads, a few frame buildings, some plywood shacks. Some of the cabins are painted up pretty, all nicely chinked with white plaster, white picket fences around the yards. Others are gone grey, grass growing up the walls, the roofs in need of new sod. Some have moosehides hung up to dry or stretched out on fleshing racks, others have smokers going, laundry hanging, guys' legs sticking out from under trucks.

Mike pulls up in front of the hotel, kills the bike, pulls off his gloves, peels down his bandana and then takes off his shades, and scrapes some of the Carcross Road out of his eyes. Teenagers in jean jackets and ball caps hanging around on the wooden sidewalk pretend not to look at him, or the bike. A bunch of kids comes running up from the lakeshore, and gathers round.

"Harley Davidson," proclaims the biggest one, a red-haired halfbreed kid about ten years old.

There's only two other Harleys in the Yukon, so far as Mike knows, but every second person seems to have the belt buckle or the ball cap, or an *Easy Rider* poster on the wall or a Ride With The Best bumper sticker on their truck. Owning a Harley is just about the ultimate status symbol. If Mike had half a brain he'd do like the guy in Riverdale with the old Police Special that he never takes off the forty miles of pavement around Whitehorse. This gravel roads thing is bullshit: choking on dust and taking rocks from passing trucks, it's like a contest between his bolts and his bones to see which can rattle loose first, but he can't help it. He just can't get on his bike and drive twenty miles one way, and then turn around and drive back. It's starting to show on the bike, though: especially the rock-dings. Much as he detests Jap bikes, there's a good deal on a seven-fifty-four he's thinking of going for, just so he can keep the chopper on the pavement. Pavement's going to get further out every year, they say.

"Hey," a little guy with a mop of thick black hair pipes up, "are you a Hell's Angel?"

Mike just grins. "Hey," he says back, "can you read?"

"Yeah," says the kid.

"C'mere. What does that say?"

The kid stands on tiptoe to look at the metal plate mounted on top of the gas tank, and starts to sound out the words.

"*If—y-ou-v-*," he looks a question up at Mike.

"Value."

"Value y-our life as m-much as I v-value? Value my b-ike you won't f-fu—" The kid looks up at Mike and laughs.

"Fool around with it," Mike finishes for him.

"No. It says—"

"Never mind," says Mike, walking away toward the bar as all the kids start to scrimmage around the new hero, shouting, "What does it say? Tell me. No, tell me, Johnny." Mike reaches in the pocket of his jeans and pulls out a crumpled five-dollar bill. He says to the biggest kid, "That's for you if nobody touches my bike while I'm in there."

"How long you gonna be?" the kid calls after him, but Mike ignores him, sticking the bill in the top pocket of his jacket as he goes through the door. One foxy little tighty leaning in the doorway tries to avoid his eyes, but he looks until she glances over and then he winks at her. The girl turns away to hide her face, trying not to giggle, and as the door closes behind him Mike catches the scurry of her friends gathering round to find out what happened.

There's windows all along the front of the barroom. That's one of the things you've got to love about this place: back in Ontario there's some kind of law against seeing the sun while you're drinking. He sets his helmet on a table by the window, where he can look at the train station and the mountains and keep an eye on the crowd of kids around his bike. The big kid's got his arms spread to block the others from actually touching anything, letting them come up one at a time to look at the paint job and try to read what it says on the tank. There's nobody else in the bar, but Mike can hear someone banging around in back. He's got a forty-miles-of-gravel thirst, and after a few minutes of waiting he calls out. "Anybody home?"

The banging stops, and a woman appears behind the bar. She's got straight dark hair and gorgeous tits, loose under a black t-shirt. And on the t-shirt, stretched over those gorgeous tits, is a pair of golden wings, and the words, Harley Fuckin' Davidson. And she's got both hands on the bar, and she's giving Mike the once-over, and she sees he's giving her the once-over back, and she tilts her head and says, "What can I do for you?" and Mike picks up his hat and gloves from the table and walks over to the bar, and takes a stool.

"I'll have a Canadian," he says.

The girl puts both elbows on the bar right in front of Mike, puts her chin on her hands so her face is about level with his, and says, "I'm Canadian."

Mike lets it hang in the air for a second, then he winks and says, "How 'bout a beer for starters?" The beer's perfect, icy cold, and they flirt while he drinks. After a while he asks, "What's your name?"

"Gale," she says. She puts her chin in her hands again. "G-a-l-e. Like the wind. What's your name?"

This time he sets his glass aside and imitates her.

"Hurricane," he says, his face about a foot from hers. "What time do you get off?"

She looks around at the empty bar.

"Soon as you're done your beer."

The walls upstairs in the Caribou were unfinished drywall, in some places pink insulation, grey-black in one patch where a hole in the poly had been letting dust and soot from the room get into the fibreglass. Mike remembered about his bike, and wondered how long the kid would watch it for five bucks.

"Hey, it's okay, you know," Gale said, tangling her fingers in his chest hair. "It can happen to anybody. At least you didn't give up." Mike looked at his watch. "No, seriously," she said. "I love head. It was great."

"Whoa," Mike said, shaking his head to clear his eyes. "What was in that joint?" He rolled to the edge of the bed, looking around for his pants. "I'd better go check up on my bike."

Mike runs into Gale once in a while. He doesn't know if she's got a big heart or a bad memory or if she's just a born optimist, but she always acts like he was the greatest stud she ever met, and she can't wait to get him back in the sack. "Hey, Hurricane," she'll say, and she always touches him: on the arm or the shoulder if they're on the street, but in the Capital she'll put her hand on his chest, or reach up and touch his cheek, and give him that look like he's a bowl of ice cream she's just about to lick clean. One Friday night in the Whitehorse Inn she came along and plunked herself in his lap and planted a kiss on his lips.

"Heya, Hurricane," she yelled over the noise of the band, "when you gonna come back and blow my house down again?"

"Very next trip to Carcross, sweetheart."

"I'll be waiting."

He wishes other people would pick up on calling him Hurricane. Now, there would be a nickname he could handle. Not much chance of a change now, but.

"So hey, Pigpen? Why's she call you Hurricane?" Big Jack asked after she jumped up and danced away.

"I don't know," Mike grinned back, "maybe after the song?"

"Fuck's the song got to do with you? You're not a fuckin' fighter."

"Or a coon," Animal chipped in.

"I don't know. 'Cause the guy's in the pen?" Mike sang against the band: *"Put him in a prison cell for some thing he never done."*

Animal scoffed, "That ain't how it goes."

"Something like that."

"Anyways, what's this 'never done' shit?" Big Jack said.

"Yeah, well."

Three times in court, Mike pled guilty every time, although he shouldn't have, only every time the lawyers said forget it, all you'll do is piss off the judge. That time in Mississauga it was because the guy was a bouncer: legal aid lawyer told him the judge would back an authority figure every time.

"Even some Nazi prick bouncer in a joint called the Brain Drain?" Mike wanted to know. At least he didn't do time on that one. Too bad he was still on probation when that crazy fag came onto him in that place in Oshawa. Probably overreacted a little on that one, but Jesus, what was the fag thinking? Did Mike look like a queer to him? Not that he hurt the poor little prick, but he

caused a bit of commotion; a couple of chairs went over and a beer got spilled on someone, and the faggot ended up on his ass on the floor. Mike didn't even push him; he just grabbed him, went to smack him one, and then changed his mind and let go, and the guy went ass-over on the floor and Mike sat back down and apologized to the people nearby. Bouncers kept out of it, but they must have made a phone call, because just when Mike was trying to buy a beer for the guy who got wet, the cops arrived, the bouncer at the door pointed at him, and they were on him like a ton of bricks. He didn't even fight back, hardly, but they had to say he did in their report, to justify the shitkicking they gave him. He did ninety days for that one and the judge called him a brute or a bully or some bullshit, and told him he was facing hard time if he ever saw him up on anything involving violence again.

Pleading guilty the last time was about the hardest thing he ever had to do; he walks into his own place and his old lady's ex-husband is there, and he's shoving her around the kitchen. Christ, what would anyone do? Mike didn't know about the guy's heart. Which was a piece of crap like the rest of him, apparently, and cacked before Mike could even get him out the door. Turns out the guy in the apartment next door had a grudge against bikers, swore he heard Mike beating up Nellie and then the husband. Nellie's word wasn't much good for anything because her social worker had her down as a cocaine addict and an alcoholic, although she wasn't either, really: she just had a tendency to get on a tear once a while. Trouble was, after her husband croaked—not an ex at all, as it turned out, she was lying about the divorce—she started hitting the bottle. By the time Mike was due to go to court, they'd taken her kids away again and she was on a full-blown toot. She showed up at his lawyer's office drunk, told three different stories, tried to bum money, and had a crying jag. The lawyer told Mike all this in the interview room at the Durham County lock-up. You want to plead not guilty, he said, with her for your only witness? Mike wound up pleading guilty to aggravated assault, because manslaughter would have meant ten years with no parole, and the lawyer told him he'd get two and a day this way. He got five, in maximum security. The second week he was in Kingston a guy on his block jumped off the tier, smashed like a sack of bottles on the concrete.

"Only two things you can't get," an old con said," is pussy and out. Might as well make do with what's available."
"Fuck that shit," Mike told him.

It was good with Nellie. When she was off the bottle. When her past wasn't haunting her: old husband, old debts, old so-called friends looking for a handout, a place to crash. Worst of all, three scared, snot-nosed kids who came and went, in and out of Child Welfare, staying at Grandma's, clinging to each other, never sure if it was safe to start trusting again. Little Shawn would be the first, burying his head deep between Nellie's big, soft, beautiful boobs, sucking his thumb, one eye open, because things can always turn nasty. Lately they'd been doing all right, the kids. Donovan had just about quit pissing the bed, and they'd all started to open up to Mike, one at a time, starting with Shawn, and then seven-year-old Carey, the oldest, always sweeping that shank of stringy hair out of her face, wanting him to help her read. Now they'd be in some foster home again, or maybe two foster homes, or three. That's the worst thing about all of it.

Some greasy little speed freak from Nellie's street family showed up one time, all smiles and smarm, with some kind of hidden threat under everything he said. Nellie acted glad to see the guy when he showed up at the apartment door, gave him a beer, introduced him. Kurt or something, his name was. But when Mike got fed up with the guy's bullshit and insinuations, and booted him down the stairs, she jumped into his arms and said, "My *man*. *That's* what I been missing." She took him by the front of his t-shirt then and pulled him into the bedroom, turning him around and shoving him backwards onto the bed and yanking his boots off.

And oh goddamn, her lips and her fingers, her brown hair in his face dangling long on his chest, belly, thighs, nipples poking him as her breasts stroked his chest, her belly round and brown, her ass a strip of white, tits white up to there and then oh God tanned in two stencilled arcs by her bathing suit and her cheeks dimpled out in that chubby smile, her lips on his, on his tits, on his belly, on his prick, oh God, goddamn, goddamn cocaine and the fuck who invented it, and me helpless, no help, behind bars, useless, couldn't be there, couldn't help, couldn't keep back the street, that slimy little prick pimp pulling her back and no Mike, no friend, not one, to kick him down the fucking stairs, and mail day getting the letter, Nellie ODed, oh Jesus Christ—bound to happen, his mom said—sooner or later, Christ—don't blame yourself, Christ, Christ, never wanted anything so bad as out of there that day, felt like I could tear down walls, break down the walls, break down, break down.

And Dinnie. His black-eyed cellmate Dinnie Boy—the old con said, *Face like a girl and a butt like two pups under a blanket, what'd you do, pay off the guards?*—Dinnie knew. That Mike cried himself to sleep that night. Stood beside his bunk. Stroked his head. Said, Cry, cry. And Mike didn't bust his face. For stroking his head. For saying *Cry: might as well. It's all you got.*

Getting out of jail, getting out of Ontario, transferring his parole, moving to Whitehorse, going to work for the railway, finding a cabin, getting settled: it kept him occupied a summer and a winter. Gale was the first woman he'd been with since Nellie. Maybe he just wanted too hard for it to be perfect: a joint of good Colombian and a wild fuck with a wild chick with beautiful tits and no inhibitions; it was like a fantasy of Nellie how she could have been, without all her low-life baggage. Like a cleansing: like cleaning Nellie, and Kingston Pen, and all that ugly old shit out of his system once and for all, making room for some clean Yukon air, some good, clean, easy headspace. Maybe the whole problem was just that he tried too hard for it to be perfect.

Sometimes Mike feels like two people: like there's him and then there's him watching him, listening in on his thoughts. If he doesn't think it to himself in plain words, then himself the watcher will never know that all the time Gale was licking and sucking and stroking and nuzzling him into half a hard-on that would wilt to nothing as soon as she straddled it, he could only get even part-way there if he closed his eyes and imagined the lips and fingers so expert, so willing, so forgiving, were not Gale's at all or even Nellie's though he tried, but Dinnie's, Dinnie-Boy's full red woman's lips that he never knew, never touched, out of pride, and never will now because that was prison and this is life.

.303

"Sky? Sky?"

"A-abe. I'm trying to sleep."

"Look. It's like ten o'clock in the morning or something."

"No, it's not, that's the midnight sun."

"Right. Come on. Listen. Do you think, like, if you could read minds, that everybody would seem twisted?"

"Or is it just you? I don't know, Abe. Probably most people would be totally boring. They'd be thinking about whether fabric softener's good for the environment. Look, if you're going to keep me awake, you better make with the cup of tea."

"Okay, I'll get up in a minute."

"Yeah, I'll bet you will. Hey."

"Mm."

"Quit for a sec. Let me get up, I've got to go to the bathroom.... So when you say twisted."

"What?"

"Twisted."

"You're going to have to speak up."

"Just a minute.... I had the water running. When you say twisted, what are you talking exactly?"

"You know, twisted. Fucked up. Come here."

"You mean like, sexually twisted, or axe-murderer twisted, or what?"

"No. Or partly. Sex, I mean, not axe murder, Jesus, come on. Or just, you know, weird shit that comes into your mind. Like what you said there. About fabric softener."

"Mm, that's nice. Fabric softener's not twisted, it's just boring. Does this mean you're going to start getting weird on me? I can't wait."

"Okay, so what would be weird? Tell me something weird you think about."

"Softer. That's nice. The weirdest thing I think about is you, Abe. But I do that a lot. Mm. Does this mean you're not going to make tea?"

***

The dream comes back almost every night. Connie looks in the mirror, and sees a man. The man could be her twin brother. He disappears from the mirror, and she turns to find him behind her. When she touches him, he disappears, but only from view. He's all around her, everywhere at once. She still feels his hands on her back. His fingers walk down her spine, her hands find his ass and she cups it, enjoying the girlish little swell of plumpness on top of the hard muscle. She searches his chest with her tongue, finds his nipple. The musk of his armpits makes her knees wobble. She speaks to him. I want to see you, she says. He doesn't reply. Please, she says.

She knows who he is. All human embryos begin life as girls. At three months, about half decide to grow a penis and start down the road to success. The man in Connie's dream is herself. He's the man she could have become, had she taken that first step. Except he was never let out into the world to develop a beer belly or a sense of authority, to learn to wear a suit or a set of coveralls as if they were armour. He wears no scars, no blemishes, no facial hair. He's perfect. She feels his body up against her. All along the length of her skin he touches her. Her pores open, and he enters. He fills her, her whole skin is full of him. No, she says, no. Don't. Not like this.

It's cold in the cookshack at night. Connie wears flannel pajamas. When she wakes, they're damp with sweat, and she's chilled. Connie wants a man. She wants to live with him, to sleep with him and wake up with him, to smell him on her body, and to leave her own smell on his. She wants to cook breakfast, to watch him make supper. She wants to have sex. Lots of sex every day, to banish the dream guy, to banish Jason.

"Dreadful, isn't it?" Connie had noticed this woman earlier, across the tiny room, leaning on Annie's built-in plywood desk in her improbable Morticia Addams dress, smoking and pouring herself short drinks from a bottle she kept in her black shoulder bag. She had just wiggled across the room—the dress being designed to permit no other gait—rested two elegant fingers on Connie's shoulder, and was talking in her ear, managing to convey by posture and gesture that she drew the line at shouting to be heard above the thumping stereo and the bellows of drunken schoolboys. "You look much too interesting for this party. Do you know somewhere we could go?"

Before that evening, Connie had never smoked weed except with Curtis, in his basement room, where his parents never bothered him. It always gave her a kind of cozy, cuddly feeling, like putting on warm pajamas and snuggling down into bed. This was something else altogether: she'd been seized by a sense of fear and excitement like stage fright times fifty. Every encounter made her nervous, and every few seconds brought another encounter, most of them with drunk guys who said crazy things and offered her beer. Never having developed a taste for beer—girls in Markham didn't drink beer—she refused the first dozen or so offered, and then finally accepted one, just for show. The party was, she couldn't deny, dreadful, but she was much too wired to go back to the Nunnery and sit alone in her room.

"Um ... ," she said. Where was there to go? There was a student pub, the Commoner, but you had to walk about a mile to get there, and it would probably be like this party, only more so. There was the common room, quiet as a library most nights, but wouldn't that seem like a boring place? With a gentle, intimate pressure on her shoulder, the woman turned Connie around and led her a few steps out of the room to where the noise was less of an assault.

"Anywhere?" she said.

"Oh," Connie said, "there's the footbridge. But—" She looked in doubt at the black dress.

"Here." The woman held out her shoulder bag. "Hold this." Everything was so unreal by then that Connie wasn't more than slightly shocked when the woman wriggled out of the dress, disappearing into it for several seconds, and reappearing in a leotard and tights, looking for all the world like she was about to turn cartwheels. She stuffed the dress in her bag without taking it back, and then said, "Back in a sec, I just have to grab my jacket."

When she returned and the stairway door closed on the noise, she turned to Connie and said, "Thank God there was a reasonable human being in there. I'm Natalie."

"Hi Natalie," Connie said, wondering what qualified her as reasonable. "I was glad to get out of there, too."

They stand on the sweeping footbridge and look back across the water at the lights of the campus. Looming at the water's edge, the tall dome of the library building appears as bands of light and darkness.

"It's like a fairy castle," Natalie says. "What river is this?"

"The Ottonabee. Look straight down at it."

Looking toward the library, the river seems to loop past in placid swirls, but below their feet, a long way below, it rushes threateningly. They stare at it till they shiver and have to look away.

"Are you a student?"

"Yes, first-year arts. You?"

"God no. I came up with a friend to visit this guy. Don't ask why she wanted me along, it would take all night—and she's been in the sack with him ever since we got here."

"Where will you stay?"

"Well, theoretically, in his room, like on the floor, but I'm not even sure where it is, and I kind of doubt they're going to come looking for me."

"Oh, you can stay in my room."

"Dahlink, how vunderful of you," Natalie says, in a perfect Zsa-Zsa accent, and reaches into her bag for the bottle she was sipping from earlier. "Care for a schnort?"

"Thanks. What do you do, anyway?"

"I'm a magician."

"Like, a pull-rabbits-out-of-hats magician? Or a wicked witch magician?"

"Vell, I don't know about vicked, dahlink, but zertainly a vitch. But actually I'm an entertainer. It started out as a comedy act, in clubs, well, in this one club, and the magic was just this sketch I used to do. But it's taken off. Maybe you've heard of me, Madame Nat?"

For a split second, Connie considers pretending, and then she shrugs no.

"Maybe you don't get to TO much?"

"Actually, I live there. Or almost."

"Almost?" The arched eyebrow, the—is that German?—accent. Connie's guessing Marlene Dietrich. "Vy, vere do you live?"

"Well, here, really, but my parents' place, where I grew up, is Markham."

"Markham?"

"Immediately east of Toronto. On the Scarborough border. Bedroom suburb."

"Dahlink, I sink zat's Green Acres, not ze city."

Zsa-zsa is back. Or it might be Eva.

"I know zis Markham. Richest town in Canada. Dahlink, are you rich?"

"I'm sure as hell not. My parents are kind of borderline. I didn't grow up real rich. Not by Markham standards."

"Zort of lower-upper-middle class?"

"Hey, lighten up, will you?"

"Dahlink, don't be ovended. I love ze rich."

The next morning Connie and Nat are sitting across from each other in the cafeteria, finding, somehow, some humour in two middle-weight hangovers, holding their heads and rolling their eyes, when the cute guy who opened the door to the North Wing for Connie appears in the food lineup, hands in pockets, elegantly slouched, chatting easily with the person next in line.

"Don't look," Connie says, "but he's right there."

"Oh my God. You sure it's Him? But I'm not ready yet. I haven't made my will, or—"

"Oh shush. The guy I was telling you about, the cute one, with the curly hair, who kind of warned me about that party."

Of course, by whatever magic it is that lets people know when they're being watched and talked about, he looks over, smiles, says some parting word, and comes over.

"Hi," he says. "How did you enjoy the party?"

"I didn't stay long."

"I didn't think you would. My name's Jason, by the way."

"Oh. Oh hi. I mean, I'm Connie."

"Ahem."

"And this is Natalie."

"Hi Natalie. I don't remember seeing you before. Do you live in the Nunnery too?"

"Dahlink, how sveet of you! But no, I'm chust slumink."

"Well, I'm delighted to meet you. Not all of the North Wing is like the Zoo, Connie. The top floor is co-ed, and people are a little more—what shall I say, mature? I'll make sure you hear about the next party upstairs. I'm sure you'll like it better. Oh look. My friend's saving my place and he's reached the food. Nice talking to you."

"Oh-oh," Natalie said, once he was out of earshot. "The Perfect Jew."

"The what?"

"Oh come on, honey, look at the guy: handsome, smart, nice manners, positively reeks of money. If it wasn't for the schnoz, your momma would love him."

"Schnoz? His nose? What's wrong with his nose?"

"Nussing dahlink, it's a divine nose. It's chust a fery chewish nose."

Jason was not, it turned out, Jewish at all. Connie's mom would have loved him, if their thing had lasted long enough for her to meet him. The black curly hair and strong nose and chin came from his great-grandfather, he said, who was Hungarian. Hungarian nobility, actually, he said, as if apologizing. The other three-quarters was pure WASP. Natalie was right about the money—father a bone specialist, mother a Rosedale socialite—and the manners!

"It's your first time, isn't it?"

"M-hm. Not yours?"

"Listen, you're sure you're okay with it? Just be in charge, all right? That's the most important thing. You be in charge. Everyone's different, right? If you don't like something, just say so. My feelings won't be hurt, I promise."

It melted her when he said that. And then she melted and melted, burst and melted and soaked into the bed asleep, and then woke up in love for the first time. Later she wished she had his words on tape:

"You be in charge. If you don't like something, say so. My feelings won't be hurt. I promise."

"I promise."

Rowan idles her machine for a minute, lets her back have a rest; Tony doesn't expect you to kill yourself, long as you get the job done. A movement over by the bunkhouse catches her eye, and she looks to see Connie hanging out sheets. There's a huge propane dryer, but it sucks up propane like mad so they don't use it much. Connie's getting pretty good at hanging out the sheets. A couple of months ago she'd have had one end trailing on the ground, like she'd never hung laundry in her life. Maybe she hadn't, it's hard to know: for a chick from Toronto, she sure doesn't talk much.

Or she talks, but not about herself. Always questions: how do you do this, why do you do that? The first time Rowan saw her, she looked like such a little know-all, an instant expert, fresh in from the city with a briefcase, or in this case a packsack, full of ideas. But she's not like that at all, once you get to know her. It's more like she's this big empty head going around saying, fill me, fill me. Oh sure, she can be a bit snooty about some stuff. Like Dago and Tony: some of those nights you could just tell she'd have loved to have a toke instead of going with Rowan down to the creek, but she couldn't bring herself to hang out with those guys, because they didn't fit with the way she figures guys should be, whatever that is.

Still, she has a cool way with her Rowan can't help but like. The way she stood up to Ida was perfect. Third day on the job, maybe, she said at supper, just like it was one of her endless questions: "So, Tony, is it some kind of camp tradition that the cook is the bullcook's boss?" Poor Tony loves Ida's cooking, he's terrified of losing her. He hemmed and hawed for a minute and then said, "In the kitchen she is." Next day, Ida tried to tell Connie how to burn garbage. Tony had already showed her, and she didn't need any more telling, but that's Ida's way; if you're doing something within hearing range, she'll tell you a better way to do it. Connie says she turned around and said, "Oh, is this the kitchen?" Apparently Ida just walked away. No doubt she was on about her third shade of purple by the time she reached the door. Anyway, you could see her after that minding her manners. That's the way to handle people like Ida, but Rowan never expected to see it in a twenty-one-year-old kid from Toronto. Cute kid, too. Not that Rowan's interested. Not this time. She's getting too old for young, straight, curious women who have just discovered guys can be assholes and think she'd make a nice safe alternative. Won't matter a whole lot after tomorrow, anyway; Connie's given her notice, she's heading back. For a while there, she was talking about maybe sticking around, but Rowan knew all along she'd never do it. The snow came down the hillsides to about a hundred feet from camp last week. That day, Connie gave her notice.

"What, you don't like my snow?" Tony said.

"On Christmas, maybe," she told him. "Not in September. Anyways, I should be getting back."

University already started, but apparently you can still get in. Rowan doesn't know about any of that stuff; it's nearly twenty years since she dropped out of high school in Grade 10 and went to work on her father's claims. First time she ever heard her mom yell at her dad. Worked out in the long run, though, she learned a lot of stuff they'd never have taught her in school. She can run just about any kind of equipment, she's a pretty good mechanic and a better welder, she can do a bit of surveying, build a log cabin, hunt, fish, handle a canoe, a motorboat, a Ski-Doo, and a dog team. Between those things, she manages to make a living. What could be better? She thanks her stars she didn't have any brothers. If her folks had had boys, they'd probably have made her into a girlie. As it was, the old man was glad to have a son, even if it was a girl.

She's looking forward to seeing her dogs again, to getting them out to the bush, getting set up for winter. Tony wanted her to work right till freeze-up, but she gave him plenty of notice that she had to be out way sooner than that. She plans to canoe into the bush before the shore ice gets too thick, and there's things she has to take care of first.

Just as she's about to get back to work, a green pickup appears over the hill, pulls up in front of the bunkhouse in a big hurry. It's too far away to see the guy's face, but after a minute she knows him from his hillbilly hat and the bouncing way he walks. It's that goof Gary, from Dawson. He goes over to where Connie's working. She has to look over her shoulder to talk to him. The way she does it makes her back arch up, the cheeks of her ass push out. Rowan looks away. When she looks back again, Connie has stopped working and turned around. There's something funny about the way she's standing. Something's wrong. What's going on? What's Gary doing way the hell out here, anyway? Suddenly Connie bursts and runs into the bunkhouse.

Rowan should really be getting to work, but she has to know what's going on. Just as she's pulling the loader up beside Gary's truck, Connie comes running out of the trailer with a gun in her hand. A .303. Rowan's .303, goddamnit.

"Hey, hold on a minute, sister," she calls, jumping down from the cab. "Where do you think you're going with that?"

"Oh, Rowan. Jesus Christ."

"What?"

"It's Dale," Gary shouts over the idling loader.

"Here, gimme that," she says, taking the rifle out of Connie's shaking hand. "What's Dale?"

"He's coming here with a gun," Connie says.

"I didn't say that," says Gary. "I said he *could* come here."

"He shot her."

"Who?" Rowan says. "Andra?"

Connie nods.

"Not dead," Gary says.

"How bad?"

"They took her to Whitehorse. She ain't gonna die. But Dale doesn't know that. He's in the bush. He probably thinks she's meat, man."

"So how do you know he's coming out here?"

"Hey, that's not what I said, man. I just said he could be. I guess he was in the Eldo the other night and he was saying some stuff about knowing where Connie was now, how he'd been asking around. Pretty heavy duty, man. So...."

"So why the hell aren't the Mounties here?"

Gary shrugs. Rowan leans the gun against the machine, climbs in, and shuts it off.

"All right," she says, stepping back down, "what do you say we go get a cup of coffee and see if we can get the cops on the phone?"

"Well, if that's what you're into," Gary says, doubtfully.

"Well, why not?" Rowan asks.

"Dale's got a radio phone in his truck, man."

"So what? Even if he's monitoring, it's not like he doesn't already know where she is."

"What if he gets here ahead of them?" Connie asks.

"I don't know," she says. "What were you going to do, shoot him? 'Cause, if you were, you should have brought the clip for the gun."

"Oh. Should I go and get it?"

"No. But Gary should. Give him the key. You stay with me. We'll go and make Ida get us a coffee, and we can decide what we'll do about the cops after that."

Ida's busy doing her prep for supper when they come in. There's a counter beside the stove, and she's standing at it, chopping an onion. Her eyes are watering, and when she wipes them with the sleeve of her right hand, it looks like she's going to stab herself in the shoulder with the kitchen knife. Connie pours the coffee. Her hands are shaking, and she spills it on the counter. Everything is always exactly in its place in Ida's kitchen, but for several seconds Connie can't think where the J-Cloths are. She hears Rowan on the radio phone.

"... Crow Creek," she's saying. "No, the other Crow Creek. Yeah. End of the Partridge Lake Road. Yeah, about twenty miles in. No. No, but ... look, I know this guy. What? He already shot someone."

Connie catches the tone of frustration rising in Rowan's voice, and turns to focus her attention. Fear has a grip on her stomach.

Her senses all seem to be functioning at about a hundred times their normal level; she actually feels her nostrils flare, thinks fleetingly of the coyote that comes down the hill in the mornings and stares at her while she burns the trash, his nose searching the breeze. When he fixes in, quivers steady on one current, she always imagines it's her he's found in the mix of odours, that he's savouring her, collecting data, passing judgement.

The angrier Rowan's voice gets, the hollower Connie's stomach feels. She's shouting into the phone now. "What? What the hell good is that going to do? You're forty friggin' miles away. Look, she's leaving for Toronto tomorrow. Just get her to Whitehorse and out of the—what? I can't hear you. You'll have to speak up. Bastard," she says. "He's doing that on purpose. CAN YOU HEAR ME? Shit."

By the time Rowan puts the phone back in its cradle and comes to sit down, Connie's squeezing her coffee cup with both hands like she's trying to wring it out. Ida comes around the counter, wiping her hands on a cloth.

"What the hell's this all about?" she snaps.

"Dale," says Rowan.

"Dale who?"

"Stoltz."

"What about him?"

"He shot Andra."

"Christ. Dead?"

"No."

"So what's this got to do with you? And what in the name of Christ are you doing in here with that thing?"

Both Connie and Rowan ignore her.

"What," Connie says to Rowan, "they won't come out?"

"Cop I spoke to's there by himself. Everybody's out searching for Dale."

"But—why don't they look here? He's coming here."

When the door bursts open, Connie dies: heart stops beating, brain activity ceases. When she comes back to life, Gary is still in the doorway and she's halfway out of her seat, so she couldn't have been dead for long. To make up for having stopped, her heart goes triple time.

"Did you get the clip?" Rowan says.

"No, no," Gary says. It suddenly strikes Connie that Gary's as agitated as she is. He fiddles with the door handle, and then says, "What room?"

"Second one," Rowan says. "Did you get the keys?"

"Uh, no. I er—"

"Connie. Connie. Wake up. Give him the key."

"Key?"

"The room key? Automatic locks, remember? You must have used a key to get the gun. Never mind, here." She fishes a key-ring out of her jeans pocket and tosses it across the table to Gary. He almost fumbles it, but recovers. "The brass key," she says. "Clip's in the drawer beside the bed. Bring the box of ammo, too."

For Connie, this situation, hideously real though it is, has taken on a quality of hallucination.

Nat, Nat, you were right. It is the gold rush. I'm at a gold mine in the middle of nowhere and there's a man in Dawson City with a gun who wants to kill me. But Nat, listen, this is the worst part: the RCMP won't come and save me. What do I do?

"What do I do?"

"Just lick your finger and stick it in the bag. Not too much. Yeah, that's about right. Tastes awful."

"Eck! Jeesh, this stuff is awful."

"Zat's fot I chust said, dahlink. Let's have some champa-gne."

"How long does it take?"

"Chust a couple of minutes, dahlink, until ze bubbles get to your head."

"No, the MDA?"

"Oh, not long. Where's your glass?"

That was the only time Connie ever tried hallucinogens. It was all too much for her: the weird pulse in the crystalline patterns of light around the street lamps, the constant sense of wonder, the sharp edge of fear underlying it all, her entire body so overwound it could snap at any minute. It was like this: the same sense that nothing is real, nearby voices booming and muffled, as if amplified to be heard from a distance, the lens of her vision so narrowly focussed that unless she's looking straight at something, it's a blur. Her hand shaking so badly, her coffee cup rattles on the table.

"All right, let's calm down here," Rowan says. "Rule number one: don't panic. Sit down and take stock, okay?"

"Yeah, okay."

"Start with the difficulties, my dad used to say." She counts them on her fingers. "One: Dale's flipped it this time, and he knows where you are. Two: cops won't come and escort you out. On the plus side, you're outa here tomorrow. Dale's gonna come back to earth long before he can follow you to Toronto. Biggest problem right now is, there's only one road out of this place."

"Yeah?"

"If we meet him on the road ... okay, we'll get Gary to drive out first. If he meets Dale we'll turn back."

"But—"

"I know. But what else you gonna do?"

Gary comes back with the clip in his hand. Rowan takes it and examines it before pushing it into its cavity in the bottom of the gun.

"Cops won't come," she says.

"Figured that," says Gary. Rowan looks up at him, surprised. "Highway and the ferry, right?" he says. "They lock them two up, figure in their fuzzy little pig brains they've got it covered. Nobody gets out alive, comprende? So, like, I figure, we vamoose, man. Case he gets around them. Down the old dusty before he shows up here, right? Get her to Whitehorse pronto, eh?"

"Right. You go first, I'll come behind with her."

"Huh? Oh. Yeah. Okay. But what if—"

"Hit him. Try and take his rad out. And your own, so he can't take your truck. Better wear your seat belt."

"Are you fucking kiddin' me, man?"

"Well, I don't know then, do whatever you figure. Try not to get shot. Get your stuff, Connie. Make it fast, will you?"

Cop Shop

Whitehorse International Airport. So-called, no doubt, because you can charter a four-seater to the nearest Indian village across the Alaska border. Or a jet to Fort Nelson, Fort Saint John, Grande Prairie, Vancouver, and Toronto, with connecting flights to places like Baffin Island and Frobisher Bay. The terminal building is a hangar. In lieu of luggage carousels, there's a kind of barn at the end of the building where the baggage cart drives in and the guys pitch your bags down a wooden ramp. You get on and off the plane on steps that lead down to the runway, just like in Casablanca, which coincidentally happens to be the name of the flea-pit where they stayed last night.

After a night at the Casablanca Motel, Connie's hair smells like an overflowing ashtray. She hasn't slept. She's booked on the milk run and won't be home till past ten at night, Toronto time. It doesn't matter, the only thing that matters is that she got out of camp alive. She rode the whole way on the edge of panic, but nothing happened. When they got to the highway, Gary flashed his lights at them and headed for Dawson, and Rowan turned toward Whitehorse. They heard on the radio this morning that Dale is still at large, so either he's hiding out inside Dawson, or he must have been lying about knowing where Connie was. Either that or Gary got the story wrong. Maybe he knows where she is, but isn't holding a grudge, although Gary was pretty specific about that: he said that Dale was still sitting on one cheek, claiming that the switchblade must have been poisoned, because the infection won't clear up. Connie wondered out loud if it could be true: she had no idea where Nat got the knife. If it came from one of her wacky neighbours, God knows what might be on it. But Rowan told her not to sweat it, because that's just the way Dale gets.

Three guys are sitting on their bags outside the hangar, singing, "Put Another Log on the Fire." They all look like Arlo Guthrie, except unwashed. One of them grins at Connie and Rowan. He has about eight teeth, and they're the colour of rotten bananas. It flashes on Connie that she'd never have believed these guys three months ago. You see rubbies on the streets of Toronto, ratty-looking old men with no teeth, but they look miserable, or if they're happy it's because they're as drunk as it's possible to be without passing out. But in the Yukon you see these guys who look like total bums, and they're having a great time, even when they seem fairly sober. It's as if the myth of the happy hobo found flesh. But why? What do they do in winter? Maybe they jump a freight to Toronto and lie around the streets looking miserable. It's true there's something here that can make people accept a life that would seem rotten anywhere else. These hippies would be in desperation if they had to live in poverty in shacks and schoolbuses back where they came from. Here, they think it's the greatest adventure. She's been doing it herself, never minding the tedium of life in camp, chambermaiding for a gross bunch of guys and taking shit from a crabby old woman—really, it was worse than any job she ever had as a student back east, but she sang while she worked every day, because this is the Yukon, and a lousy job here is some kind of adventure. It seems like it's got something to do with the light, which is a different colour from any light she's ever seen, paler and yet brighter than the sunlight in Ontario, not so much golden as sharply white. Or the constantly changing rhythm of the light, each day since the midnight sun solstice six minutes shorter than the day before, heading toward the dark days of December to start all over again. But it takes more than that to explain the way the place seems to lift people's spirits higher than you would predict from looking at their true situation. She suffers a moment's regret that she has to leave before figuring out what makes the Yukon special, and flashes for a second on Tony shaking her hand at the end, smiling knowingly the way people here love to do, and saying, "You'll be back." The infuriating thing about it is, he was probably right. She doesn't feel finished with the place quite yet.

Connie's just reaching for the door when Rowan takes her arm and spins her around and starts walking away in the other direction.

"Don't panic," she says.

"What?"

"Don't look, but Dale's in there. As soon as we get out of sight of the window, run like hell for the truck."

"Hey, change your mind? Right on!" the toothless guy calls after them, and he and his friends all laugh.

It's a good thing Rowan insisted on carrying Connie's pack, because she'd never have been able to run with it herself. Her legs seem to have a hard time taking her own weight. In the truck, she sits with her eyes closed, her fists clenched in front of her. She tries not to clench them too hard; she has to feel like there's a bit of squeeze left in them, because when they can't get any tighter, that's when she's going to explode. Her lips are moving. She tries to stop them, but they're out of her control.

Not like this not like this not hunted by a madman not in the middle of nowhere not gunned, gunned down—

"Okay, sister, get a grip on yourself."

"Sister," Connie says. Speaking helps her to control her breathing. "Sister," she says again, and laughs. "My best friend in

Toronto calls me that. But only when she's doing Bogey. Like 'shishter,' you know?"

She hears her own voice. It sounds hysterical, but Rowan's not listening. She's pulling out onto the highway, craning to see better in her rear-view mirror.

"Shit," she says, and then tears out into the intersection. A car has to brake hard for her. Typically, the driver doesn't even honk.

"What?" Connie asks. "Is he coming?"

"Could be. What's he driving?"

"I don't know." There were a couple of vehicles in the yard at Dale and Andra's place. Connie tries to get a picture of them in her mind. "I can't remember."

"Black seventy-nine Chev three-quarter-ton?"

"Could be." They're going much too fast. Connie grabs the armrest on the door to steady herself.

"Four-by-four, white boat rack?"

Boat rack. White. A black pickup with a white metal frame on the back.

"Yes. Yes, oh God, it's him." Her feet come off the floor, her hands go to her head. She hears herself whine like a jet engine.

"Hey, hey! Get a grip on yourself. We're heading for the cop shop. We're all right. Don't sweat it."

"Come on in, bud, have a seat, I'll be right with you. Jill's just putting the finishing touches on dinner. Grab us a couple Cokes, willya, while I finish up with old shitty-bum here. Maddy? Madeleine? If your show's over, you can turn off the TV now. Maddy? Do you hear me? They'd drive you nuts sometimes, Abe, believe me. Maddy, you turn that thing off right now, or I'm gonna give it to Uncle Abel. He's looking for stuff to pawn, you know.

"So, here's the sitch. I talked to the lawyer, and he can get you a deal. He says they'll drop the assault if you plead guilty to mischief. Hey man, you can't expect to trash the soup kitchen and totally walk. He can get you probation, if you agree to take counselling, and live under my care. Come on in here, bro, we can talk while I do this. Never mind, you can hold your nose. They used to make me do this for you, you know that? Cloth ones, too. Ten years old, I could change a whole diaper without taking a breath. Says it would be better if you had a job. I agree. I mean, it's not like you've got any place left you can borrow money, he-said-significantly, if you catch my drift.

"Okay, tiger, you're on the road again. Try to make that one last at least till after dinner, willya? Then it's Mommy's turn. Is it ready yet, hon? Come on, Abe, let's go chow down. Moose roast tonight, made it special to cheer you up. I dunno. I hate to say no hope, you know what I mean? But she sounded pretty definite on the phone. Anyways, you can hear it for yourself tonight. Said she'd call back around seven-thirty. Pass the spuds, please. Look at those. Garden fresh. Wouldn't the old man be proud of those? Anyways, I was thinking maybe a winter in the bush'd do you good. There's that old line shack, top end of the creek. Right on the edge of the line. Bet you the dyke's never even been that far out. Hey, what? That's what she said herself. Seriously. Would I shit you? She come in to look at the line that time, and she's wearing a shirt that says, no kidding, it says Queer Nation on it. So I says, 'How come you're wearing that?' straight out, you know me, and she says, "Cause I'm a dyke.' Just like that. Honest, this is no shit. Oh, excuse me. No poop. Sorry dear. I see so much of the stuff these days. But she's okay, you know. Knew her way around in the bush. You know how you can always tell right away. Other one, the girlfriend or whatever, was kinda clueless.

"Anyways, I says to the lawyer, 'not much he's qualified for,' which is true, you know. I mean, what the hell you gonna do? What the heck, I mean, with your back broken? But I says to him, like, what if he went in the bush for a while, come out and got into the vocational school, learned a sit-down job? No better way to dry out than a winter in the bush. Eh tiger? Here, let me get the snot off your face before it mixes in. Yuck.

"He says that might work, he'd have to check it out. I think it could work out. Amount of stuff you'd need, a one-eighty-five'd be plenty big enough. About an hour airtime, cost you about four hundred bucks. Stereo survive the slide? How much would that fetch? Hey, partner, you'd be hawking 'er anyway. Disability cheque won't pay the rent. Get there in the next three weeks, you can get a moose, smoke a bunch a fish, get some berries. What? So get a little moose, Jesus, your back ain't that bad. Ah, what the hell, she ain't gonna bother you way out there. Nobody in their right mind uses the number of shacks the old man had. Who traps on foot anymore? Nah, she's got a dog team. Took her a whole winter just to widen the trails out so's she could use them. I could hear the o.m. spinning in his grave when she told me that."

"Nat, how come you never have guys up here?"
"Dahlink, I chust get so tired."
"But, don't you ever feel—you know?"
"It gets too complicated, C. I'll take my chances with Big John."
"I don't know how you can do that."
"It's easy, come on, I'll show you."
"No! I mean, no. Thanks. It doesn't appeal. I dunno, it seems so—disconnected."
"Dahlink, of course it's disconnect-ed. I have ze nine-volt reshargable model. A girl can't be too careful nowadays."

"Ladies, could you just step in here, please?"
"He just drove by. If you'd looked out the window when I pointed, you'd have seen him."
"If you'd just take a seat, we'll take a statement."
"I already made a statement." Rowan's voice rises on each word. "My statement is a man's trying to kill her, and he just drove by. If you get on the radio now, you can catch him."

The cop hesitates.

"You people are already looking for him. It's Dale Stoltz. From Dawson."

"Just wait here, please."

The cop is only gone a few minutes. Connie's starting to work her way through her anxieties, pushing each of them in turn down to a realistic level. She's not going to catch her plane today. Accepting this helps. There are always more planes. Nobody's going to shoot her in the police station. She's not going to die here. Not today. She's still very anxious about Dale, about being in a police station, but that's okay. She can name these things. She can keep control.

Connie's greatest anxiety is the anxiety itself. It can take over. In school, they always thought she was on drugs. She'll start to hyperventilate, all her muscles will clench up. No matter how many times it happens, she always thinks she's dying. The panic spirals upward until something external snaps her out of it, or until she accepts death. After that she usually calms down and realizes it was just another attack, and then it's over. Except that she feels completely battered for about three days.

"You okay?" Rowan asks.

Connie nods. "You?"

"Yeah," Rowan says. "I'm okay. I just get frustrated with assholes like that. Christ, he could have friggin' caught him if—"

The cop comes back.

"Have you got him yet?"

"Not yet." He smiles, complacent. Around here, they still pretty much always get their man. Whitehorse, Faro, Mayo, Dawson, they're all one-road towns. And the whole thing funnels down into the Alaska Highway, one road in or out of the whole territory. After the cop takes their statements, he leaves.

"Not exactly what you had in mind, I guess," Rowan says. Connie looks at her, puzzled. "When you came to the Yukon."

"Not exactly," says Connie. "But my friend Natalie told me it was still going to be the gold rush up here."

Rowan laughs. "This the gal gave you the switchblade?"

"No. No. She didn't. She's the one who called me sister."

"Oh, right. What was it you said about that?"

"It's when she does Bogey. 'Lishen shishter,' you know."

"Oh, Bogart, yeah."

"She's an impressionist. And a comic. And a magician, kind of. It's part of her comedy act. She's really good. She just plays little clubs right now. Kind of tacky little places, actually. Some of them are even strip joints. Except they have comedy nights. No strippers. Or not till the show's over. The comedy show, I mean. But she's great, you're going to hear of her one day. Madame Nat. Great stage name, huh?"

Connie talks about Natalie to fill the empty space in the air while they wait for the cop to come back. The room is panelled with the kind of stuff they make office dividers out of, and it has one of those ceilings people put in their basements, with big white cardboard tiles in some kind of metal frame. It's sure to have hidden microphones, probably even cameras. Rowan obviously hasn't thought about this, or she wouldn't have made that crack about the switchblade. It's a good thing she didn't say anything to the cop. Connie certainly didn't. She came close to panic when he asked why Dale was after her. She said it was because she knew he was a wife-beater, but she didn't think he had believed her. He comes in again.

"Did you get him?" Connie says. The cop looks uncomfortable at this question. He came into the room with his mouth open, like he wanted to get the first word in, take control of the situation right from the start, but Connie got the jump on him.

"Er—"

"Jesus," says Rowan. "Where the hell can he go?"

The cop doesn't answer, but it looks to Connie as if he has some guesses he's keeping to himself. What's he thinking? There's always cops all over Whitehorse, it's one of the things you notice about the place. And it's a distinctive-looking truck. Where could he hide it? Could he have sunk it in the river, or in that crazy lake at the south end of town, the one that's the city's water supply, and the float plane dock? Somebody would have seen him. And then she knows.

"Shit," she says.

"Yeah," says Rowan.

"He's in the bush, isn't he?"

The cop says, "We put roadblocks at the South Access, Two-Mile Hill, and the bridge into Riverdale. It's possible he may have crossed the bridge before we got there. He's not on Grey Mountain, and he doesn't appear to be in Riverdale. We're checking the Long Lake Road right now."

"What if he beat you to the South Access?"

The cop doesn't exactly shrug, but his face more or less does.

"Jesus," says Rowan.

"I am not staying in the Casablanca tonight," says Connie. It was bad enough last night, but now they know Dale's actually out there, she cannot possibly sleep in a motel along the highway, with the bush all around stretching for hundreds of miles.

"I think I can find us a place where it's safe," Rowan says.

"We'll need a way of contacting you," says the cop.

"We'll phone you when we know where we're going to be."

He's not too happy about letting them go without a contact phone number or anything, but Rowan insists she doesn't know for sure yet where they'll be staying, and she'll let him know. In the end he has no choice but to let her go. Connie doesn't understand why Rowan's being so standoffish with the guy now, she's the one who was determined to be under police escort.

They walk to the truck in silence. When they close the doors, Connie speaks first. "Why did you do that?"

"Assholes. They're friggin' useless. I know a place we can stay tonight, even if we have to sleep on the floor. Least we'll know Dale won't be coming in the door."

"But couldn't you at least tell them where we were going?"

"Don't think Pigpen would like that too much," says Rowan.

"Who?"

"Guy's place we're heading for."

The place they go to is south of town. There's no roadblock up, but they meet three cruisers, spaced out along the highway.

"He's not going to be doing any driving, anyway."

The place they go to isn't far down the highway, but it's a long way in on a dirt road. It's a fairly typical log cabin, low-roofed and not many windows. The yard's a bit of a mess, though not outstandingly so by local standards: there's a partially dismantled truck, and a few tools lying around it, and a dozen or so empty beer bottles. There's a lean-to against one side of the cabin, with a messed-up stack of firewood along the wall, and a gleaming motorcycle all by itself in the middle of the yard. Two piggy-looking brown and black dogs come out, stiff-legged, and walk around the truck, growling.

"Just sit where you are," says Rowan, unnecessarily. They wait in the cab until the door opens, and a big guy with a grey ponytail comes out and speaks to the dogs. Rowan opens her door and jumps out.

"How the fuck are ya?" the guy says, and comes over and bear-hugs Rowan, slapping her on the back. Connie gets out uncertainly. The dogs come round to sniff at her. They're wagging their piggy little tails now, but Connie doesn't trust them. She's never trusted dogs. Her mom says a German shepherd jumped up and barked in her face when she was three and scared the life out of her.

"They won't hurt you," the guy says.

"Pigpen, this is Connie."

"It's Mike," he says, and stalks around to shake her hand. He's a big grinning bear of a man. "Pleased to meet you, Connie. Real little fox you got yourself this time, Rowan. Come on in."

As they're all turning and crouching to go through the door, Connie doesn't see Rowan's face when she says, "Connie's a friend, Pigpen. From camp. Needs a safe place to stay tonight."

"Oh yeah?" says Pigpen. "Bit of trouble?"

"You heard about Dale? Dale Stoltz?"

"That's that guy shot his old lady?"

"Yeah. You know him, Dale Stoltz. Carpenter from Dawson. Builds log houses."

"Oh, yeah. Scrappy little prick, eh? Yeah, I know him. So he shot his old lady? He still with that broad with the big tits, what's her name?"

"Andra."

"Yeah, Andra, that's the one. Used to work at the Edgewater. She hurt bad? Hear they medivaced her out."

"That's all we heard, too. But he's after Connie. And me, too, by now, no doubt."

"What'd you do to Dale?"

Connie feels herself blush. It's a bit embarrassing on the one hand, but on the other, she knows in advance Pigpen's going to love it.

"I—stuck a switchblade in his ass."

"Yow."

"Not, you know, up his ass," she hastens to explain. "In his cheek. The right one."

"Gettin' a little out of line, was he?"

"Actually, he was beating up on Andra at the time."

"Hoo," says Pigpen to Rowan. "Got yourself a feisty one."

"I told you, Pigpen—"

"Oh, yeah. I forgot. Hey, listen, can I get you ladies a beer?"

Why doesn't Connie hate this guy? He's a sexist jerk. Although it's downright quirky the way these redneck guys around here just seem to accept Rowan for what she is. She tries to imagine macho biker types like Pigpen or Tony, back in Ontario, having lesbian buddies, treating them like one of the guys. She supposes it might be possible, with a woman like Rowan, a tough gal. Brutal gang rape seems a lot more likely, though. *Huh huh huh, show her what she's missing.*

And those are the kind of guys who would look her over like that and say, "Real little fox you got yourself," and Connie would be disgusted, as well as scared. But she's not scared of Pigpen. She even kind of likes him, in a way. He'd be very handsome if he'd just trim his beard. His clothes are actually quite good, if you don't mind contemporary cowboy, and he's clean, despite the name. But anyway, there's something genuine and endearing about him. Maybe after a summer with Tony and Dago, she's just getting acclimatized to northern men. Perish the thought. What would Natalie say? Natalie would say she's nuts for even being here.

"Listen," she says. "How do you know Dale isn't going to come here tonight?"

"I'm a pretty hard guy to sneak up on," says Pigpen.

"Oh, that reminds me," Rowan says, and gets up to go out. She hesitates at the door. "They okay?"

"Sure," says Pigpen. "They know you from before. No problem."

Connie was thinking those dogs would never stop Dale. They're not even big. They scared her, but all dogs scare her. But if Rowan's worried about them—

"What kind of dogs are they?" she asks.

"They're pit bulls. And nobody gets through that door without my say-so."

Rowan comes back in carrying her gun.

"Oh-ho," says Pigpen. "This is gettin' serious."

"Just didn't want to leave it in the truck."

"Hey, nobody goin' in that truck tonight. I promise you that."

"True. But anyways, I sleep better when I can see my gun."

"Me too," says Pigpen. "'Nuther beer?"

Animal Friends

"Abe?"

"Hey, babe."

"Abe, what's going on down there?"

"Uh, well, the bluff came through the wall of the house."

"Yeah, I heard about that. That's not what I mean."

"Yeah. I know. But then I got the guys to help me fix it up, and then—"

"What guys?"

"You know, Pigpen, Big Jack, Backhoe Mike."

"Oh, Abe, you know you can't drink with those guys ... Abe?"

"Yeah, I know."

"Abe, is it true you're going to jail?"

"Uh...."

"Uh, what?"

"Probably not."

"Probably?"

"My brother's got this idea." He tells her about the trapline, about drying out. He realizes just at that moment that she doesn't know anything about him. He doesn't know much about her, either. The first time they went out they talked about John Lennon, Vietnam, health food. They went to the Kopper King and she tried to teach him how to dance to this hippie band, kind of a cross between bluegrass and rock and roll: people's elbows in his ear, workboots stomping all around him, a pissed-drunk guy standing in the middle of the dance floor with a beer and a smoke, smiling all around and trying to put his hand on people's shoulders. They smoked a joint with three of her friends, two guys and another hippie chick named Ruth, in the men's washroom of the bar. Guys came and stood at the urinals and Ruth passed the joint to them, and everybody acted like it was the most normal thing in the world. Abe watched to see if they took it with the same hand they pissed with, but nobody did. The next time they went out, they didn't go out. Abe knows every inch of Sky's body, what she likes to eat, her favourite albums, what politicians she hates most. He knows she can swim like a fish, never learned to ride a bicycle, but has a motorcycle licence. He knows her mother was one of the original hippies, lived in a commune for a while, shacked up with a burned-out old biker, spent half her life on the road. Sky knows Abe grew up in the Yukon, that his father was a trapper, that he broke his back in Faro, that he drinks too much. That's about all. That's what makes this conversation so hard to have: face to face, they know each other like a foot knows an old sock; from a distance, they're strangers. He struggles to explain.

"It's like something you do, you know? Go in the bush to dry out. My uncle did it. Worked for him. Lot of guys—"

"So what do *we* do?"

"We?"

"You and me. Us."

"I, er, thought..."

"What, that I'd dump you?"

"I guess."

"Well, I thought so, too. But I don't know. I still might."

Abe thinks about this for a minute. "Maybe I shouldn't go," he says.

"Why?"

"I, ah, didn't think you'd, like, want to see me. So when Frank said bush, I figured, yeah. What the hell. But if..."

"You want to go to jail instead? What, so I could come see you on visiting day? Couldn't I visit you in the bush?"

Abe hadn't thought of this.

"I—I don't know. I guess so."

"How do you get there?"

"In a plane."

"What does it cost?"

"Couple hundred, I guess. Might be more with skis, I dunno. Or you can walk it. Or Ski-Doo, I guess."

"Hm. Well, you never know. But don't go to jail, because for sure I won't visit you there."

"Sky?" Abe's not sure what he's going to say. Not thanks, exactly, but that he's grateful, glad, something. Relieved is the truth, but how do you say that, exactly?

"Yeah?"

"I'm sorry about this."

"Yeah. Me, too, Abe. Quit drinking."

"So here's the situation. I need to go to Dawson." Rowan sets a bag of groceries on the bare plywood counter. She's been to town while Connie was still sleeping, which is not fair, not only because she's had a shower somewhere and Connie feels like the bottom of a shoe—make that the bottom of a cowboy boot—but because Connie had to take a pee this morning and she had to get Pigpen to walk her to the outhouse, and wait nearby to walk her back. He said it would be okay once he'd gone out there with her and told the dogs she was cool, but Connie would never have been able to leave the outhouse if he hadn't been there. "I called there today," Rowan says, "and the chick who's looking after my dogs has to fly to Halifax, because her dad's about to die. I have to go and get them. Might be able to take them up to the claim. Don't know what Tony'll say, though."

"Oh, Rowan, I totally forgot. You're still supposed to be working."

"Don't worry about that. They can put Chuck on the loader for a couple days. He's underworked anyway."

"Yeah, but can you afford this?"

"Hey, I wanted to quit last week and Tony talked me out of it. I've got a bunch of shit to do before freeze-up. Come to think of it, I don't know why the hell I'm going back. Anyways, thing is, I've got to go to Dawson."

"Have they—?"

"Dale? They're never going to catch him now. Mounties are all from friggin' Saskatchewan or someplace. They're hopeless in the bush."

"So what's he going to do, hide in the bush forever?"

"No fuckin' way," Pigpen calls from the other room. He sticks his head around the door. "He's out there, man. I been listening to the radio. They haven't said fuck all about his old lady. Just that he shot her. All he knows, she's dead, right? He ain't fuckin' hangin' around the Yukon."

"But they're looking for his truck everywhere."

"Dump the fuckin' truck, eh? Fade into the bush, come out someplace else, find a ride outa here. He ain't hangin' around. It's either that or—" he shrugs with his face.

"I've got to go see what I can do about my ticket," Connie says to Rowan. "Could you run me over there? And maybe someplace I could get a shower?"

"Yeah. I got some breakfast stuff here. How about we eat and then I'll run you down to the Y. Grab a shower before you deal with CP Air."

"Sure," says Connie. "Good plan."

In the truck, Rowan talks about Dale.

"I just hope he didn't friggin' shoot himself."

"Shoot himself? Why would he?"

"I don't know. But they do, eh? I mean, you hear about it all the time. Some guy shoots his old lady, shoots himself. Or disappears. Ends up bearshit."

"Ew," Connie says. "He didn't strike me as the type."

"He's not. But then, he loses it, he's not himself anymore. It's something out of whack in his brain."

"Oh." Connie doesn't like excuses like "something out of whack in his brain" but she doesn't have the strength to make an issue out of it right now.

The washroom at the YWCA is dirty, not in the way of a washroom that hasn't been cleaned; it smells of disinfectant, but there's grime on the walls that's been there for so long the janitor probably doesn't even see it. She closes her eyes. The water feels clean so long as she doesn't think about, or touch, the walls.

Driving down Fourth Avenue, Connie sees Dawn, Natalie's sister, walking by. Looks like she's wearing the same granny dress she had on last time she saw her. She's walking arm in arm with a guy Connie met back in June, too, looking like she owns the world. It seems so innocent, she wants to open the window and yell at them, Do you know where you are? Do you know how dangerous it is out there? Please, please, she's thinking, put me on that plane. And yet—

The woman at the airline counter is sympathetic, but she's new at the job, and she doesn't know if she's supposed to give Connie another seat for the one she paid for and missed. She doesn't think so, and she's too busy to find out right now. She asks for a number where she can contact her.

"I'll be right over there on that chair," Connie says, "guarding my luggage."

"Oh, it won't be today, honey. We're overbooked for today as it is. This time of year, everybody wants out." She smiles and shrugs. "I doubt whether you'd get on, even on standby, for at least a week."

In the parking lot, Connie experiences an overwhelming urge to kick something. She looks around and sees a chip bag. It makes a very unsatisfactory target.

"Listen," Rowan says, "I don't know what you're going to do but ... I hate to dump you like this, but if I don't get down to Dawson tonight, my dogs won't get fed. I told Alice I'd be there, so she won't have set anything else up. Must be about, what, eleven o'clock? Seven hours to Dawson in this thing. I better drop you someplace and get on the road."

"Dawson," Connie says. "My paycheque. I never picked up my pay. Shit. I forgot all about it."

"Want me to mail it to you?"

"No. I want to go back for it. I've got nowhere to go around here. And anyway," she says, brushing the soft, newly washed hair away that's tickling her face in the wind, "I never got a chance to say goodbye."

"To who?" Rowan says. "Dago? Tony? I thought you hated those guys."

"No, I don't hate them. They're okay." She hears with Rowan's ears how her tone dismisses them, sees how it makes her look. Condescending. Strictly from Toronto. It makes her feel a little sheepish about saying the next part. "Actually I was planning to say goodbye to the coyote."

"Which one?" There's a laugh in Rowan's voice. Not a malicious one, though.

"There's one that's been coming every day when I burn the garbage."

"Made pals, did you? Give him a name?"

"No."

"Hey, don't be so sensitive. Lots of people give them names. I had an old wolf named Boris used to come around my main cabin all the time. First I thought he was after the dogs, but he never took one."

"What do you mean, took one?"

"They eat them."

"Seriously?"

"Yeah. Easy meat, eh? Not often they get dinner chained to a tree. But anyways, for some reason this guy didn't eat dog. Against his principles or something. Or maybe he was too old to kill one of my guys. They're pretty big dogs. Tried to trap him for a year, but he was way too smart for that. Set snares, the whole bit. Then I just gave up on him. He robbed my traps a couple times, but I figured if I couldn't catch him I might as well learn to live with it. So I called him Boris, I don't know why Boris. Friggin' wolf was so smart, he knew exactly when I decided to give up. Before I gave him a name, I'd never see him if I had a gun on me. After that, he'd hang around, get like fifty feet away from me, armed or not, didn't make a lick of difference. Knew I wasn't going to shoot him once I gave him a name."

Connie is amazed and charmed by this tale. She would have been embarrassed to have given the coyote a name, even if she hadn't told anybody about it.

"Well, I never got quite that close with this coyote. It's just, I don't know, something I want to do. It'll feel like saying goodbye to the Yukon, I guess."

"Well, all right. Let's hit the trail. I got to go out there tomorrow anyway. I've got a cheque coming, too."

"Are you sure it's okay?"

"Sure, why not?"

"I don't want to impose."

Rowan snorts. "No sweat. Nobody home at Alice's. Tons of room."

After they climb into the truck, Connie says, "What finally happened to him?"

It takes Rowan a second but she catches on. "Boris? Died of old age. Froze, actually, I guess, when he got too skinny to hang on. I found him lying in front of my cabin door one morning. I took his hide. Don't know what I'll do with it. Most of it's totally ratty. Nice piece on the back, though. Might make part of a hat or something."

Connie shivers, and Rowan notices.

"Hey, I figure that's what he wanted. Stole a bunch of fur from me, gave me a bit back in the end."

The sun strikes them in the face as they pull onto the highway. All the motorhomes are heading south.

The ferry lineup is all the way down Front Street. Stuck halfway, Connie begins to fret. She knows Dale can't be in Dawson, but still, she feels trapped here. Rowan's pulled up tight behind the car in front, and there's a motorhome just about touching their back bumper. If he came driving along in the other direction, there'd be no escape. To distract herself she watches a beautiful blonde hippie girl working her way along the lineup, going to each car window in turn with a cardboard beer-flat of something for sale. It's not until she's on the third car ahead that it becomes recognizable as jewellery, laid out on a folded sarong or something: mostly earrings, by the look of it.

"Starting to thin out a little." Rowan nods to indicate the street behind her. Connie looks around. Near where they're parked there's a big wooden storefront kind of place with coin-op showers and a laundromat and a little restaurant where you can get coffee and snacks. Next door, the Klondike Visitors' Association parking lot is almost empty. Further up the road there is a handful of shops with kitchy false fronts, and people are wandering in and out of them.

"How do you mean?" Connie asks.

"Friggin' crowds."

"Like in the ferry lineup, you mean?"

"Well, yeah, especially that."

"How long does it get?"

"Oh, it'll go all the way down the street here."

Connie laughs. "We have longer lineups than that in my grocery store."

Rowan looks at her and shakes her head. "To each her own," she says.

"I guess it's easy enough to get on in wintertime."
"On what?"
"The ferry."
Rowan's laugh explodes out of her nose. "In winter? What do you think they do, put it on friggin' skis?"
Caught again. Connie's been sitting here feeling just a bit superior to all these tourists. She, at least, has been around long enough to get a feel of the place, to pick up some of the local jargon, to actually work here. Now she's exposed again as one of those dumb southerners with no concept of winter.
"This freezes?" she says, looking at the broad, swirling, muddy river surging past, and trying to imagine it frozen solid.
"Oh Christ, yeah. Ferry only runs four months."
"What do people do in the winter?"
"Ice bridge."
"What?"
"Ice bridge. Berm up the snow, eh? Two berms, ice road in between."
"Berms?"
"You know. Like windrows? You got snowploughs in Toronto?"
"Of course."
"You know the ridges they leave?"
"Oh, yeah."
"Like that."
"And that makes a bridge heavy enough for cars?"
"Cars? Oh Christ, haul a D8 over there on a low-boy."
Connie knows now that a D8 is a particularly big bulldozer. She decides to let low-boy pass. By this time she feels like a tourist herself. *Christ, I was just about ready to go back and ask the people in the motorhome how long they'd been in the Yukon. Tell them the one about the sourdough.* She laughs out loud.
"What?"
"It's hard to explain."
The girl with the beads comes up to their window. She gives them a Raphael smile and shows them the tray of jewellery.

Rowan shakes her head, but Connie sees a necklace that would go great with Nat's magician's costume. It has one of those glass Moroccan money beads, tubular, and swirled with colour, broken off ragged on each end, flanked by two claws, and then symmetric rows of little red glass beads, all on a leather string. She moves across the seat and leans past Rowan to point.

"How much for that one?"

"That's eighty dollars."

"What are those things?"

"Bear claws."

"Will you still be here tomorrow?"

She shrugs and smiles one of those superior I'm-too-hip-to-predict smiles and Connie just about decides to forget the whole business, when the girl starts fingering the claws, and says, "They're very powerful. They're from a winter bear."

"What's that?" Connie asks.

"A bear, in the wintertime. When they should be hibernating."

"Why does that make them powerful?"

"She chose her own time to die."

"That that old sow griz came into town last winter?" Rowan says.

"Yeah," says the girl. "Strange, wasn't it?"

Rowan shrugs. "I hear she was pretty skinny. Old sow, eh? No teeth left. Game Branch figured she'd never have survived the winter. Must have woke up when she ran out of fat. They're totally disoriented when they wake up in wintertime. Only thing weird about it was no one got hurt. Friggin' dangerous, winter bears."

"What happened?" Connie asked.

"Charlie Mulroony came out of the Downtown, saw her walking down the street, went and got his ought-six out of his truck, and blasted her." Rowan laughs, shakes her head. "Right in front of the bar. Crazy bastard."

"Why did he shoot her?"

"Well, somebody was going to have to do it, eh? Can't just let her wander around. But he might have been smarter to have let the cops do it. They were gonna charge him, eh, but he talked his way out of it. Said the kids were going to be getting out of school in another ten minutes, and he didn't have time to go back in the bar and call the cops. Had a point, actually. Turned out, they even let him keep the bear. Don't know what good she was, old sow like that, not much for fur probably." She laughs, and says to Connie, "Kind of like skinning old Boris." Then, "Where'd you get the claws?" she asks the girl.

"Charlie gave me them."

"Wow. He must have liked you a lot."

"Yeah, I guess he must." The girl smiles, and Connie has a flash of Ida saying, "That's the way things are, sweetie." Connie looks at the necklace. Maybe the old bear was just disoriented. But then why didn't she hurt anybody? Connie likes to think she might have come into town looking for a merciful death. She'll tell Nat that's what happened, anyway, and not spoil the magic by saying the bear was probably just mixed up, like an old lady lost downtown. She looks in her wallet. Twenty-seven dollars.

"Could you loan me some money till we see Tony?" she says.

Rowan reaches in her pocket and pulls out a small roll of bills. "How much do you need?"

"I've got twenty-seven. So, what's that, fifty-three?"

"No can do. I've got about thirty bucks on me."

"Are you coming back to Dawson after you see Tony?"

"Passing through. I was kind of hoping to get all packed up first, and then just come back and pick up the dogs, head right in to Whitehorse."

"I'm going back to Whitehorse soon, too. I can hold it for you," the girl says. "Here, here's my phone number." Connie's surprised when she pulls a business card out of her beaded rawhide purse. Sky Blue, it reads. Registered Massage Therapist. "That's my real business. I just do this for fun, so I can travel around a bit."

"That your name?" Rowan says.

"Yeah, it is. What's yours?"

"Rowan. This is Connie."

"Nice to meet you," says Sky.

"I really want the necklace," Connie tells her. "For a present for a friend. I can give you this much now, to hold it for me."

"There's no need," says the girl. "I can hold on to it for a while."

"No, I want to. It's only twenty bucks, but I'll feel better if you take it. I get my pay tomorrow, I won't need it before then. Take it."

Sky's still reluctant, but she takes the twenty. She starts to put the necklace away in her purse, and then changes her mind. Holding it in her hand, she walks around the front of the truck and comes to Connie's window. Connie rolls it down, puzzled. Sky reaches up and puts the necklace around Connie's neck. "Just pay me when you get to town," she says. Her face is close when she speaks. Connie feels her breath on her cheek.

"I—" she says, and then stops. Sky is already walking away. The ferry lineup is moving forward. It looks like they'll be at the front of the line for the next crossing after this one. Sky turns and waves. Connie watches her in the mirror until the angle of the road makes it impossible to see her anymore.

The noise and chaos are beyond belief. It sounds more like a hundred dogs than seven. When the truck first pulled up, they were standing on their doghouses, or beside them, barking toward the driveway, but when Rowan got out and they saw her, they went completely nuts. They don't bark or howl or make any normal dog noises, they scream. It's the most bizarre sound Connie has ever heard. Rowan strides up to the nearest one. It's huge and hairy, but it leaps up into her arms and she holds it there for a second and then drops it to the ground. It crouches down and dances around her feet, while she claps her hands at it, and then it jumps onto the doghouse. She hugs it and lets it lick her face, and then goes on to the next dog. The first one jumps off the doghouse to come after her, but she sends it back, and it stays. She repeats the performance until they've all been petted and almost all are on their houses. The doghouses are unpainted plywood cubes, and most of them have holes that appear to have been chewed into them. One dog keeps jumping off the house and then jumping back on again as soon as Rowan looks his way. She shakes a finger at him and then waves to Connie to come over. Each dog has a perfect circle pawed into the dirt around its tree, as far as its chain will reach. Between these is a path that looks relatively safe. Connie takes a breath, clenches her fists at her sides, and begins to thread her way toward Rowan. One huge grey dog leaps off its house as she goes past and she freezes, but the dog turns and scrambles to get inside, as if it was Connie who was the great fanged, shaggy monster. Rowan shakes her head.

"Virgil, Virgil," she says. "So shy."

Another, slightly smaller, dog jumps off its house and leaps at Connie. Its chain's too short to reach, and before it even snaps taut, Rowan has barked a command and the dog is back on the doghouse, but Connie's heart stops anyway. When she reaches Rowan, all the dogs are on their houses except Virgil, who is still inside. Every once in a while a dog frantically whines without opening its lips, trying desperately to resist the urge to bark. Rowan quiets it with a finger to her lips, or a word.

"Pet this gal," she says. Cautiously, Connie reaches her hand out toward the top of the dog's head. It sticks its muzzle up toward her hand, and she pulls back, frightened. "She won't hurt you," Rowan says. "Feel this, come on." Connie puts her hand out, lets the dog lick it, and then strokes its head. It feels like angora. "This is Kitty. My number one." Kitty puts her head against Connie's chest and snuggles up. Connie's nearly pushed backwards off her feet.

"What's that mean?"

"My top leader. Incredible dog."

"You mean, she's the boss of all these huge dogs?"

"Nope. That'd be me. She just runs out in front and goes where I tell her to, and they follow."

"Oh."

"Come on, I've got to put feed to soak."

Alice's place is a well-built log cabin, two storeys, a lot bigger windows than most. It's between two wide, fenced pastures. There's a barn at the back of one of the fields, and some kind of big open shed in the other one. There's a wooden trough along the edge of the fence. It looks like a real farm, the first one Connie's seen in the Yukon, except there's no animals. Other than the dogs, of course, which are in the only patch of forest on the property, a stand of lodgepole pines about twice the area of the cabin.

They pack in three blue jerry cans of water from the truck. Rowan carries two as if they weighed nothing, but Connie's hangs against her leg as she tries to walk, and makes her stagger.

"How do you do that?" she says, as she dumps the jerry can down on the plywood floor of the porch.

"Country food."

"I thought all food came from the country."

"Hell no, most people's food comes from the store. You know, Ida's a good cook and all that, but I've been really looking forward to getting back on a proper diet. Stuff I know isn't covered in chemicals."

"I read that they're finding DDT or something in caribou now."

"I know, wouldn't that just piss you off? But it's trace elements, eh? I mean, beef is pumped full of crap these days. Shouldn't eat that shit, you know. Gives you cancer." While she's talking, Rowan is mixing together the most disgusting concoction Connie has ever seen. There's a pinkish brown slop, which she explains is dog food Alice left soaking this morning. Another bucket contains a lump of partially frozen, coarsely ground, fibrous-looking meat. Horsemeat, as it turns out. Not the horses that used to run around these corrals, but blocks of meat from a factory in Alberta, the unconsumable leftovers of a packaged meat industry that ships to France and Japan. Rowan steps outside, comes back in with an axe and, wielding it like a toilet plunger, works at the meat until it softens. As she picks up the bucket of dog food to split it into two pails, Connie's stomach turns. Not long ago, she would have gone away, either outside or on into the cabin, but now she just turns her head, takes a deep breath, and looks back. Connie has made a decision. She's going to help feed the dogs. There are going to be three buckets when it's all put together, so she's going to come along and help carry them. She's terrified, but that's part of the reason she's going to do it. Everybody says sled dogs aren't vicious; Rowan swears none of these dogs would ever bite. Knowing this, she's got to be able to make herself go close to them without fear. And Kitty was a sweetheart—although Connie has always believed that people's dogs pretend to be nice when their owners are around, just so they can get you alone and attack you. But it's become a matter of pride, something she has to do before she leaves the Yukon. She's already thinking about how she'll play it when she tells Nat about this.

The dogs stayed quiet for about ten seconds after Rowan and Connie went into the porch, and then burst into manic barking again. The racket increases as Rowan pours the food. By the time they get back out with the buckets, it's pandemonium out there. They scream and leap and claw at the ground. Around each dog there's a concentrated cloud of dust, and a big general cloud hangs over the whole area. Evening sunbeams slant in through the dust and make patterns among the trees.

"You don't have to help if you don't want," Rowan says, seeing Connie coming out behind her with the third bucket.

"I want to," Connie says, taking a deep breath and hoping she doesn't look too much like Sally Fields. Whenever she does that, that screwing up her courage thing, Nat always calls her the Flying Nun.

"It's all right. It's clean."

"I'm sorry. It's just: I think I might gag."

"I didn't gag. Last night. On you."

"I think I might just not be ready, Jason."

"I understand."

"Come on. A couple of months ago I was a total virgin."

"Listen, it's no problem."

"Yes, it is."

"No."

"It is, I can tell."

"No pressure. I just thought, you know, maybe you wanted to try it."

"I do. I will. Really. Just—don't rush me. It's—you know—kind of, new."

"I understand."

"Will you quit saying that? You make it sound like I've got a problem."

"Not a problem. Just a little hang-up. It's perfectly clean, you know.

"I'm sorry, like I say, I'm just not ready yet."

"I—right. It's no problem. Let me show you something different, okay?

"Uh, okay. What is it?"

"You'll see.

"So how do you get them to do it?"

"What?" Rowan's taking it slow on the Crow Creek Road. She's able to glance over at Connie, no idea what she's on about. Connie realizes she's treating Rowan like an old friend, trying to do what she does with Nat: start in the middle of a conversation and expect her to just pick up the thought.

"Oh, sorry," she says. "The dogs."

"Do what?"

"Mush, or whatever."

"Pull, you mean?"
"Yeah. Pull."
"I don't know. They just do it."
"In the blood, I guess."
"Yeah, that's part of it. But a Lab'll do the same thing. Collie dog, anything just about. I mean, you tie it up to a sled, and if it wants to go anywhere, it has to pull the sled with it. So any kind of dog that likes to go can learn to pull a sled. Half the dogs on the Iditarod are more hound than they are husky."

"Have you ever done anything like that?"

Rowan laughs. "The Iditarod? With my guys? I'd be needing bug dope by the time I got to Nome."

"They're slow?"

"Oh Christ, yeah. You ever seen a racing dog?"

"No."

"Quarter, maybe a third the size of my guys. Short coats so they can run fast and not overheat. Way higher strung."

Now it's Connie's turn to laugh. "Higher strung?"

"What? You think my dogs are nutsoid? They were just happy to see me. It's been a while, eh? They're not always like that. All business out on the trail. Racing dogs are, too, once you get going, you know, but I've tried them on the team, they'd drive you friggin' nuts. You can't get them to sit still while you check your traps. They've got so much jam, they don't start to settle down till you're running them fifty miles a day. On the trapline you do maybe twenty. They just never get over being wired up. I had three of them one time. Thought maybe they'd speed the big guys up, get around the line that much quicker? They ran me round the friggin' bend. Good dogs and all, but I couldn't handle it. Traded them all to a guy in Dawson after one year. That's how I got Kitty. She was too heavy-coated for him. She's a bit wound out compared to the other guys, but she's worth it. Never quit, that dog. You got something like that up front, you'll always go, no matter what."

Connie still hasn't spoken to Rowan about the trapline. She

doesn't know what to say about it, what to ask. She can't say, how could you, but that's what she wants to know. How can you? Are the animals still alive when you find them? Are they suffering? What do you do? Do you have to shoot them? Club them over the head like in that horrible Greenpeace commercial? She loves the idea of Rowan on the trapline, a woman in the bush, doing it for herself. But to set a steel trap, catch an innocent animal by the leg, make it wait there in agony for you to come and get it, look in its eyes as you take its life—how can you?

Rowan manages to time it so that they're pulling into camp while the guys are sitting around having coffee. It's sunny and not too cool out, but they're sitting indoors because of the blackflies, which appeared suddenly overnight and are now unbearable. You can't be outdoors without repellent, and even then it only half works.

"Well, will you look what the Cat pushed up," says Dago.

"You miss me, Dago?" says Rowan.

Tony looks up and nods, his mouth full of sandwich. After he swallows he says to Connie, "Come for your pay?"

"Make that two," says Rowan.

"You too, eh?" Tony says. "Couldn't talk you into a couple more weeks?"

"Alice had to leave. Her dad's dying or something. So I've got the dogs to deal with now. Anyways, I was cutting it pretty fine for getting my moose. Guess I'd better pull the pin. You'll be okay?"

"C'est la vie, eh?"

"That's what I figured. Cat work must be just about done. Get Dago moving the piles."

"Hey," Dago says, "I guess the squarehead's really lost 'er this time."

"Dale?" Rowan says.

"Fuckin' A. Where you think he is?"

"I guess he's in the bush around Whitehorse somewhere," Rowan says. "He'll come out when he comes around."

"Not this time, compadre. This guy's fuckin' gonzo. Either he already took the big one"—he shoots himself with his finger—"or he's still lookin' for her." He nods toward Connie.

Tony shrugs, and then looks at his watch. "Got your cheques in my room," he says, and gets up to go. Rowan and Connie get up, too.

"Well, fellas, it's been another good one," Rowan says.

"What are you gonna do?" Dago asks Connie. Connie hesitates. Up until now her only plan for survival has been to stick close to Rowan and let her take care of the details. She doesn't know how much longer she can keep doing that.

"I don't know for sure. I missed my plane, and I have to wait a few days for another one. Just lie low, I guess."

"Yeah, like real fuckin' low. Lower than a snake's asshole," Dago says, and grins. He gets up and offers his hand to shake. "I better get back to work," he says. "Take 'er easy, eh?"

"Yeah. You take 'er easy, too, Dago."

"Seeya on the next shitpile," he says to Rowan.

"Take care, Dago."

The guys all get up and clump out the door, saying their goodbyes as they go. Connie and Rowan are leaving last when Ida speaks.

"Worked with that Andra girl once, over in Elsa. She told me something about this Dale character." She pauses for encouragement. Rowan and Connie stare at her, waiting. "Said when he gets something in his head, he never quits. She didn't want to go around with him at first, but he wouldn't leave her alone. Says he's like that about everything. Mark my words, that guy didn't shoot himself. He's out there, and he ain't gonna quit."

"Well, uh, thanks, Ida."

"Don't mention it. Take care of yourself."

"Yeah. You too, Ida. Bye now."

Tony's waiting when they get out. When he hands over the cheques, he grins. "Just as well you're packin' it in," he says to Rowan. "No bullcook anymore, we're gonna have to get rid of some of these guys or I'll end up muckin' up after them myself."

They shake hands and Tony turns and crunches away across the gravel, toward the loader. Connie never noticed before how small his head looks, with the shoulders of his green quilted vest hunched up around his ears.

"Do you mind waiting a bit?" she asks.

"What, for the kiyoot?" Rowan says. "No problem. Can I come along, or did you want to be alone with him?"

"Oh, give me a break. It's just something I want to do before I go. Just don't bring your gun, I'm sure he knows what they are."

"I have no doubt of it. Smart little buggers."

They go around behind the cookshack and climb partway up the hill, and sit for a while on a couple of tree stumps at the edge of the bush, listening to the engines roar. Ida doesn't come out to burn the garbage. Now that she's on her own, she'll be getting one of the guys to do it after supper. The time when the coyote usually shows up comes and goes, but he doesn't appear.

"Okay," Connie says, "let's go."

"Happens like that."

"Yeah. He just seemed so wise, like he knew what was going on all the time. I wanted to see if he knew I was leaving."

"What were you gonna do, ask him?"

"I would have known."

Rowan doesn't respond for a moment, and then she says, "Okay, bush woman, you want to get outa le shithole?"

"Sure," says Connie. "Let's go."

The Bush

Leather hinges are only good for so long. They rot, the squirrels eat them. Abe remembers the last time the hinge was replaced on this door. He helped the old man with it, the summer before he died. He's covered in bug dope, but the blackflies swarm around his head anyway. He's eaten about a hundred of them, and pulled a few out of his eyes. A beer would sure go nice right about now. He turns to the bucket of water beside him and scoops a drink. Two things he has to keep his mind off if he's going to survive out here: one is booze and the other is Sky. He lines the strip of leather up along the edge of the door and sets the first of the roofing nails. Sometimes it's impossible not to think of how a beer would taste, or how good a couple of shots of Jack Daniels would feel hitting the bloodstream. Other times, it's impossible not to think about Sky.

He didn't tell Sky he was a virgin when they met. He was too embarrassed. It didn't take her long to figure it out, though. She was so cool about it, too. He wasn't humiliated when she announced, "You're going to need some lessons." He was excited.

He's doing it again. He promised himself he wouldn't think about Sky. What if it's over? He may never have another woman like her, even if he doesn't really know her. They spent almost all their time together in bed. Not to mention on the floor, in the bathtub, in among the bushes by Ear Lake, and in an abandoned car in the alley next to his mom's house.

A shaft of pain runs up his back as he lifts the door and sets it into the doorway. He pulls a wedge out of his hip pocket and shoves it into the gap beside the door. Unsure if the wedge is enough to keep it in place, he holds the door up with the fingers of one outstretched hand as he reaches for his hammer with the other. He just manages to get a grip on the handle, but when he goes to straighten up, he is pierced by a sharper pain, and then finds himself stuck. With a sudden wrench he manages to pull himself up and flop forward against the door. He drops the hammer at his feet, turns, and leans for a minute, and then slowly stretches out his arms. He cut short on his stretches this morning, eager to get to work. Maybe better not do that again.

The plane dropped him off yesterday on this little pothole lake with no name, out on the edge of the line. The shack is just out of sight of the lake, down the creek about a hundred yards. The sod roof has held up pretty well, although a mouldy smell inside indicates water getting in somewhere. The dirt floor was littered with squirrel shit and pine cones, but when he cleaned it up, he found that it was still fairly hard-packed underneath, and not too dusty. He remembered then his father making him sweep that floor for an hour as soon as the cabin was built, and then again every time they came to it and every morning they woke up there, to harden it up.

The only trouble with this little lake is that it doesn't have any trout in it. There's pike, which he doesn't mind, but he'd rather have some lakers. How far is it to Ashcan Lake from here? Long way. He could walk there and back in one day, probably, but he wouldn't be able to carry much fish back with him. He could get there in the canoe easily enough if his back was better, but he's not so sure he could pull it up over the beaver dams. There were three of the old man's canoes to choose from, one at Mom's and two at Frank's place. Abe chose the lightest one, a sweet little fifteen-foot Chestnut. It would be the perfect one-man canoe if the one man didn't happen to be crippled. But he doesn't know how well the canvas would stand up if he had to drag it over the dams without taking any of the weight off. And coming back with a moose on board would be way harder, even if he took three trips. Still, it's something he's going to have to face. He didn't argue with Frank about how bad his back is, but the truth is, getting a moose is going to be torture. Not as bad, maybe, as trying to live for a winter on beans and rice, but bad. Very bad.

Rowan pulls a heavy sack out from under a shelf in the porch, and opens it, releasing a strong odour of fish. "Fish meal," she explains, scooping a can of powder into one of the dog buckets.

"Vitamins?" Connie ventures.

"Yeah, that too. But it's mostly for flavour. To get 'em to drink the water."

"Why don't they just drink it?"

"I don't know, but they don't until they're just about totally dehydrated, and by then they've usually knocked it over or pissed in it."

Connie's almost as fascinated by the dogs as she is terrified of them. They do all the goofball things that people's pet dogs do, only at fever pitch. They frisk around and play, they jump on their houses, they bark their heads off. The males run over and piss on their trees at the slightest provocation, even if they have only two drops of urine left with which to signify their defiance, excitement, lust, or perceived dominance. To signify submission, they pee right on the spot, crouching low and dribbling, males and females alike. And yet they have this weird kind of majesty, too, and there's this romance about them: dogs that have to sleep outside in the dead of winter, working animals tough enough to face the wilderness, and yet they have to be pampered in these curious ways: flavoured drinking water, special vitamin supplements. Little booties to protect their feet from the snow. She picked one up off the floor of Rowan's truck yesterday—Jesus, was it only yesterday?—on the way to the airport from the Casablanca. It was green, shiny, like a cute little waterproof, thumbless mitten.

"Dog bootie," Rowan said. "Most of my guys don't need them unless the conditions are pretty extreme."

"Like what?"

"If you get fresh snow and then it drops to forty below? It gets like sandpaper sometimes. It's rare. I hardly ever use them, but I always carry them on the sled."

Rowan is packing. Considering she describes Alice as her ex, a lot of her stuff seems to come out of the bedroom. Seeing it accumulate for sorting and packing in the middle of the cabin floor reminds Connie that she has to decide what she's going to do herself. Rowan seems to read her mind.

"I can run you down to Whitehorse tomorrow. I have to make a run for supplies."

"You must be getting tired of all this driving."

Rowan shrugs.

"Well, I want you to know I appreciate your going all that way for me."

"Yeah, well, you can do the same for me someday, somebody ever comes gunning for me."

"Do you think he's still coming?"

"Well, it's kind of hard to say, isn't it?"

"What do you think about what Ida said?"

"What, that he never quits? Yeah, that's Dale all right. But this is different, eh? Sooner or later he's going to come to his senses. We just have to stay out of his way until he does."

"We?"

"You don't think he's pissed off at me, too, by now? Anyways, I can take you to the airport tomorrow, and if you can't get out of here right away I'll run you up to Pigpen's."

"Pigpen's?"

"What? Pigpen's harmless. And he'll help you out: run you to the airport in the morning, whatever. I can just as easy take you to a hotel, if you want." Her tone says Pigpen's place would be a lot safer. Connie considers this. She would never have believed that the path of safety would lead to a night in a rundown cabin at the end of a dirt road alone with a crazy biker and two killer pit bulls. She sets the matter aside. There's plenty of time to think about where she's going to stay.

At loose ends while Rowan sorts her gear and packs, Connie hangs around the cabin, picking up books, putting them down, staring out at the mountains. Late in the afternoon she wanders outside and stands watching the dogs. Used to her now, most of them don't bother to bark. They lie on top of their houses, each with its own little cloud of blackflies, and stare. Once in a while they shake, or paw at their heads. Kitty, well to the back, jumps down and starts to whine at her. The noise she makes is bizarre, somewhere between a scream and a moan, a restrained version of the noise she makes at feeding time until Rowan tells her to shut up. At the same time her front feet—Connie has learned that mushers never say paws—make jerking motions up from the ground, as if it takes all her strength to keep from jumping straight in the air. All this noise and body language says, please, please, pet me, come over and pet me. Some of the other dogs are joining in the noise, unwillingly it seems, as if Kitty's enthusiasm was dragging them along. Kitty's plea is so compelling, but where will Connie find the courage to slip between the other dogs? She looks at the path she would have to take. The first obstacle is the hand's breadth of unclawed ground between Virgil and his brother, Homer. They're two of the most enormous dogs she's ever seen, although Rowan insists that half of it is hair and they're really smaller than a big shepherd. This is no comfort to Connie when they both jump down off their houses at her cautious approach. Virgil dives into his house, but Homer throws himself at his chain and barks. Connie is sure she hears the chain ringing as his weight hits it. Rowan was doing some repairs to dog chains earlier today, so it's a fact that they do break. What if that chain broke right now, what would Homer do? Would that insane leaping turn out to be what it looks like, just an overexuberance of friendliness, or would the loss of the chain's restraint turn him into a wild beast? If he took it into his head, she thinks, he could kill and eat her like a rabbit.

By now, all the dogs are off their houses, and most of them have joined in the barking. She glances back at the house to see if Rowan's watching out the window. She doesn't see her, but the window's in the full glare of the sun, she could be standing right in the middle of it, watching, and you'd never be able to tell. Anyway, it stands to reason she's got to be looking; she checks out the window whenever they bark. This thought gives Connie the courage to approach them a little closer. The closer she gets, the more they bark and scream, until, a few feet from Homer, she's deafened by it. Someone could be yelling her name from ten feet away and she'd never hear them.

She glances back once more to see if Rowan might be there. She's not, and this gives her an odd kind of confidence. If there was any real danger in going in among the dogs, she'd come out and stop her. She decides she can go at least as far as the path between Virgil and Homer, because Virgil won't come out of his house anyway. She'll stick close to his side. She passes Homer with her arms tight to her sides, making herself as small as possible. When she's two feet away from him, he stands right up on his back legs, leans his weight against the chain, and tries to reach her with his front feet. Even when he does this, it's so obvious that his intentions are friendly, she feels foolish about her fear. Still, the fear only diminishes slightly, and she comes to the next dog wondering what she's doing in this situation. This one she doesn't know the name of. It crouches on the ground and stares at her with a fixed eye she can't interpret. Because the dogs are randomly scattered among the trees, there isn't another very close, so she can take a fairly wide path around him. He follows her all the way around at the length of his chain, eyes fixed hard on her, vibrating with who knows what kind of nervous tension. That leaves only two more dogs between her and Kitty. Approaching, she realizes that the patch of undisturbed ground between them is about four inches wide. By straining sideways at their collars, the dogs can touch muzzles. In between making lunging dashes toward her, they do this. They look like a pair of hockey fans, pausing in the middle of screaming at the ref to give each other a kiss. It's so incongruous she has to laugh. Laughter pushes the fear back even further, and she baby-steps up to the point where their muzzles meet. Both dogs shove their faces at her to be petted. Reaching out her hand, she lives each fraction of a second in vivid detail, thinks fleetingly of inching toward Jason's cock, his hand on the back of her head, thinking simultaneously, *I'm committed now, it's going to happen,* and *Never, never will I be able to do this.* The dogs' soft muzzles are amazingly strong. They shove them hard under her hands and then thrust backwards, pushing her hands to the tops of their heads. When she begins to stroke them they press against her in a kind of frantic ecstasy, their bodies tensed to leap if she should try to quit, but their heads melting into her in perfect relaxation. Again, she thinks of Jason.

By now, most of her fear is under control. She notices that, physically, the excitement she's now experiencing feels almost identical to the fear. Heart pounding, she pushes past her two new-found friends to where Kitty is screaming at the top of her lungs, demanding her share of the attention. She walks up and imitates Rowan's gesture and command, pointing and saying, "Up on your doghouse." To her surprise, her delight even, Kitty obeys, and stands on the house waiting for the praise and affection that are her reward. At this height Kitty's head comes level with Connie's. She walks up and puts her arms around her the way she has seen Rowan doing and the dog returns the embrace by pushing the whole of its body against her and licking her ear.

"Ew," Connie says, and laughs. She rubs Kitty's head and

thumps on her rib cage and then stands back and claps her hands to make her jump from side to side on the house. While they're playing, the noise of the dogs rises to a peak, and then suddenly stops dead. Kitty turns her attention to something over Connie's shoulder. She looks back to see Rowan standing behind the cabin, her finger to her lips.

"Hey, don't get them too wound up," she says, grinning. "The neighbours are going to complain." Connie's not sure whether she's kidding or not. There's another driveway about half a mile up the road; it's quite possible that their place is close enough for the dogs' racket to disturb them.

Kitty hardly seems to notice the blackflies swarming all around her, but Connie does. They land on her face and crawl over her neck. "Okay, this is goodbye, Kitty," she says. Giving the dog one last hug, she starts across the dog lot before Rowan can go back inside. She wants the sense of security her presence gives, but more than that she wants Rowan to see her pass between the dogs without fear. Without too much fear.

"I'm putting supper on," Rowan says, when Connie comes within earshot. "Will you eat a whole moose steak?"

Disappointed that Rowan doesn't seem to be impressed with what she's done, Connie follows her in the back door, suddenly realizing how hungry she is.

"Honey," she says, doing Mae West—*since when did I start to do impressions?*—"I believe I could eat a whole moose."

Untying her air mattress and sleeping bag from her pack, Connie thinks how she was expecting to be done with this stuff by now. She had been looking forward to shoving it in the closet in her parents' basement, not bringing it out until next summer, when she might take a trip with the folks to a nice noisy government campground with a beach nearby. She's reaching in the pocket of the pack where she keeps the air pump when Rowan comes out of the bedroom. She's wearing olive drab pajamas that look like army surplus.

"Look," she says, "don't take this wrong, but there's no need for you to sleep on the floor. This bed's enormous."

What do you mean, she thinks, don't take this wrong? How do I take it? What would constitute taking it right when a lesbian friend offers you half a bed? "I, er..."

Rowan laughs and holds her hands up in a gesture of innocence. "Just a place to sleep," she says.

"Sorry," Connie says. "Thanks."

"Hey, don't be sorry. I don't blame you. A girl can't be too careful these days."

Connie giggles.

"What's so funny?"

"The last person who said that to me was talking about her cordless vibrator."

Rowan shakes her head in a way that clearly says she doesn't understand these weird city ways. The bed is a queen-sized futon, and there's barely enough room to walk around it in the small bedroom. Connie tries to imagine where all Rowan's stuff was that she pulled out of here today. Still embarrassed, she waits to see which side of the bed Rowan will take before getting in. By this time of year the midnight sun is a thing of the past, and when Rowan snuffs the candle on the floor by the bed, it's dark in the room.

"Goodnight, sister," she says over her shoulder.

"Goodnight, sister," Connie replies. She's never called anyone sister except in irony before, but under the circumstances it seems like the appropriate thing to say.

"Hey," Rowan says, "you were pretty cool with those dogs today."

"Thanks."

"Didn't think you had it in you. We'll make a musher out of you yet."

Rowan drops off to sleep almost immediately. Connie never does that. She lies awake for at least twenty minutes every night, usually filtering the day's events and occasionally, when she's sleeping alone, masturbating. When she does, she never drags it out; a few minutes of gentle touching while she thinks of something sexy—sometimes it amazes her afterward what can constitute a sexy thought, but she never questions it at the time—and then a quick stroking to orgasm, and then a swift drop into sleep. Out of the question tonight, of course. Tonight she thinks about the dogs, and about what a momentous thing she achieved today. She's never petted a dog without its owner present, and even then, it's never been any great pleasure to her. Even the occasional mop-dog or cockapoo that she's known without actually fearing, she's never enjoyed their company. She loves Kitty. She has never understood how anybody could love a dog before, but now she knows. Kitty returns love with such purity, such intensity; Connie's never known anything like it. Even her mom judges, everyone does, but when she petted Kitty, there was nothing there but undiluted love.

What are they like when they're pulling a sled? she wonders. She's seen a clip on TV of an Inuit guy, running alongside the team with a big whip. The whip is to guide the dogs, the commentator explained. Rowan doesn't own a whip, she says. And you don't run alongside these guys. ("They're slow, but they're not that slow.") You stand on the runners, where they stick out the back of the sled. There's a handle that you hang onto, called the driving bow, but you don't do much driving with it, besides "wrestling it around the corners sometimes, or keeping it up on a sidehill." You don't steer the team with it, nor by cracking a whip at them, either. The lead dog responds to commands. There's commands for stop, go, turn right, and turn left. That's about all they can handle without getting confused. When people talk about smart leaders, Rowan says, they're not talking about Lassie or anything.

It's strange lying beside Rowan. She's slept with women before, but none of them were lesbians that she knew of. If Rowan feels about women the way Connie feels about guys, you'd think it would be hard to get to sleep with Connie right beside her like that. She wonders if she should be insulted. The night they sat by the creek and Rowan explained about her and Alice, she said, "I don't go with straight women." Connie must have looked puzzled because she went on to explain: "A lot of them to want to try it once, just for curiosity. But not with this sister: I've been down that road."

Connie thinks about straight women being curious about lesbian sex. Is she? Certainly she has fantasized about it, all alone at night. But then, she often fantasizes about things she'd never actually do. Some of them are a lot stranger than going down on a woman. She thinks about that. Would it disgust her? Probably not as much as doing it for Jason, the insistent bastard. Funny how that sprang to mind in the dog lot today, that same hesitation. She doesn't think she would feel the same with a woman. She's neither as attracted nor as repelled by the idea. Maybe it doesn't disgust her because she already knows how it would taste. Assuming, that is, that all women taste more or less the same. Certainly she knows her own flavour. Jason made sure of that. It's kind of smoky, salty, the hint of urine not nearly as nasty as she would have thought. On the other hand, she's not more than mildly curious about the giving side of cunnilingus. Okay, maybe a bit more than mildly. But she's not lesbian, or bi or anything. She's not attracted to Rowan, not attracted to women at all the way she is to men. She doesn't look at their bodies and wish she could touch them. She never dreams of a woman at night.

Jason soaps Connie's foot carefully, dunks it in the bathwater to rinse it off, and then puts the toes in his mouth. It tickles, and she giggles. Face to face in the tub, they splash and laugh. It's late Saturday night, far past the chance of a parent invasion, and nobody in the North Wing is going to say a word about them taking a bath together. It's heady, knowing that people can hear them, and it's okay, nobody's going to say anything. They sip champagne in the tub and he almost breaks the long-stemmed glass climbing out and wrapping her in a vast, soft, white towel that definitely does not belong to the college.

She wears his housecoat and he wears a towel to go down the hall to his room. They walk, his arm around her neck, kissing. In the room they drop together to the bed. She floats above the bed while he crouches and kisses her thighs, moves up, starts to make that tiny circling motion with his tongue that always makes her moan. Again she thinks of the people through the paper-thin walls, hearing them, knowing. It excites her to know they can hear, can tell from the sound of her moans how great it feels, how loved and valued she feels when he—oh—does this, and then he's moving up, he's going to enter her and she rises toward him but he turns away, moves his hips up the bed, oh God he wants me to—I don't know if—maybe—

He sits up, leans over, and kisses her: tender, perfect kisses that flit over her lips like dreams of kisses. She half rises to meet his lips, and then lowers her head to kiss his nipple. His cock strains toward her as he shifts position, turning his hips to push it toward her face. She thinks maybe tonight she can do it. It means so much to him. And it's true, as he says, it's only fair. She moves toward it, kisses his belly along the way, the soft black furze around his navel, and then she's there. But how? What should she do? How to start? She kisses the pinkish-purple tip, and pulls back, uncertain. Is she really supposed to take it in her mouth? Once, in grade school, she saw a girl pretend to do it with a popsicle, sliding her mouth up and down, sucking so hard her cheeks caved in. Is that what you do, really? Jason moans, a hint of frustration, and she moves back to try again. She puts her lips to the tip again, and this time lets a little bit of it slip between. Words flash across her mind, playground words, washroom wall words, but she pushes them aside. He does it for me. It's no different. But she can go no further. She circles the shaft with her hand and begins to stroke it, moving her mouth over the tiny bit of flesh she's been able to make it accept, feeling like in a minute, maybe, she'll be able to go farther. And then Jason moans and puts his hand on the back of her head, and ever so gently pushes down, lifting his hips as he does, pushing his cock deeper in to her mouth. She tries to accept it, knows she should *accept it, because it's the 1970s goddamnit, and everybody's equal, and if he can do it for her then she can do it for him, and she wants to do this but it feels wrong and she doesn't know why but it has to feel right, but it doesn't, it has to stop, so she pulls her head back, but Jason doesn't seem to understand that she wants to stop now, he has hold of her head and he won't let go and he's pushing it down and his hips are thrusting up, and she's choking, panicking. She starts to gag and to try to speak, to tell him to let go, but he doesn't let go, what's the matter with him, doesn't he see she's choking, and then he suddenly goes all stiff, pumps a couple of times into her mouth and then, just as he goes slack, two terrifying spurts of something gooey, something awful, inside her mouth, and he lets go.*

Remembering, reliving it, Connie wants to call out to her more innocent self of last year, the way she sometimes wants to shout a warning to unsuspecting victims in movies. Bite him, sister, she thinks. Bite it off. But at the time, she didn't know what had happened. She didn't even blame Jason till after he dumped her. It was just her first blow job, and it was a bit traumatic. Jason was sweet about it, afterwards. She put her head down on the bed and sobbed, still choking a little. Jason stroked her head, so so tenderly.

"It's okay," he said. "You'll get used to it."

She didn't understand why it mattered to him so much. They had lots of sex, great sex, he even said so himself. But every time, the hint was there that it wasn't enough. On the little narrow bed in his residence room (she wasn't about to take him to the Nunnery, to become the talk of the afternoon soap-opera circle), they discovered dozens of sexual positions, rolling from one to the next sometimes without disengaging, like sexual gymnasts. She grew to know the smell and taste of her own juices from Jason's lips and fingers. And always, every time they made love, at some point, usually just when she was starting to think this time would be perfect, he would shift around and place his cock near enough her mouth that she might take the hint. She was willing to try again, because he was so sweet and tender with her, and because it annoyed him when she wouldn't at least try, but every time she came near, she panicked. She could imagine that hand like a clamp on her head, the terrible sensation of choking. It was just because she was too slow last time. If she got down to business she was sure he wouldn't do that again. But what if she got it wrong, and he grabbed her head again? She'd go from floating on a cloud at the centre of heaven to feeling scared, and pressured, and finally ragged and miserable. She thought Jason would understand, he was so kind and thoughtful about everything else, and the first time was so awful, but the longer it went on, the more she tried to find other ways to make up for this one lack, the more obsessed he seemed to be with oral sex. She tried to talk to him about it but he wouldn't listen, wouldn't even admit that he was pressing her.

"It's okay," he'd say. "There's no pressure." But of course there was. Constant pressure, through his body language, the turning up of the hips, the constant proffering of himself on his back, or on the edge of the bed, pantless, erection crying out for attention, the frustrated way he would respond to the pressure of her hand. It began to tell in the sex: his consideration waning, her pleasure diminishing. One day it all ended in frustration for both of them, and Jason barked at her and she walked out. She waited for him to call, to come over to her in the cafeteria or the common room, or catch up to her on the footpath one day, to apologize, to ask her to forgive him. She'd made up her mind that when he came back, she'd take a deep breath and tell him that she'd be willing to give him oral sex if he'd promise to keep his hands off her head till she was finished, but it never happened. She began to wonder if he was afraid to try, for fear that he'd offended her too deeply. After nearly two weeks she had decided to give it another two days, until the Friday, and then she would approach him. That morning she came down to breakfast, and Jason was sitting with a girl, a girl she'd seen around the college before, red-haired and perfectly tanned, her loose breasts bursting out of a peach Wallace Beery shirt. They sat together, side by side instead of across from each other, and he turned toward her and put a slice of orange in her mouth.

Last night, Connie dreamed about Dale. She'd forgotten that until just now. She woke up in a panic, even though in the dream Dale wasn't threatening her. He was stroking her hair and telling her that he forgave her, that the stabbing was no big deal, he was glad she did it because it stopped him from hurting Andra. In the dream, Dale cried and swore he would never hurt Andra again. She unbuttoned her shirt, put him to her breast like a frightened baby. Connie's pretty sure it was actually a scene from a movie, although she can't remember which one. Something old, she thinks. Nat would know.

"Nat, Nat, I was going to be there, really I was. I would have been home by now. Safe."

Connie is aware that this thought, the thought that she could and should be in Toronto right now, sitting beside the bricked-in fireplace in Nat's apartment, drinking something exotic, maybe smoking a joint, doesn't bring her the pang it ought to do. In fact, as she pictures it all, the whole idea of returning causes a kind of low-level depression to seep into her heart. When she tries to picture Toronto, she can only see it on a rainy day, or after a heavy snowfall has turned to slush: grey, bleak, and chill. She realizes what it is that's been building in her all day. She doesn't want to go home. She wants to see the Yukon in winter. She wants to go dogsledding, huddle in a cabin at forty below, experience ice fog. She wants to be able to say as she's leaving the North that she knows what it's really about.

"Nat, am I nuts? Forty below? I hate cold. I have no clothes for winter. I'd spend all my money and have nothing to show but frostbitten ears, like Rita's cat. But..."

She thinks about Dale, about his anger. How does anyone get that angry? What goes on inside his head when he thinks about killing her? A shiver runs up the length of her spine and down her arms. She can actually imagine him pointing a pistol at her, in the middle of the Whitehorse airport, firing, the bullet coming at her, hitting, smashing her to splinters, ending her life. Life slipping away. Worse, she can imagine Dale imagining it, relishing the thought, his bullet, in his mind, entering her. It's rape; she'd never thought of it before, but she sees it so clearly: it enters you like a broken bottle, tears you to pieces. She shakes herself. Quit that, she thinks. You'll never get to sleep.

She considers for only a tiny moment the possibility of touching herself, taking that small comfort that always brings on sleep, but it's impossible with Rowan lying beside her. Even though her breathing is heavy and regular and there seems to be no chance she'd wake up. What would she do if she did wake up, and Connie was masturbating? Would she pretend she didn't notice? Say something, make a joke? Or would she reach over and put her hand on top of Connie's? Kiss her neck above the collar of her flannel pajamas? Offer to help?

No, I can't. It's impossible.

But it takes such a soft caress, such a tiny motion of her fingers. And Rowan's starting to snore. What could it hurt?

Abe wishes he didn't do this every night. Even in front of himself, it embarrasses him. Not until afterwards, of course, because at the time he's too focussed on whatever it is he's fantasizing, but almost immediately afterwards he feels ashamed. Not like he's committed some great sin or anything, but just—silly. Like it's something he should have given up years ago, like wetting the bed.

It wouldn't be so bad if it was normal stuff that occurred to him while he was jerking off. When he knows he can't help doing it, he always tries to steer his mind in the direction of something regular, something a guy can think about and not be ashamed: a squad of cheerleaders, something like that. And then, he'll lose himself, and when he's back, he's been kidnapped by female buccaneers and they're forcing him to scrub their decks, naked, and he's higher than a kite. Sometimes it's like he's two people, and the regular one comes in and catches the weird one at it and takes back over and makes him concentrate on the cheerleaders.

Sometimes the struggle between the two halves of him kills the whole feeling, and it goes soft in his hand, which is what he, or half of him, wanted, but it leaves him feeling like shit anyway. Sometimes, after all that struggle, the crazy side of him takes back over and he tries again. Not tonight, though. Tonight he's started thinking about Sky, only not in that way. Or he's thinking about sex all right, but not fantasizing, not even remembering or doing anything that makes him horny: just wondering. He wonders why he needed someone to teach him what to do. Who tells a dog? Although, when he considers it, he already knew about the part that dogs know. The thing he didn't know about was how to make it fun.

Abe never had a girlfriend before Sky. He spent so much time in the bush, he didn't actually know any girls until that one year his mom made him go to high school. There, the girls made him so nervous, he never managed to say more than a few words to them. When he'd pass by a bunch of them in the hall, they'd laugh and make smartass remarks, most of them too quiet to make out, but you could tell from the tone they were nasty. He told Sky about this, and she laughed.

"They liked you," she said.

"Yeah, sure."

"Well, of course they did. Look at you." They were on the old legless bed at the time, naked, taking a break and finishing a bottle of wine. She made him get up and look in the mirror with her. They stood side by side. "Look how cute you are," she said. "Nice ass." She gave it a pat. "Nice and fit." She ran a hand over his shoulder.

"I was skinnier then."

"You were probably even cuter. Look at your blond mop, and those dimples. I can just imagine them at seventeen."

"I looked goofy."

"You just thought so. Cute guys who don't know they're cute are the best kind. I bet they were mad for you. Especially when you blushed."

"Get real."

"Okay, how's this? Real enough?"

Before Abe even realizes he's started again, it's all over, and he's looking around for something to clean up with. He hates having to get out of bed to find something; getting up from lying down is the hardest thing for his back. But the toilet paper is over on the table three steps from the bed. Hauling himself out of bed, he feels a moment of disgust. Oh well, at least it wasn't about anything too weird.

The road between Dawson and Whitehorse is starting to be familiar territory. A few highway lodges, three tiny communities squatting around the ends of bridges, dusty gravel road through the bush that everybody seems to drive as if it was the 401. Connie's learning to watch for the bursts of mountain scenery, and even to appreciate the long stretches of raggedy-looking forest.

Rowan pulls into a gravel side road and stops the truck.

"What's up?" Connie says.

"Got to drop the dogs." Connie must look puzzled. "Let them out for a pee," Rowan explains.

The dogs are in a kind of condo-camper on the back of the truck called, appropriately enough, the dog boxes. Each dog has its own box with a door. The doors have breathing holes in the middle and most of them have tooth marks around the edge of the hole. One or two are chewed almost to nothing, and have some kind of metal screen screwed on to patch up the holes. When the dogs get in and out, straw spills onto the ground. Rowan goes around and unloads them, opening the door, and then assisting each dog as it leaps out.

"They tend to stove themselves up jumping out if you don't kind of break their fall a bit," she says. Kitty and three or four others are allowed to run loose. The rest get chained up to the truck. "Come on, get on with it," Rowan tells them. "We don't have all day." She gives them about five minutes to stretch their legs and go to the bathroom, and then starts putting them back in. At one point, Connie hears a scrambling noise from the other side of the truck and Rowan's voice saying, "Goddamnit, Virgil." She feels like she should offer to help, but there's not much she could do; the dogs would be way too heavy for her. When only Kitty is left running around the truck, Rowan says, "You want to put her away?"

"Okay," Connie says, although her whole body tenses up.

"Just put one hand under her belly, and one under her butt. That's it, now don't strain yourself, just lift easy, as if she was light."

As she braces herself to take the weight, Kitty suddenly leaps straight up into the box and Connie falls over backward. She lands on her butt on the gravel, not very hard. When she looks up the dog has turned around in the box and is lolling her tongue out at Connie, grinning. Rowan is laughing so hard she has to put her hand on the truck to steady herself.

"Did you do that on purpose?" Connie says.

"No. No. Scout's honour. She just needs the confidence of a little boost. You were just lifting too hard."

"Did you know she was going to knock me—"

"—on your can? No. But it was worth it. How do you like sled dogs now?"

"Better than mushers. Are we going now?"

"In a sec." Rowan opens the tailgate and pulls a shovel out from under the boxes. There are a few dog turds on the ground around the truck, and she flicks them off into the bush. "Okay, we're on our way."

Connie loves Fox Lake and Little Fox, stretching away toward the distant mountains like a long, bony finger. South of there they come to the bleak, flat, burned-out forest that leads into Whitehorse, mile after mile of grey, limbless trees and charred stumps, all of it tangled up in lying-down logs so thick the fireweed can only peek through in patches.

"This has got to be the ugliest place on earth," she says.
Rowan looks surprised. "The burn? Huh."
"You don't think so?"
"No. I kind of like the way it looks."
"Seriously?"
"Yeah."
"It looks like death."
"Yeah, but also life."
"How?"
"Lodgepole cones don't open till they're cooked. That's how new forest gets started. You look in among all that tangle, you'll see the poplars coming up, making leaf mulch every year for the pines to grow in. Tons of fireweed. Moose like it. Rabbits are ecstatic. All that deadfall to hide under, food everywhere you look. Plenty of rabbits, so hawks and coyotes are happy. Lots of easy wood, so the woodcutters are happy, customers are happy. And in a few years, after the poplars really take? Beautiful. I mean, really amazing."

It still looks bleak to Connie, but maybe a little less so. She starts watching for moose.

A couple of moose came into camp one day, a cow and her yearling calf, everyone said, although they looked about the same size to Connie. The names seemed to fit—they were bovine enough, staring stupidly at the open cookshack door where Connie stood sweeping the dust and gravel back out onto the ground to be carried in again at coffee time, but when they suddenly turned and slipped back into the bush, she forgot about cows. They were taller than horses and ran like deer and they vanished into thick bush like shadows.

"You're pretty quiet today," Rowan says.
"Yeah. Just thinking, I guess."
"Worried about Dale?"
"Well, yeah. And that's going round in my head with . . . oh, you know, what will I do when I get home? Is the airline going to give me a break? Will I find the girl with the necklace? And . . ."

"What?"

"Well, to tell you the truth ... I wish I didn't have to go. I have this one friend I'm looking forward to seeing ..."

"That'd be the one who didn't give you the switchblade?"

"Hey, that room could have been bugged, you know. But yeah. Nat, the comedian I told you about. Other than to see Nat, I don't want to be in Toronto anymore than I did when I left."

"Couple months from now it could be fifty below right here."

"Yeah. Wild."

"Uh oh."

"What?"

"I don't think this is a good time for you to start catching it." Connie laughs. "What, Yukon fever?"

"Yeah, whatever it is. If they don't catch Dale, which they're not going to now, you're going to have to get out of here."

"What if I just hide out somewhere?"

"Like where? Dawson? Whitehorse? You can't hide around here in winter, girl. Not from someone like Dale."

"Jesus, what is it about this guy?"

"Knows the country, good in the bush, and he's stubborn as a mule. I'm starting to think Dago was right, and Dale's really lost it this time. If he's still alive, you'd better not be around."

"Well, Jesus, if the guy's such an evil genius, how the hell do I know he won't have my parents' house staked out, or my friend's apartment, when I get back to TO? How do I know he won't be at the airport in Edmonton? Or fucking Whitehorse for that matter."

"Hey, whoa, take it easy. I'm on your side."

"Sorry. I just hate this feeling of running away. It feels really insecure. Like, if the RCMP can't catch the guy, where's safe? It also feels ... really ... powerless. Like, I don't want to go but I have to because of this jerk? I just want to say fuck that, but I can't. And then I think, what if they don't give me another ticket? It didn't sound likely, you know. It sounded more like, sorry, that's what bookings are for. So then what do I do? Spend all the money I saved for a flight I don't want to take? I'm just ... really wound up about this."

They've reached the Mayo cut-off, and Rowan pulls up to the stop sign to turn left onto the Alaska Highway. She turns to look at Connie.

"You sure are," she says. "What are you going to do about it?"

"I don't know. Go home, I guess. Figure something out. I'm sure it'll all make sense, looking back."

"How old did you say you were?"

"Twenty-one. Why?"

Rowan pulls out onto the highway behind a passing motorhome. "Last comment just seemed a litle wise for twenty-one."

"What's age got to do with it?"

"Yeah, guess you're right. Listen, if you want to put off going just for a while, I'm going in the bush till Christmas."

"You mean, like, now?"

"Yeah," Rowan says.

"Jesus. You don't come out at all?"

"Shit no."

"How far is it?"

"From the highway, about forty miles."

"How do you get there?"

"Canoe."

"So how do you get back out again if the lakes are frozen?"

"Dogs."

"Wow. Are you sure?"

"About what?"

"That you wouldn't mind?"

"I wouldn't offer if I didn't mean it."

Connie's mind races over the possibilities. What does she have to go home to? It's not like Nat's pining to see her or anything. And what can she tell her? She had all these good stories about the Yukon that she couldn't wait to tell, but now it seems as though what made the stories funny was a screwed-up perception of her own, and now she feels differently enough that she wouldn't be able to tell them. She could never talk to Nat about Pigpen, because she couldn't explain the fact that she likes him. Anything you could say about the guy would make him seem like a total jerk. Same with Dawson, it sounds like such a stupid place when you try to describe it, but Connie's coming to realize she loves it there. She's thinking maybe she could come out of the bush and go and stay with Rita until spring. This whole Dale business has got to have resolved itself somehow by then. She imagines the canoe trip.

"Do they all fit in the canoe?"

"Who? The dogs?" Rowan laughs. "Not friggin' likely. They swim."

"Seriously?"

"Yeah. And run along shore. They love it."

"This sounds incredible. I don't see how I can miss it. You're sure now?"

"I told you."

"Yeah, I know. But, er..."

"What? You're not a lesbian? Shucks, what a disappointment. Look, this is not about that, okay?"

"Okay, sorry."

"That's what you said last time. Don't be sorry. Just, if I was coming onto you, you'd know, all right? And I won't be." There's a long pause while Connie tries to think of something to say to that. "And don't be offended, either," Rowan says. "It's not that you're not cute. I'm just not into—"

"—straight women, yeah, I know. That's okay. It's nice to get that straight. So to speak."

"Yeah. But you have to kick in for grub."

"Sure."

"And help with the chores."

"So long as I don't have to skin animals, or anything like that."

"Up to you."

"Okay, it's a deal."

"Right on, sister."

"Right on."

Bull Moose

Abe stands in the doorway of the cabin, looking down at the Chestnut lying tipped over on its side by the shore of the nameless lake. Nameless Lake, he thinks, good name. He's starting to wonder if he thought this thing all the way through. Sure he can bone the moose out so he can carry it. Sure he brought the lightest canoe he could find, although picking it up still makes him feel as though pain is his heartbeat. The old man travelled all over this area in that Chestnut, but he was always fit and strong, any time he was worried about the canvas he could just carry the damn thing. Maybe Abe should have tried to get his hands on a Grummond or one of those Coleman things, something he could drag over the portages. Or maybe he should never have gotten into this in the first place.

It was easy enough back in Whitehorse, talking to Frank and saying, oh sure, I can handle it, I can get a moose, one way or another, but now he finds he can't think of any good hunting spots that he can get back from with a moose in the canoe. Or half a moose. Or a quarter. Well, maybe a quarter, depending on the beaver dams. Sometimes you can get right through to Ashcan Lake from here. Just this side of Ashcan there's a place where the creek runs through a big willow swamp, and a higher meadow behind that, with a pup running through it down to the creek. Between him and Frank and the old man, they've taken half a dozen moose out of that hole over the years. There's hotter spots around, but none that Abe can get to. He throws the last few gritty drops of coffee onto the ground and goes back inside.

Kitty's swimming for all she's worth, just ahead of the boat. There are two other dogs coming up right behind, and the rest are crashing through the thick bush along the shore, diving into the water to get around fallen trees and then leaping back to dry land as soon as they can.

When the paddle dips into the clear black water, two little whirlpools form before and behind the blade. When she lifts it again and returns it forward for another stroke, the water runs off the end, and joins the swirling wake. Waves like folds in a blanket roll back from the bow of the canoe. Connie was surprised to learn that it's the stern paddler who steers. Sitting up front, all she has to remember is to turn her body into the stroke, so that she doesn't wear out her shoulders, and to lift the paddle gently so as not to splash water on all the gear packed into the middle of the boat. Oh, and to keep in the middle so she doesn't rock the boat. This is the second of four lakes in the chain that leads to Rowan's cabin. The portage at the end of the first lake was nightmarish: Connie stumbled under the weight of the canoe, her shoulder bruised and tender from the constant pressure of the inverted gunwale, her eyes, ears, and nose full of crawling blackflies, dying to stop and brush them off, stubbing her toes on tree roots and scraping her arms on branches. When they did finally reach the next lake and she walked into the water to set the canoe down, her feet sank into about a foot of disgusting black sludge that gave off a smell like a sewage lagoon.

"Oh yeah," Rowan said, "I forgot to tell you, it's all loon shit along here." Already sick at the feel of the stuff, Connie's stomach turned. She dropped the canoe and floundered back to shore.

"Ow, hey," Rowan complained, laughing, as the canoe flopped sideways in her hands. "It's a figure of speech. It's just muck."

"Sorry."

"That's okay. Natural reaction. Everybody calls it that. Just got to watch out for leeches."

"Leeches?" Connie has never seen a leech. They were spoken of in cottage country, but everyone knew where they were to be encountered, and no one went near those places. She associates them with obscure blood diseases, witches, doctors with unwashed hands.

"Come on, Christ's sake, you've got pants and shoes on. Let's get this thing loaded." They had brought the cargo up first and piled it along the shore, ready to load once the canoe was launched. Connie's getting a big kick out of all the nautical terms, attaching this real, physical, knowledge to the names she's only read in books before. Pigpen's canoe, which Rowan borrowed because her own isn't big enough for the two of them and all their gear, has a fibreglass hull, with wooden gunwales (pronounced *gunnels*, she was delighted to discover) down the sides. It's long, seventeen feet, Rowan says, and broad. It has three spars, but no seats, which is because it's a freighter. You're supposed to kneel to paddle it, but Pigpen has stuck in a couple of boxes with cushioned lids. The boxes are lined with styrofoam, *so your ass don't warm the beer up*. It has plenty of freeboard even with a full load, which means it doesn't sit too low in the water. The food is packed into big, rubberized, drawstring sacks called dry-bags. As well as their packs, there's a sack each of potatoes and carrots, two cardboard boxes of cans and dry foods, two kinds of flour, and four bags of dog food. The dog food is wrapped in garbage bags rather than dry-bags and has to be handled carefully to avoid tears and punctures. It looks like it would feed all these dogs for about a week and a half, but Rowan says it has to last two months. When she comes back in after freeze-up, she'll haul an extra sled with more, but for the most part she and the dogs have to live off the land when they're in the bush. Fish, berries, and wild mushrooms. Flour for bannock and oats for breakfast. Moosemeat, fresh for as long as she can keep it, frozen over the winter, dried for spring. That's why she's here in the fall: to get her moose. Yesterday, in the supermarket, Connie asked why she says "get my moose."

"As opposed to what?"

"I don't know, 'get a moose,' or 'kill a moose,' or something. Why 'my'? I mean, you don't come to the supermarket and say, 'I'm going to get my ham today,' you say, 'I'm going to buy some ham.'"

Rowan thought about it for a minute. "I don't know," she said. "Everybody says it."

"It just sounds funny. It's like there's this moose out there waiting for you to come and shoot him."

Rowan considered this while she bent to pick up a bag of powdered milk from the bottom shelf. "Yeah, that's it," she said, and smiled, so Connie couldn't tell if she was kidding or not.

There's a creek between the second and third lakes. Depending on what the beaver have been up to, Rowan says, there can be enough water in it to float down easy, or you might have to carry your canoe the whole way. This time it was half full, and they managed it with only one portage of about a hundred feet, although it was necessary to step out into the icy water a couple of times and drag the canoe over the dams. Somewhere Connie had read that the beavers weave the sticks together, and she had formed an image of a tightly woven lattice, bellying out in the current like a sail in the wind. A real beaver dam, it turns out, is more like a pile of sticks and mud all gummed together, except for the upper layer, which is a bunch of loose sticks that sag under you when you step on top of them to drag the canoe up, and make a hideous sound when they scratch against the fibreglass. In one place they had to unload the dog food and pack it on their shoulders, two trips each, shin-deep in water, to a place downstream where they could set it on the bank, just so they could pull the canoe over the dam. By the time she got back into the boat, Connie's feet and ankles were numb.

With her pant legs soaked and chafing and her back and shoulders bruised and tired, her hair full of tiny, crawling, itching misery, her wish that she had caught the plane back to Toronto was so intense she could almost touch it, as though that moment of decision to stay in the Yukon, to go in the bush, was there just behind her, just out of reach, and if she stretched out her hand she could take hold of it, change her mind, be warm and comfortable in an airport limo in heavy downtown traffic, only minutes away from Nat's living room, where the steam heat bangs in the pipes and the Glenfiddich is kept in the cabinet above the kitchen radiator so that it's always just slightly above room temperature. Now, with the sunshine warm on her back and the flies left behind ashore, she luxuriates in small gains: her pant legs are nearly dry, the sun feels like healing medicine on her shoulders, and Rowan promises there are no more portages.

A ghost gives a long, breaking moan from the far end of the lake, and from the opposite shore a demon cackles a reply. Connie shivers. "Loons?" she says over her shoulder, identifying a sound she's heard only on TV.

"Awesome, ain't it?" Rowan says, although her tone sounds more comfortable with the sound than awestruck by it.

"It's—"

"Yeah, I know."

"What are they saying?"

"Nothing too earth-shattering, I wouldn't expect. Something along the lines of, 'This is me over here, is that you over there?' I guess."

"Oh, no, it must be more than that?"

"You figure?"

"Well, why would it be so complex?"

Rowan chuckles.

"What?"

"Well, how do you think we sound to them?"

"Not nearly as musical as they sound to us."

"Although," Rowan says, "most of the time they hear me coming, it's this." She strokes with her paddle.

Connie's been thinking of the paddle's rhythmic splashing as music already, but she meant it in a vague way, a metaphor or something, for the pleasing sound, but when she stops and listens to Rowan paddling she realizes that it really is music in the literal sense. She believes she could still remember enough of her high school music theory to write it out, at least as percussion, although she thinks the two different sounds the paddle makes entering the water might actually be the first and third of a minor chord. Maybe not, though. When she left Grade 13 she vowed to keep up with her music, no matter what, but at Trent she let it drift, the way she let everything drift that year, and then Jason came along. Jason managed to convince her, without ever putting it into words, that the trombone wasn't quite suitable for her. Or, more precisely, she now understands, for a girlfriend of his. On the day that she saw Jason and the redhead together, she took her horn out of its case, oiled the slide, blew out the spit valve, and played "April Showers." She couldn't get rid of the feeling that this was no longer an independent act, that she'd given it up for Jason's sake and from now on every time she played, it would be because Jason had given her permission to play such an unhip, unfeminine instrument by dumping her. She put it away in its case. Stashed it in the basement next time she visited her parents. It's still there.

"But what I meant was," Rowan says, and her voice brings the present moment rushing up.

"What?" Connie says.

"What I meant about the way we sound is that a lot of the time we're not saying much more. We stick in a lot of words, but listen to what people say when they meet. Hi, how are you, good, yourself, pretty good. What you been up to, not much, how about you, oh you know, same old shit. What does it mean?"

"Yeah, I know," says Connie. She often thinks about this: small talk. It's one of the things that makes her not much good at parties; she'll be talking with someone over the food table and suddenly get an image of seagulls all walking around on a beach and squawking at each other, apes grooming together. She resumes paddling again after a minute or so of sitting still and a dull pain follows the sweep of the paddle, riding across her back from shoulder to shoulder.

It must show, because Rowan says, "Why don't you take a rest? It's already been a hell of a long day for your first canoe trip."

"I'm okay."

"Hey, who's the skipper on this boat? I'm going to need you in working order when we put to shore, sailor. Now ship that paddle."

"Aye aye, sir," Connie says, and her body sags with relief. It's a long way down to the end of the lake, too far to make out the cabin that Rowan says is on the left-hand side, and she's been trying to wish away all the endless paddle strokes that lie between her and a rest. "Thanks. I don't want to make extra work."

"Oh, hey, forget it, you've already pulled your weight and then some. You're actually a pretty amazing paddler for a first time out. You sure you're from Toronto?"

"Suburb of. If I'd been about five years older, I'd probably have learned to canoe at the cottage, but by the time I came along, it was all water skiing."

"Your folks had a cottage?"

"Not mine, but a lot of my friends. None of it was bush anymore, though. Lakes like this, kind of, in the Muskokas, but with cottages all around the whole shore. Everybody talked about how a few years ago there used to be loons on the lake and bears coming in to the yard and all that, but we never saw any of it. We laid on little patches of beach with our bathing suits rolled down to our nipples and read teen magazines and watched the guys go by in their motorboats until they'd stop and ask us if we wanted to go skiing. You'd see people in canoes once in a while but it was totally uncool."

"Were you a rich kid?"

"Kind of, I guess."

"Big house?"

"Biggish."

"Servants?"

"No. Well, there was a cleaning lady."

"No shit?"

"That was later on. But she wasn't a servant. She was freelance. She did about four houses or something. Insisted on cash."

"Go to private school?"

"No, but my little sister did. We kind of got richer later on when my mom went back to work."

"Same thing happened with us."

"Oh yeah?"

"I went to work on my old man's claims when I was sixteen. Mom was pissed off at first, but then she decided it was a good time to go out to work herself. Been running the business end of the mining operation for years. Took a couple courses and started doing other people's books and stuff. Ended up selling real estate, made a bunch of money. They were millionaires on paper by the time they retired."

"Are they still?"

"Actually, they're kind of vague about that. The old man likes to whine about how he didn't get his price when he sold out, and the equipment was getting worn out so he lost on that, and on and on. But they're living pretty good on what's left. Mom says they'll be laughing unless they live past ninety, and then they'll have to sell the house to keep going. Funny, eh? When I heard they were worth a million, I thought they'd be in luxury forever."

"Might depend on what you call luxury."

"Yeah. Guess it might."

Without looking over her shoulder, Connie can tell Rowan's

doing the same thing she's doing: looking around the lake and gloating over the luxury of it, the canoe slipping through the black water, the weird echo-chamber cooing and cackling of the loons, the lake's surface a shimmering mirror reflecting the green and golden hillsides, the snow-sugared mountains, the only disturbance the dogs hustling along the shore, diving in and climbing out of the water, occasionally stopping to whine when their path is blocked by dense bush and they know they will have to jump into the cold lake again. Even Kitty has tired of keeping up with the canoe, and is swimming across the bays, getting out and shaking herself off on the points before leaping in again.

"You can see the cabin now. See it?" There are three dark spots on the still-distant shore, ahead and to the left, randomly spaced apart. Each of them could be anything or nothing, a bear, a cabin, an upturned tree, or just a dense patch in the spruce forest. "At about ten o'clock." This must mean the dark patch in the middle. Staring, Connie can just make out that it's up off the shore a little, but still can't reconcile it into any discernible shape. She takes up her paddle and tries an easy stroke. The pain is dull and comfortable, like stretching after a strenuous game of tennis, and she leans in just a little more, finding the spot where it hurts too much before backing off. Rowan tells her again that she doesn't have to paddle, but this time she wants to. She says it's just for the sake of stretching, but the truth is she's in a hurry to reach shore. She wants to see the cabin she's heard so much about, the one built by the crazy old Scottish guy with the silver pigtails who never owned a vehicle or a Ski-Doo or even a pack dog, let alone a dog team, never drove a motorboat, walked everywhere unless he paddled. Maybe she feels some of the old character's spirit in her, making her want to lean into her stroke and reach her destination. There's no exact moment that she can pinpoint when the dark shape becomes a cabin, or when she can make out the tall grass growing on top of the sod roof, the old-fashioned mullion windows, the stout dock at the foot of the hill, the wooden staircase leading up to the door. They pull up to the dock and climb out. Rowan ties the canoe off at both ends to a couple of posts that have been carved into the shape of capstans.

"Float plane dock," Rowan explains. "Fanciest friggin' dock in the Yukon. Story goes the old guy built it so his wife wouln't feel so isolated. Try to get her to stay."

"Did she?"

Rowan laughs. "Only plane ever docked here was the one that took her out. Or so they say."

On the hillside leading down to the lake there's a fenced area bigger than the cabin where wildflowers grow thick and tall against the grey boards. "Garden," Rowan says as they climb the stairs, she with her pack on her back, a sack of dog food on her shoulder and a drybag under her arm, Connie struggling with just her own pack and one of the boxes. "There's still some chives in among all that somewhere. And those are raspberry bushes on the west side."

"I guess you're never here in summer to look after it." Connie's breath comes short, but not as short as it would have been a couple of months ago on a climb this steep.

"Probably wouldn't anyway," Rowan says, setting her load down by the cabin door. "Got no interest in it. Guess I'm more of a hunter-gatherer type."

Amazing how warm it can get sometimes in the middle of September. Rowan watches Connie set her paddle down carefully behind her and begin to unbutton her shirt. It's the fourth layer she's shed since this morning's fog cleared from the lake, and they went out to feed the dogs. Oh no, please, Rowan thinks, not topless. Alice used to do this, her naked back flexing and rolling as she paddled. One bug-free day they turned back to shore and blessed old Hector's dock before heading out again to catch a fish.

Sure enough, naked shoulders shrug out of the shirt. Rowan closes her eyes for a second, and opens them to find Connie stretching her arms out wide and leaning back as far as she can, offering her body to the sun.

"This is incredible," she says. Her skin is rose pink, her nipples are brown.

If Rowan was on her own she'd be out hunting today, but it was pretty easy to see that Connie needed a day to recover from the trip in. They're only paddling as far as the island in the middle of the lake, where the big trout feed in the channel. All Connie needs to do is sit still while Rowan paddles over there and then let her line out, and she'll catch a nice fish for supper, but she's got to be up there paddling for all she's worth, the twinge of pain visible with each stroke. You've got to admire her spirit. And the way her back flexes from left to right as she leans into her stroke.

I hope this was a good idea, Rowan thinks. As recently as two days ago she was sure she could be Connie's friend and nothing more, that there was no risk involved in inviting a beautiful twenty-one-year-old to spend six weeks in the bush with her, that when she made the offer she was just being friendly and that she didn't have any real stake in the idea. What the heck, they'd been in camp together longer than that and she'd never taken more than passing notice. Even at Alice's place, the night she pretended to sleep while Connie brought herself off beside her, she thought, hey, no big deal, I can handle this. Last night she lay awake remembering, wishing she could just have turned over and joined in. She tries to remember if she was still doing that at Connie's age, but she doesn't think so. She never did it much to begin with.

Most of the time, Rowan can't see what all the big deal is about sex. She likes it well enough when it comes along, and doesn't miss it that much when it doesn't. That's why she wasn't worried about this arrangement. It's curious that the first thing people identify her with is who she has sex with, when sex is a lot less important to her than to most people she knows.

Connie, for instance. For all that Connie rejected every guy in camp, every guy she's met since she came to the Yukon by the sound of it, she moves like a constant invitation to flirt. She's forever tossing her head back and showing off the way her thick hair plays with her neck, or stretching her shoulders so her breasts crush against the inside of her shirt. Whatever she's doing, her ass seems to present itself like it was born for the touch of a hand, and her eyes flirt unconsciously with everybody, man or woman. One evening in the cookshack she leaned forward, chin on hands, to ask Tony a question, something about logging. He got the full close-up treatment: big hazel eyes and little pouty mouth and the tiny hint of cleavage above the open second button on her bush shirt, and everybody in the room except her seemed to notice the way he crossed his legs and licked his dry lips, and finally got up, visibly limping, and left the trailer. Connie looked so innocent you could almost believe she didn't know what everyone was laughing at.

Even with that Sky chick, when they tracked her down at the shack where she does her massage thing, Connie was outrageous: leaning close, touching her arm, sitting down and looking up at her so she got the full effect of the big brown eyes.

"You know," she said, holding the bear-claw necklace out toward the other girl, "I'm not going to be seeing my friend as soon as I thought. You've got almost exactly her colouring. Could you just let me see it against your skin, so I can picture it on her?" And that Sky, she went right along with it, flirted right back at her in her own hippie way. Why do they do that, straight women? Rowan pushes aside the thought that she might have been a little jealous of the speed with which they began to flirt with each other. She doesn't go for that stuff anyway.

But the topless canoeist treatment is a bit much. Connie seems to have taken Rowan at her word: she's not into straight women, and that's the end of it. Well, it is the end of it, it's true; Rowan has no intention of getting involved with Connie. Still, that doesn't mean she's made of stone. She's going to have to find a nice way to tell her to keep her shirt on.

A-bel Walk-er, A-bel Walk-er. Goddamn that old bastard anyway, giving him a name like that, a name you can't walk or paddle without thinking about, thinking: of course I can do this, I'm Abel Walker. I can do anything. Wonder if Frank's name was supposed to shape his future, too? Frank Walker. Doesn't work. He's frank, though, you have to give him that. Told old Hector straight the day he left, You're a goddamned old tyrant, he said, you know that? Sixteen years old. I never lifted my hand to you in your life, says the old man. No, Frank says, but you never cut me an inch of slack, either. You're not going anywhere, says the old man. Hector, Frank says, always knew it pissed the old man off when he called him Hector, you can't stop me. Remember it clear as yesterday, five years old sitting on the front step, Frank on the dock. Getting in his own canoe. Old man on the top step. Poor old Hector: brought his boys up to be able to look after themselves, feed themselves out of the bush, fix their own clothes, not to depend on women for everything—didn't expect them to think for themselves, too? Channel in the creek up ahead runs through the tall grass like the pictures in that kids' book Mom used to have.

When he paddles up to the meadow, he sees that the path of the creek is different from what he remembers. It used to flow directly across the open space, but now it wanders around near the edge of the bush. He follows along until he comes to a place where something has been coming down to the water to drink. He pulls up close and climbs out, holding onto the stern rope. There's nothing around to tie to but willow bushes, so he pulls the canoe up onto the trail.

He takes the gun case out of the canoe and opens it, picks up the .30.06, and pushes the clip into place. He follows the path to the edge of the bush, maybe fifty yards away, and then scouts around among the trees for somewhere to camp. There's moose sign all over the place. Early in the morning he can walk down to where it's open toward the high meadow, and call. There's bound to be bulls up there. Send me a little one, please, first thing tomorrow morning. Although it's not actually going to be so bad, getting it back to the cabin. So long as he comes down close to the water. If he does that, and he's not too big, I'm okay. Once it's in the canoe, I can get it home without taking it out of the water. God bless the beavers this year. Be three trips, though, even for a little guy. What did the physiotherapist say? Light exercise, no lifting.

He goes back to the canoe for his tent and sleeping bag. He's got some bannock and cheese with him, and a bag of figs, and a dried fish. He can eat without cooking, and turn in early.

Fog parts like a white curtain ahead of the bow of the canoe. It's the eeriest feeling, slicing out across the water, nothing to tell where they're going but faith in Rowan's ability to keep a straight line. The creek flows on out of the lake, just around the bend from the cabin. There's a willow swamp a little way downstream, Rowan says, with a game trail leading down to the creek. They need to get there early in the morning if they want to call in a moose.

Call in a moose, trick it into thinking you're another moose, and then shoot it: how? In the head? The heart? Carve it up in the stink—is there a stink?—of blood and guts. Me? How can I do that? Not shooting, of course. Still—watching, being there, taking part. What does it look like? Seen death before, birds that flew into windows, bugs in their thousands. Not killing, though. Except some of the bugs. And then the lake trout yesterday, flopping and gasping in the boat until Rowan clubbed it on the head with a stick—"pass me the fish-bonker there." But never anything that bled. They're so huge. And those soft eyes.

"Hey, Rowan?"

"Yeah?"

"How much does a moose bleed when you shoot him?"

"Depends how quick he dies."

"What?"

"Yeah. Once the heart stops pumping you've just got seepage."

Nat, I know, I know. I can't believe it, either. But it's starting to make sense. It's not like I was ever a real vegetarian or anything. I wear leather. And I would always eat meat if it was really scrummy. So this is just a kind of honesty, right? I mean, it's not like meat is born cut and wrapped. Something has to die before I can wear leather boots. Okay, all right, shut me up, I'm rationalizing my face off.

"We can't talk too much when we're hunting, okay?" Rowan says, her voice hushed. "Just what has to be said, and keep it low. You know how voices carry over water."

The plan is to paddle out to the willows every morning and evening and make noises like a cow moose in heat. They'll call and then wait quietly for a couple of hours. Eventually, Rowan says, a bull will come to check it out. She demonstrated the cow call last night in the cabin. It's a bit like the bawling of cattle, but shorter, more guttural. The dogs leapt up and started barking at the ends of their chains, looking all around. Rowan did a bull call, too—"just to play with their heads"—a grunt like a constipated linebacker, and then called out to the dogs to shut up as they frantically ran around their houses, leaping on top to sniff the air, and then off again when they found no scent.

A vague shape in the darkness to the left is just discernible as the bank along the mouth of the creek. The still water suddenly comes to life as it funnels down into the channel. It takes effort to paddle strongly enough to make any difference going downstream. Connie's leaning into her stroke, getting up a rhythm, when Rowan says, very softly, "Connie." She turns and looks over her shoulder, and Rowan is motioning her to settle down. "Just drift."

The morning sun has begun to penetrate the fog. Connie ships her paddle, pulls her fingers out of the fingers of her gloves, tucks them down inside the palms, and rubs both hands together.

"*Connie.*" It's a whisper this time. She turns around to see Rowan putting her fingers to her lips. "*Sh.*"

Out of the grey, colours begin to resolve themselves. Orange and gold leaves on the willows. Patches of blue sky. A white bird that dips and turns. Once it begins to go, the fog dissipates quickly. Willows ringed with dense spruce forest to the right, spruce forest all the way to the riverbank on the left. It looks as though, if you lost your boat, there'd be no way out but to swim. She feels oddly claustrophobic until they round another corner and the view opens up wide. The creek runs through a broad marsh of hummocks, willows, and buckbrush. Straight ahead, at the end of the marsh, it takes a sharp turn to the right and back into the bush. Beyond, there's a short rise to another meadow that looks like tall grass and wildflowers. After that there's another rise to a high plateau, and a grand sweep of mountain ridge, thick with snow on top, and snow-dusted most of the way down its slopes. She's so awestruck that for a moment she doesn't recognize the loud bawling noise that comes from just ahead. Her heart's done about four backflips before she even realizes it's a cow moose. In heat.

She turns to look at Rowan, who puts her finger to her lips again. They keep going until they come to a trail that leads to the water's edge. Rowan signals to Connie to plant her paddle in the water—points and then pantomimes, and punctuates it with her *keep it quiet* gesture—and drifts in backward to the path. She's been carrying the gun next to her, propped up on the gunwale, the handle part between her feet. She picks it up, half stands, and then steps out of the canoe onto the trail. The canoe rocks and she steadies it with her hand. She signals to Connie to come out, and once again to be quiet. Once Connie's standing beside her on the trail, she ties off the canoe to a clump of willows, slowly working it under the base of the bush and then fishing it back out, silently. She motions for Connie to stay put and then turns down the path. As soon as she can see around the corner, she pulls up short, and turns back to signal Connie to come on. When Connie comes up beside her, she, too, stops short when she sees the green canoe. Rowan looks like she's going to laugh, but she doesn't. She motions Connie to follow her. A little farther down the trail, the willows open up on one side enough that they can see the edge of the woods. Rowan points, and Connie sees a man, standing on a slight rise, looking in a pair of binoculars. Rowan seems to be straining to listen for something, so Connie tries to listen, too, but all she can hear is the water running past. Time ticks by while they squat on the trail and watch the man with the binoculars watch the horizon they can't see over the high willows.

The man lets the binoculars hang from his neck, puts his hands up to his mouth, and makes the cow moose call again. It's still ringing in the air when he seems to start, and stare in their direction. Rowan leans her gun against a bush, signals the guy to hush, and then turns her open hands toward him in a shrug of innocence. He looks completely puzzled, seems at a loss what to do for a moment, but then takes up his binoculars. When he lowers them again, he signals for Rowan and Connie to come over to where he's standing. He uses the same two-palms-down signal Rowan uses to mean *keep it quiet*.

The trail wanders a bit, and it takes a minute or so to reach the place where the man is standing, still looking down his binoculars. When they come close, he leans over so his head is next to Rowan's.

"You after a big bull?" he murmurs. Rowan nods, and then the man nods toward the willows. "Too big for me," he says. Rowan lifts her own binoculars to her eyes, looks and nods. Connie has no idea what she should do, so she stands, awkwardly watching Rowan and the man looking up the valley. And then she hears it: the crashing sound in the willows. The man turns and bends to pick something up from the ground beside him. It's some kind of bone, with a flat part on the end. He rubs it up and down the trunk of the tree beside him, and then knocks it against a willow bush. There's more noise from the bushes, this time closer, and Connie sees the moose, still a good distance off, coming in at an oblique angle, turning his head this way and that, listening, looking, scenting the wind, still suspicious.

"Keep very still," Rowan says, just above a whisper. When the bull's head disappears for a moment behind a big willow bush, she turns to look at the guy, asks him a question of some sort with her eyebrows, which he seems to understand.

"It's your moose," the guy whispers. Rowan nods, turns, puts her hands up to her mouth, and makes the bull call. Then she nods toward the bone, and the guy bangs it against the willows. There's a crashing noise from the direction of the moose, and suddenly he comes charging forward, head up, ready for battle. Although he's searching all around for his rival, he doesn't see Rowan raise the rifle, slide something back and then forward again, squint down the length of it. At one moment he turns broadside to them, about twice as far away as across a city street, and then Connie's ears are shattered by the loudest noise she's ever heard.

Oh my God he's hit he's stumbling what's that noise he's making, like the end of the world, his world, great monster thing crashing down oh God he's getting up again listen to him it hurts him, he's like a baby, he doesn't understand, panic, pain, it hurts like hell I can't stand it, what is that thing in my chest, hurting tearing me I'm dying where's it coming from not like this not like this not like this.

The gun barks again, strangely quieter the second time, and the moose, on its knees, kicks over sideways and stops moving.

"Good shooting," the guy says, and Connie loses control.

"Hey, sister." Rowan's hand on her back, like a voice calling to her from a distance. How long has she been lost, taken over by violent sobs? Rowan's hand doesn't stop the crying, but now Connie's present, called back to her body. She can feel the presence of the man beside her, a vibration of extreme discomfort. Rowan's hand tells her she understands, knows the context, loves, forgives, but the guy knows nothing except that this chick, who, he's probably guessed by now, is from the city, has burst out crying at the sight of a shot moose. Embarrassed, she begins to struggle for control.

"I—I'm sorry," she says, half turning toward him, but not meeting his eyes. It takes a moment before he answers.

"I pissed myself the first time," he says. Now Connie looks up. "I was four," he explains, and they both burst out laughing. It's several moments before Connie realizes Rowan is laughing, too.

"That's the easiest hunt I ever had," she says, taking her hand away from Connie's back and offering it to the guy, who, Connie now realizes, is very young, maybe even a teenager. "Rowan," she says, and they shake hands.

"I figured. I'm Abe," says the guy.

"Oh," says Rowan. "Frank's brother?"

"Yeah," says the guy. "Abe Walker."

Walker. Old Hector Walker. This must be his son. There's some kind of subtext between him and Rowan, a tiny double-take on Rowan's part at hearing his name, a hint of sheepishness from the guy. Who, on a second look, is probably Connie's age. And very good-looking. He has the kind of narrow, handsome features that could be Jewish or Spanish, or possibly Indian, but his hair and beard are blond and wispy and his eyes are pale blue.

"I'm Connie," she says, trying not to stare.

"Hi Connie," says Abe, and shakes hands. She pulls her glove off and feels his hand, cool in hers.

"Why didn't you want him?" Rowan says, and Connie turns in surprise and then realizes she's talking to Abe about the moose.

"I'm looking for a little guy," says Abe. "I was calling him in, and then just before I saw you there I got a look at him, and I was just going to let him go."

"If he would go."

"Yeah. Well, that's why I was glad to see you come along. Why don't I help you clean him out? Get him out of the way."

"Sure."

They go about the job without saying much to each other. Every once in a while one of them will get Connie to pass them something—water, the sharpening stone, Abe's thermos, Rowan's bone saw and game bags from the canoe. When she turns to come back from the creek, Rowan's standing up, her gun in her hand, casting her eye over the bushes. There's something protective about the way she stands, and Connie's heart freezes.

Dale.

But then Rowan takes one last look around, and disappears, squatting back to her task on the carcass.

"What was that about?" Connie asks when she gets back.

"What?" Rowan says, looks up, and then catches on. "Oh. Pays to keep an eye out for bears. Smell this a mile away."

Of this Connie has no doubt. The guts, it turns out, do stink. It's all lying on the ground beside the hollowed-out carcass, partially contained inside a white membrane, though it hangs sickeningly out of the end. Rowan has pulled a folded scrap of polythene out of her vest pocket and spread it on the ground. There are bloody things lying on it.

"Actually," Rowan says, "that's something you could be doing. Just keep an eye out for anything moving in the bushes."

Okay, so now I'm on bear patrol. Right now the biggest animal I've ever seen outside a zoo is lying here on the ground with his guts torn out and his skin coming off, and people hacking at him with knives, and I'm keeping watch for bears. How big could these bears be? How many might show up? How fast do they come? Couldn't we just build a fire? I thought wild animals were afraid of fires.

"You're going to get eaten to death up there."

"So I'll wear bug repellent."

"So you'll be eaten by mountain lions."

"There's no mountain lions in the Yukon."

"How do you know?"

"I've been reading."

"Bears then."

"I'm sure you can just stay out of the bear areas."

"It's all one big bear area, kid. That's why the wages are high."

Okay, Nat, you win. You can stop proving it now, I admit it, you were right: there are crazy murderers and wild animals all over the place.

Connie stares at a patch of willow where she thought she saw a movement. "How do I know if it's a bear?" she asks.

"Big furry thing," Rowan says without looking up.

"With claws," Abe adds.

"Ha ha. How do I know if a movement in the bushes is a bear?"

"Because after the bushes move, a big furry thing comes out." Interesting how comfortable those two are together when they're mocking Connie for a dumb city chick. Great ice-breaker. She goes back to scanning the bushes without speaking. "They don't sneak around," Rowan goes on, mollifying. "If a bear comes along, you'll know it. Watch out for moose, too. Another bull could be just as dangerous as a bear."

Great. More things to worry about. But a bear doesn't come along, and neither does a moose. Connie's neck gets sore from looking around. Ice broken, Rowan and Abe talk while they work.

"—size of that hindquarter."

"Well, yeah. Look at that rack."

"Good to get these big guys cleaned out of here."

"Why?" Connie asks.

"They attract trophy hunters," Rowan says.

"Oh."

"This guy's a record bull, for sure."

"You take the rack?" Abe asks.

"Oh yeah," Rowan says. "Friend of mine makes carvings out of them. Trades me needlework."

"Don't do your own?"

"No. You?"

"Oh yeah, my old man made sure of that. Cook, clean, sew. 'Never be dependent on a woman, lad.'"

"Guess he was quite the character."

"Know him?"

"No, but my father did. Talked about him some."

"Yeah, guess a lot of people did."

They're like variations on a theme, these two. Children of the bush, people whose parents had the whole world to choose from, and chose to bring their children up in the middle of nowhere, raise them into these oddball creatures, Rowan and Abe. Not that Connie knows anything about Abe. Yet.

"So, where are you camped?" Rowan asks.

Abe glances over toward his tent as if to say that's his camp right there. She flashes him a look that says *get real*, and he smiles.

"In one of your cabins."

"My cabins?"

"Other end of this creek. Back Lake, we used to call it. Back end of the line, eh?"

"I know it. Squirrel house."

"Yeah, I cleaned it up a bit." Rowan doesn't speak. "But if you don't want—?" Again she doesn't reply, and Abe keeps working, waiting.

Eventually she looks over at him and asks, "Staying long?"

"Guess that's up to you." This time it's Rowan's turn to keep silent and wait. "I was thinking about staying till break-up."

"What for?"

"Nothing. Look, if you don't want me there—"

"Long trip out for a guy with a bad back."

Abe looks sheepish.

"When's the plane coming for you?"

He shakes his head, grinning at Rowan's ability to see through him. "Soon as it's clear." He stands up then, and stretches, the first time he's done that since they started on the carcass. He stretches every direction, taking his time over it, and then squats back down. He doesn't ask Rowan how she knew about his back. He acts as though it was completely obvious and he's embarrassed even to have tried to conceal it, but Connie never noticed. She watches him now and sees that he holds himself stiffly, turning his whole upper body in order to turn his head. She watches him turn over the bit of the moose he's working on, the back leg and half the ass. He winces. She wonders now how she could have missed it.

"That why you were looking for a small moose?" Rowan says. "Account of your back?"

He laughs. "Don't miss much, do you?"

She laughs back. "I try not. You're not after my fur?"

"No. Just—hibernating. If that's okay."

Rowan doesn't say anything for a while. It's not until the moose is quartered and wrapped in cheesecloth that she stands and says, "You wanna split this moose?"

Abe looks doubtful.

"Look," Rowan says, "I was ready to spend days on this hunt. I'm going to be home for friggin' lunch. Thanks to you."

"Yeah, but—" says Abe, scratching the back of his neck and squinting.

"What?"

"Well, I appreciate it, but aren't you feeding a dog team?"

"I got a net in for them. And we can always get another moose, need be."

"We?" Abe says, his finger hovering between himself and Rowan.

"Yeah."

It's miraculous how good these two are at non-verbal communication, Connie thinks. It's as if they'd known each other all their lives.

Freeze-Up

"Hey," Rowan says, "check this out."

Connie's just waking up, sticking her arms out of her sleeping bag to stretch. After a quick eye-rubbing, a trial squint, and a follow-up rub, she's able to make out Rowan standing by the window with that I've-been-up-for-ages look. With an effort Connie pushes herself into consciousness, wriggles out of the bag, and puts her feet on the floor, quickly recoiling when they hit the cold wood. She leans forward and finds her boot liners, puts them on, and stumbles to the window.

"Hope you put the axe back in the stump last night," Rowan says, as Connie stares astonished at the suddenly unfamiliar landscape. Overnight, a foot of snow has fallen. There's not a single cloud, not one wisp of white, in a morning sky slowly fading from pink to blue. Rowan doesn't believe in getting up before first light, an expression she uses as if it articulated a specific time, like seven-thirty, instead of an ever-advancing moment when there's enough light from the window to find your liners, throw a couple of sticks in the fire, and start making coffee.

"That's quite a dump of snow," Rowan says, moving to the stove. "Must be ten inches anyway. Did you stick that axe in the stump?"

"Of course I did," Connie says. She can't manage to quarter the spruce logs yet, but she's learned to split the straight pine into kindling and the slightly bigger chunks for cooking Rowan calls stovewood. She takes pride in doing it well, and remembering to stick the axe back in the stump is one of the first lessons she learned. She'd left the axe with the blade on the ground, the handle propped against the woodpile. She thought it looked good that way.

Rowan had picked it up and stuck it in the chopping block. *It could get knocked over there. You've got to watch out for stuff like that. One of these mornings you're gonna wake up and there'll be a foot of snow.*

Now that it's arrived, Rowan seems to be lifted in spirits by the snow, almost as much as Connie, who's been feeling a bit blue during this new season of which she was previously unaware. Four seasons are enough for the rest of the world, but the bush has to have two extra, freeze-up and break-up. Bracketing the winter months, these are the seasons of isolation. Lakes and rivers are the roads of the bush, and once they begin to freeze or thaw they're impassable until the process is complete. Now that she's in the middle of it, this winter in the bush business is different from what Connie had imagined. It's all very pristine and everything, but there's only so much time you can spend appreciating the wilderness. Once the chores are done for the day, there's Rowan's company or there's her own.

After they met him on the moose hunt, Connie had been expecting to see lots more of Abe. When she and Rowan helped him ferry his share of the meat home, it seemed to her that the two cabins were quite handy to each other. It was more than a week later that he did show up at Rowan's. Connie was splitting wood when the dogs started to bark towards the water. Watching the small shape out on the lake resolve itself into a man in a canoe, she got the feeling there was something funny about the way he was paddling. When he was close enough to make out his features, she could see that each stroke was causing him pain. It was excruciating to watch him wince and try to grin at the same time. After that, he didn't come back. Connie couldn't think of a casual way to ask Rowan to take her visiting, so she waited for Rowan to suggest it herself, but she never did, and then one morning there was a ring of ice around the lakeshore, sticking several feet out into the bays. Carrying the canoe up and putting it on the rack, Connie felt stranded.

There are some bush trails in the area, but most of these end beside water, either at a canoe launch surrounded by untrustworthy ice, or at what will be a crossing as soon as the channel freezes over hard enough to walk on. Rowan and Connie have been hiking around in the open pine forest, looking for grouse.

Hunting has been a struggle for Connie. Everybody here takes the attitude that if you eat meat, you can't bitch about killing the animal, which is true, she guesses, but now that she's seen wild moose she can't help thinking they're worth more than some dumb cow in a field. Since she does eat the meat—loves the meat—she doesn't feel like she can reasonably cavil, but something close to panic takes hold of her when she thinks of that bull moose, the most powerful, the most *alive* creature she's ever seen reduced by a couple of loud bangs to a pile of, as Rowan put it, *groceries and guts*. Although she's aware of the twisted moral logic involved, she feels less troubled about grouse hunting. There isn't the same sense of destroying a magnificent beast. The grouse—*spruce chickens*—are fussy, panicked little creatures that fly into the trees in a great flurry of wings and noise, and wait brainlessly there for the bark of the .22, whereupon they fall. Some drop instantly dead, hitting the earth with a soft thump. Others flip around on the ground like spastic gymnasts, using up the nerve impulses in their dead bodies, but they're always dead when Rowan picks them up and checks her shot. She tries to shoot them right behind the eye, and usually succeeds, widening the eye socket on one side and creating a quarter-sized chunk of blood and splintered bone on the other. Connie was appalled at the grinning—she hates to think it, but, boyish—way Rowan showed her this the first time. Later, eating the red-meat grouse breasts stuffed with lowbush cranberries and wild onions—*can't do 'em up this way unless you get a head shot*—she began to appreciate Rowan's obsession with marksmanship.

Connie might even—although it's still hard to imagine—try shooting a grouse. She's already amazed herself by accepting Rowan's offer of shooting lessons, using a piece of plywood for a target leaning up against the bank of a hill. Drawn on the plywood in black marker is a picture of a grouse, roughly life-sized.

"*Okay, pull it up tight into your shoulder, that's how you keep it steady. See that little ball on the end there? Line that up on the target, and right in this vee here.*"

Palms sweating, Connie squeezed the trigger and the .22 gave a sharp pop.

"*Hey, that's pretty good! Looks like you missed his head by about an inch. That's damn good for a first shot. Try another one.*"

To her surprise, Connie loved shooting. She turned out to have a knack for it. She emptied a ten-shot clip, hitting the plywood every time. She leaned the rifle against a tree and ran up with Rowan to check the target. The fresh wood around the new holes distinguished them from Rowan's old shots, peppered around the head. Seven of Connie's bullets had hit the grouse. Two of the shots were in the neck and the rest were in the head. There were two in the perfect kill area. Rowan and Connie threw their arms around each other, doeskin shirt to doeskin shirt, and danced a jig of extravagant joy, kicking up the sand with their hiking boots and whooping like a couple of old sourdoughs who'd struck it rich.

"*Holy Annie Oakley! I can't believe it. You swear you never fired a gun before?*"

"*I never even saw a gun before I met you.*"

"*We'll make a bushwoman of you yet, girl.*"

Less exciting, but satisfying in its own way, has been berry-picking. The lowbush cranberries, tart but succulent, the mossberries bitter and sweet, tiny wild raspberries and strawberries. To get the fat blueberries that leave their mouths purple and black and make the best pies, they have to hike up the hillside behind the cabin. On these expeditions Rowan's been carrying the .303.

The first sliver of sun appears in a cleft between mountains on the far side of the lake. Standing by the window, Connie's beginning to feel the chill through her flannel pajamas. "I guess this means winter is really here," she says, moving closer to the stove.

"I guess," Rowan says. "Doesn't help any with the ice, though."

"Oh no?" Connie had imagined that this sudden and sure sign of winter would mean the whole package was only days behind—ice, snow, forty below, short days, aurora borealis, the works.

"Insulates the ice against the cold, eh? Takes longer to thicken up. If it had turned cold for a few days before this hit, we'd be travelling. This way, could be a while yet."

This news takes a lot of the joy out of the snowfall for Connie. Still, it is a beautiful morning, and by the time they've had coffee and bannock and scrambled powdered eggs with grated cheese—not one of the world's great delicacies, but a good belly-filler—the sun's above the horizon and she's looking forward to going out and making footprints in all that white perfection.

"Here," Rowan says as, booted, coated, scarfed, tuqued, and mittened, Connie reaches for the door handle. "Gonna hurt out there without your shades."

As soon as she steps out of the shadow of the cabin, Connie sees why the sunglasses are necessary. Even with them on, the glare from the snow is like an assault for the first few seconds. After her eyes adjust, the picture makes her stand and stare in wonder. A million pinpricks of light shine from everything in sight, from as close as the trees in front of her face, to as far as the mountains across the lake. She's heard snow referred to as sparkling before, but had always assumed it was a figure of speech. Down at the lakeshore, sparkling snow obscures the dock. The branches of the trees droop under its weight, the doghouses have almost disappeared in the drifts. Some of the dogs are lying inside, some are out frisking around in the snow, but at the sight of Connie, and of Rowan coming out the door, they all leap up and start to scream with the kind of enthusiasm they usually reserve for feeding time. Approaching, Rowan shushes them, and laughs.

"What's with them?" Connie asks.

"Think they're going running," Rowan says. "Smart enough to recognize snow, but they don't know the ice isn't safe. Kitty knows, though."

Kitty's nose pokes out of her doghouse, unmoved by the excitement.

"Smart dog," Connie says. "Guess that's why she's the leader."

"That, plus she likes to go."

"Don't they all?"

"Yeah, but," Rowan says, and then stops to think. For a minute it looks like she's going to explain, but then she shakes her head and says. "Wait a couple weeks, I'll show you. Come on, let's go look around for tracks. Nothing like first snow for seeing what you got hanging around."

Abe can feel the snow settled around the cabin before he opens his eyes. Maybe it's the quality of the dim light from the window, or maybe because the clatter of the creek, barely audible from inside the cabin, is subtly altered by the muffling blanket, but without looking he knows, can picture the triangular prism of white on the window ledge, the nearest branch of the black spruce leaning under the snow's weight to kiss the dark glass.

The need to piss keeps him from dawdling in bed. He fights through the first and worst pain of the day to struggle out of his bag and to his feet. Two barefoot steps take him gingerly to the door where his boots stand ready. Naked but for these, he opens the door, and although he knew, although he's seen this happen more times than he can count, he has to stop for a second to stare. It's a different landscape from the one the sun set on yesterday afternoon, different from how it's going to look in a day or two when it's tracked up by Abe's boots and the feet and the shit of a hundred small critters, mouse, martin, weasel, claw-footed grouse with their shredded-wheat droppings, whiskey-jack wing prints like etchings on the snow, shards of kindling and bark around the woodpile, a path beaten to the outhouse, a thousand blemishes soon to come.

It's a few degrees too cold to stand admiring the snow in the nude for long. Abe steps out and makes the first marks in the white perfection: six boot prints on the path to the pee tree, and a yellow stream of piss that washes the slight peak of snow down from the spruce's gnarled trunk. *Goddamn, that's yellow. Need to drink more water.* The trouble is, if he drinks more water at night, he'll have to piss sooner in the morning. *Already getting up while it's too goddamn dark in the shack to make coffee.*

Back inside, he hurries to dress, to chase away the slight chill on the surface of his skin. It's not what you'd call cold out—he checks the thermometer on the outside window frame and sees that it's thirty degrees, just a touch below freezing—but there's a feeling in the air, a kind of stillness, a density you don't usually get when it's this mild, so he knows that colder weather's on its way. *Going to have to start keeping the parka by the door at night. Colder weather'll be nice, get the lake frozen over, have someplace to travel.* There's a bush trail he can hike that takes him to a ridge that overlooks Ashcan Lake, where he can look across the half-frozen water at Rowan's cabin, the cabin where he spent nearly half his childhood. He did it once, but the sight of the place depressed him, and the thought that Rowan, or worse, Connie, might look across and see him standing there, the tiny outline of a spy, a peeping Tom, or just a lonely crippled guy who should have known better than to strand himself in the bush for a whole winter without company or help, made him blush, all alone, so hot that his face burned for much of the way home.

Abe's made the most of freeze-up. With nowhere to go, he's had lots of time to get things done. He's built a woodshed between four trees, using log poles and a tarp for the roof. It's full of wood, half of it split. There's a small stack by the cabin door, ready to go in the stove, except that this morning it's covered in snow. The cache that he built with his father ten years before only needed a little repair. He keeps his dry meat and fish up there, and the flour and beans. It hurts to put the ladder up and pull it down again to keep the critters out of the cache, but he only has to do it once a day. There's not much left to do now, not that many chores involved in maintaining one man in a trapper shack with no traps. It hadn't occurred to him how much musing time he'd have out here—even more than he's accustomed to. Sometimes he doesn't enjoy the places his mind goes.

Frank and Abe are driving down to Lewes Lake in Frank's one-ton. Abe just got out of hospital and his brother's taking him fishing. Madeline's standing up between Abe's legs, stretching up to see over the dashboard, and little Billie's on the seat, holding onto the four-speed stick shift. The Carcross Road is loose gravel and washboard, and just wide enough for two vehicles to meet and not click mirrors if everybody keeps their act together. Frank drives it at about forty-five, down to forty on the curves, talking the whole way, oblivious to the occasional cowboy in the new '78 half-ton four-by-four that'll ride his ass around the blindest corners and barrel by at the hint of an opportunity. To the east the mountains rise up close to the road, but to the west there's a broad river valley and then a long ridge of white-striped peaks all the way to Carcross.

"You don't look so bad to me, partner. What they say you did?"

Abe explains about ruptured disks, pinched sciatic nerves.

"They don't understand why I'm not flat on my back."

"They never treated a Walker before?"

That's the thing about Frank. He has no respect for the old man, but he has that same family pride, as if the name really means something. In some ways he's the old man, part two, but if Abe tried to tell him that he'd turn, spit out the window, and then change the subject.

Lewes Lake is completely surrounded by white chalky hills with practically no vegetation on them. There's a signpost by the crossing on the railroad tracks explaining how it got to be such a weird moonscape. Maddy insists on having it read to her, but gets bored before Frank's halfway through. It was the White Pass engineers, blowing up beaver dams or some such shit to stop flooding on the tracks. Worked a little better than they anticipated, though—dropped the water level forty feet.

"Must have shit when she started to go," Frank says. "I mean, pooped."

The fishing isn't so good in the fall, but Frank knows the spot where the small lakers always bite. With a little bacon on the hook, and just the right action on the line, they catch their limit in a couple of hours. Frank wants to keep fishing, Abe thinks it's too dangerous so close to the road.

"Shit, Frank says, "bush pigs show up, we'll just tell 'em we're Indians. Might as well get something out of it."

Frank always mocks Mom's Indian pretensions.

"It's friggin'—Maddy, cover your ears—it's fuckin' bullshit, ain't it? The old lady grew up in like downtown Toronto, right? Never seen an Indian till she was older than you are. Finds out she's got a Native granny up north Ontario some place, meets her a couple times, runs off to the Yukon and marries an Indian. Guy gets drunk and puts his snowmachine through a soft spot in the lake, she ends up with his trapline, which I want to tell you a lot of people in Teslin were mighty unhappy about, especially when the old man ended up on it. Somebody screwed up there, eh? Like big bureaucracy SNAFU, *that going through. Those lines are supposed to stay in the family. I mean the real family. That's why I never stopped for a drink at the Full Moon when we were going to Watson Lake that time. Remember that? Yeah, I'm not so sure the Walkers are real*

welcome in Teslin. Well anyways, I guess the point is Mom never did have much sense about men."

"She managed to land the old man."

"My point exactly, buddy."

It takes half an hour of fishing before Frank starts to talk again.

"I know you loved him, bud, but there's shit you should know."

The Mounties first heard of the old man's death from an anonymous phone call. A woman. Abe doesn't know what to say, what to feel. Was it the old man's fault? He tries to tell Frank he doesn't see that it was such a big crime.

"If Mom wanted to keep him to herself, she could have stayed with him."

"Yeah, right. We were about to starve if she'd of stayed in the bush, you know. She had to go to town to get a job. She wanted the old man to come with her, and he said no, neither him nor us. We'd survive off the land. What the hell was that all about? I mean, everybody loves the bush, but you don't live there, you go in the bush, and you bring something back. And don't talk to me about trapping. That line barely covered expenses at the best of times. The year she left was the year they'd used up all their credit. All that crap about doin' it nature's way, on foot? Couldn't have afforded to put gas in a friggin' snow-go if he'd wanted to. Although, maybe if he'd tried it he'd have gotten some goddamn fur. I hiked that line with him for three days one time, we took two marten. Didn't even cover the tobacco he went through. Took so damn long to get around that line on foot, the wolves cleaned the traps out before we ever got there. Sonofabitch would of starved to death, and you and me with him, if it wouldn't have been for Mom sending Jimmy Jack in with a skimmer full of grub. I don't know about you, but I was sure sick of squirrel before that grub arrived."

Abe goes to the window and checks the temperature. It's minus ten. It comes to him he's mounted the thermometer in exactly the same spot the old man always put them, in all his cabins, half-way up the kitchen window frame to the right-hand side. It drives him nuts to think that all the stuff his childhood was based on, the whole self-reliance pull-your-socks-up shit that he lived with every day of his life on this crazy trapline was bullshit, that the old man couldn't have made it on his own. That he lived on handouts from his wife.

Dog Mushing

It's Kitty that makes it seem like magic: Kitty and Rowan, and the way they work together. The rest of it's just noise and fuss. Always the first dog in harness, Kitty leans all her weight into the line, keeping it bowstring taut as Rowan and Connie go to fetch the others. The dog lot is pandemonium. Even when Rowan puts up her hand for quiet, the level doesn't drop a bit, so she yells, "Shut up," and for a few seconds it's silent. "Do this," she tells Connie, showing her how to hold the dog back by its collar until its own forward motion lifts its front feet off the ground. "Walk him on his back legs like that," she says. "If you let him get his feet down, he'll drag you flat." At this moment the spell breaks and the dogs all start to scream again. Connie manages to walk the straining dog across to the sled, but when she tries to snap the tug-line onto his harness, he gets his front feet on the ground and yanks her off balance. Rowan runs up with another dog, snaps its collar to a neck-line, and grabs Connie's dog by the harness. "Okay, I got this guy, go grab another one," she yells. Every dog except Kitty starts screaming and leaping at the line as soon as it's in harness. Soon the sled is coming up off the ground, and the tree it's anchored to is swaying. "Jump in," Rowan shouts. This is insanity. Connie considers backing out, but this is it for transport around here. One of these days she's going to want out, and if she can't handle this, she's going to have to walk. Kitty is still calmly leaning into the line, looking back over her shoulder at Rowan while the rest of the dogs are busy winding themselves into a frenzy. Connie takes a deep breath and climbs into the sled. When she's snuggled down inside the caribou hides, Rowan pulls the snow-hook. There's a sudden silence as Kitty turns and leaps into action and the team surges forward.

Who would ever have guessed it would seem so fast? The bottoms of the trees rush past Connie's face at a terrifying pace. The trail down to the lake is steep and makes two sharp bends around trees. When the dogs disappear around the first bend, Connie is certain the sled will hit the tree, but at the last second it swings out and misses neatly. As it does, she sees another bend straight ahead, the front half of the team already gone around the next tree. This time the sled hits the narrow trunk a glancing blow and tips up on one runner for a couple of teetering seconds before righting itself just in time for the final ten-foot plunge down to the ice. The sled hits the ice with a bang, and then swings out sharply as the dogs make a nearly right-angle turn onto the trail. Connie comes six inches out of her seat and lands again with a bump, which could have been nasty if Rowan hadn't remembered at the last minute to throw two pillows in the sled for her.

"You okay?" Rowan says, leaning over the driving bow to make herself heard through Connie's parka hood. Connie's okay. Now that the dogs are running on a flat lake trail, she can see what a machine the team really is. Maybe it's the contrast with the chaos of a few minutes ago that makes it all look so incredibly smooth; the dogs are loping in perfect step, looking straight ahead, all their concentration on the job. Nothing she's ever seen compares to this. *Nat*, she thinks, *Nat, it's*... but there are no words in her vocabulary for what she would tell. *Magic* springs to mind: the whole thing, the cold rushing air, the glide of the sled, the beauty of the team in action take her breath away, make it all seem like some mystical experience. Then one of the dogs at the back starts to look over his shoulder and hang back.

"Get up, Virgil," says Rowan. The dog takes a few more steps and then squats, locking up his legs and letting the rest of the team drag him by his neck-line while he calmly takes a shit. Connie ducks down behind the caribou robe, out of the sight and the smell and the possibility of flying debris, until Rowan says, "All right, Virgil, get up," and she feels the rhythm of the sled shift. Glancing up, she sees that Virgil is back in step with the team.

"Jesus," she shouts over her shoulder, "they don't even stop for a shit?"

"No way," Rowan says in her ear. "You'd be stopping every five minutes. Rest of them can do it on the run. Virgil's the only one that has to squat."

After a while the dogs begin to slow down. "Notice the way their gait changes?" Rowan says. Watching, Connie realizes she's never seen dogs go so fast without actually running. It's not quite as coordinated as when they lope, they're not in step anymore, and some of the machine-like quality has gone out of it, but they are rolling down the trail in what's basically a speed-walk. "They can trot like this all day," Rowan says, and Connie believes it. They look as if this is what they do for rest. After a few minutes, though, Rowan says, "Whoa now," and brings the team to a halt before planting the snow-hook in the trail and tromping one foot down on it. "Trail's not hard enough to hold that for long," she says. "I'll stand on it till you get around here."

Connie looks up at her. "Me?" she says. "Drive?"

"Sure," says Rowan. "It's way more fun than sitting in the basket." Connie still looks doubtful. "Come on," Rowan says, "I'll be right there in the sled."

When Connie's standing with one foot on the runner and one on the brake, pushing down on those two iron claws like she's trying to drive them right through to open water, Rowan says, "Okay, without getting off the brake, bend down and pull the hook, and hang it on the crossrail. Let me know when you're done."

The line from the snow-hook runs up right behind the back pair of dogs, or wheel-dogs, as Connie's learned to call them. As soon as she releases the tension on the line, the team surges forward. She drops the hook and plants both feet on the brake, but the sled's still moving till Rowan says, "Whoa now," and the dogs stop. "Hey," Rowan says to Connie, "don't drop that hook like that when you got a passenger on board, okay? If they do take off it can bounce around pretty good. You all set? Got that hook secure? Let your foot off the brake." And then, to the dogs, "Okay, let's go."

They take off running again, but this time slow down to a trot almost immediately. The motion of the sled seems slower from a standing position, and after a while she starts to look around. They're already halfway up the lake, heading back in the direction they arrived from in the canoe, weeks ago. While Rowan's been out with the dog team working on the trails, Abe's been teaching Connie to cross-country ski. Her expectations of how fast you can cover the trail being based on skiing, she's suddenly surprised to realize how far they are down the lake. The sky is doing its incredible cloudless brilliant blue thing again, and the snow is a perfect blanket, marked only by the dog trail and a few scattered animal tracks. She's getting so she forgets to be amazed half the time.

Rolling easily down the trail like this, Connie finds herself thinking more clearly than she has in weeks. There's been so much to remember, ponder, desire, scoff at, fear, that her mind seems to have been jumping around as if every thought was a hot coal she could only step on for a few seconds at a time. She's never felt so strong, physically, but mentally she's exhausted. She's been retreating more and more into her half-remembered, half-imagined running dialogue with Nat. Sometimes it worries her that she spends so much time occupying her mind with what is essentially a fantasy, but this worry is just another of the problems her mind shies away from and into the dialogue. Now, with the cool wind in her face and the quiet poetry of a rolling dog team on a silent, mountain-ringed lake in her vision, she sees that the Nat dialogues are not a sign that she's losing her mind at all; they're a cataloguing system. She's been using them to filter the Yukon, the bush, and her life, with all its unpredicted twists. While she's been fretting that her mind's refuge was a step on the road to madness, it's been working in spite of her to help her sort things out.

She knows now how it is with Rowan and her. She started to get it when Rowan asked her to wear a shirt around the cabin as well as outdoors. At first she thought it was some kind of country-girl reticence thing, but she sees now—sees it right now, for the first time, although it comes at the end of weeks of Nat dialogues on the subject—that Rowan is fighting off a strong attraction to her on the grounds that she's too young to get involved with, too transient to get attached to, and basically a tourist as far as loving women is concerned, all of which are true, which is something else she's just realized. When she accepted the invitation to come and live in the bush with Rowan, she only half believed the strictly buddies business. Pushed to the back of her mind all along has been a sexy little fantasy about having one youthful lesbian affair to remember and cherish after she realizes her other, much less sexy, little fantasy about settling down with a good, honest, interesting man, and raising sweet, handsome children in Markham. She brings this fantasy out and looks at it now, sees it for what it is, a dark little bit of cruelty she's been keeping tucked away in the boggy part of her unconscious. It's not just that she'd be willing to cause Rowan pain to give the middle-class woman she secretly expects to become a few exotic memories; Rowan's pain is essential to the whole fantasy. It's not about having a lesbian affair at all, it's about always knowing there's a broken heart somewhere that longs for her, fingers that ache for the feel of her skin.

All this clear-headedness is frightening, but it's too strong to resist now. Having scraped the overburden from the Rowan thing—she smiles at herself for thinking in mining images—she's cleared up something about Abe; the Nat dialogues have been dominated by adolescent rhapsodizings over this sweet, gorgeous guy whom fate has thrown her way, plagued by expressions of doubt, timidity, lust. Really, she sees now, it's not all that complicated. She wants him. She doesn't want to be his pal anymore, she hasn't thought about whether he's The One: she just lusts after him. Come to think of it, she's probably been pretty transparent about it. She thinks of Tony, who couldn't look at her sideways without getting a hard-on, Dago leaning over trying to see down her shirt, guys in gas stations, bars, grocery stores. Guys who know her like a sister and guys she's never seen in her life, lusting after her like a bunch of drooling goons, she thought, still thinks in a way, except now she's a little more understanding because surely, she sees, Abe knows she checks out his ass, just the same way she knows when just about every man she passes checks hers out. You just know when someone is looking at your ass. Although maybe it's different for men, maybe it's part of that whole oblivious male pattern they're all caught up in, she thinks, and then catches herself in the contradiction. Well, whatever. She wants Abe, and she's guessing she's probably given the secret away by now. So what's his problem? He seems to like Rowan better than her. Once in a while he skis over in the daytime and spends some time hanging out with Connie while Rowan's out working on her trails, training her dogs: "getting things ready for trapping season," she calls it, although Connie guesses it's got more to do with just being out in the bush by herself, with no one to explain things to, no convoluted relationships to weave through. More often Abe comes by in the evening after supper. He says it's to sit in the rocking chair, for his back's sake, but what he really seems to love is talking to Rowan about a hallowed class of characters they call the old-timers. The expression almost demands capital letters, but not quite. At first she thought they meant hockey players over forty, but it turned out to mean old Yukoners, mostly men, who had some quirk, usually a bizarre one, that qualified them for the title of "quite the character." Usually it would be Abe who would say it, in response to one of Rowan's stories. "Oh, he was quite the character, that one," or, "Wigwam Harry, now that was a character." Rowan knows more stories, mostly because she's older. Probably for the same reason, she's less impressed by them, too.

"Character?" she'll say. "Friggin' nutcase."

At the head of the team, Kitty is coming up on a fork in the trail. One fork follows the shoreline around a large bay; the other, better travelled, goes from point to point. The dog's ears perk up and her head comes back, a completely readable request for instructions. "Gee," Rowan says from the sled, and Kitty dives into the softer snow of the right-hand trail, obviously proud of herself. One of the dogs behind her balks at going the longer, softer way around, pulls determinedly in the direction of the better trail, but Kitty gives an extra hard tug and drags him around by his neck-line. Instantly the whole team leaps down the trail, loping for about four steps before they notice the extra weight of the sled as it ploughs through the soft snow and settle into a straining trudge.

"Why did we come this way?" Connie asks.

"Workout for the dogs. When I start setting traps I need to have some of the top end run off them. You've got to be able to hook up without all that palaver like we had this morning. Get 'em settled down so you can walk away from your sled and know they'll just sit there."

"They get like that?"

"Oh, yeah, eventually. Do it six days a week for a couple of months, it gets to be like getting up and going to work."

Connie tries to picture these dogs lining up in harness like a bunch of bored factory workers getting on the bus, but after this morning's performance it's a hard image to hold in her mind. The bay isn't as large as it looked, and they come back to the hard trail in less than ten minutes. Kitty's ears go up hopefully, but there's no reason to give her any command; it's obvious the trail goes straight ahead, and not back and to the left. The dogs pick their pace up a bit when they get back onto the hard trail, but they're still moving a little slower than before they turned off. After a few minutes Rowan says, "All right, git up now," and they break into a lope. Connie begins to see a pattern; the lope lasts a few steps and then one by one they abandon it for that fast walk that Rowan calls a trot, although it's only slightly similar to a trotting horse. She watches the dogs for a while and then turns her attention to the surroundings, the mountains like a dozen different shapes of breasts, the pale blue of the sky. She's in something approaching a trance when Rowan speaks.

"Okay, stop them here. Drag the brake and say whoa." The dogs come obediently to a stop and this time stand patiently awaiting the next command. "Keep your foot on the brake," Rowan says. "We're going to do a come-around turn." Before Connie can ask what that is, Rowan calls out, "Kitty!" Kitty's ears go up and she looks back. "Gee come." The dog snaps around to the right and starts running toward the sled. As she passes each pair of team dogs, she snarls and they hang back, falling into place behind so that, miraculously, the whole team turns around and runs past the sled, spinning on the axis formed by Connie's foot planted firmly, in near terror, on the metal claw of the brake. They end up stretched out perfectly, pointing back the way they came.

"Wow," Connie says.

"I know, amazing, ain't it?" says Rowan. "That takes a real lead dog."

During the Nat dialogues there's one theme Connie always likes returning to: the pride she takes in conquering her fear of these dogs.

You should see me, Nat, I'm amazing. I feed them and play with them, and handle them and I'm not even slightly scared of them. And they're this big, and they're the craziest things you ever saw.

"Don't go in the lion's cage tonight, mother darling, the lions are ferocious and they bite."

That's not even one of Nat's, that last thing, it's something Connie's mom used to sing around the house, but it has a kind of Natalie feel to it, so Connie gives it to her anyway. Maybe she is going crazy.

Magic Mushrooms

"Do you ever think about dying?"

Abe doesn't answer. He's concentrating on the snow. He can't believe Connie can actually talk, in the face of the scene in front of them. It's a perfectly symmetric pattern of coloured diamonds glittering in the sunlight from one side of the lake to the other. It's interrupted by a dark band of forest that starts at the shoreline and ends halfway up the hillsides all around, and then it starts glittering again from treeline to the pale blue sky, which is doing its own diamond-pattern thing, except with whorls in it, like fingerprints. Maybe she doesn't see it. They say it affects everybody differently.

"Can you see that?" he asks.

It takes Connie a minute to answer, but finally she says, "Yes."

Abe thinks about this. How did she know what he meant by "that"? How did she know she's not seeing something totally different from him? What it feels like, what Abe is not sure he wants it to feel like, is that the mushrooms are causing some weird kind of mind-melding thing, and they're having exactly the same hallucination, and passing it back and forth between them. Sky used to talk about this, but Abe never experienced it till now. If he tries, he can just manage not to believe it's happening. After a minute, the struggle to ignore what seem to be telepathic signals coming from Connie begins to make him nervous, and he gives it up. Immediately he starts to feel a wave of mind-power, a clear message reminding him to respond to her question.

"No," he says. Connie collapses in laughter, bent double over her ski poles. Something must be buggered with the telepathy, because Abe can't figure out what's funny about him not thinking about death.

"No, what?" she says, just managing to get control of herself.

"No, I don't think about dying."

"That was ages ago. Come on, let's ski."

Pigpen gave Connie the mushrooms, told her not to tell Rowan where she got them. Abe didn't get that one when he first heard it; Rowan didn't seem like the kind to make a big deal about a few shrooms. It turns out, though, she's got a thing about drugs in the bush. Some people do.

"Are you fuckin' zooed?" was what she said, walking in and finding the two of them giggling like fools in her cabin, in the middle of a sunny afternoon. "Look like you're on acid or something."

"Shrooms, actually," was what Connie said. "Want some?"

Rowan looked at her for a minute and then said, "No, I'll pass." She didn't exactly shake her head, but she spoke in a kind of head-shaking way. "Listen, I've got work to do on my traps. Why don't you guys go for a ski or something? If you're going to be hallucinating, you might as well do it outside where it's pretty. I don't want you hanging around in here giggling at me all afternoon."

That's why they're out here, standing on the lake with their skis on. It's twenty below, which is perfect for skiing, once you get moving, but they're not moving. Rowan had them hustled out the door with their skis waxed in jig time, but they lost all momentum after she closed the door behind them. They managed to make it down to the lake, but since then they don't seem to be able to move.

The thing, the totally telepathic thing, about all of it is that Abe is certain they have the same problem about the trail, because the only really nice ski trail, the only trail that Rowan doesn't run her dogs on, the only perfect pair of side-by-side, uncontaminated, cross-country ski tracks, is the trail to Abe's cabin. And neither one of them wants to suggest they go that way. There's a big block of shared consciousness of where that trail leads, and it's parked right across the fork. Abe giggles.

"What?" says Connie.

"Mental block," he answers. She gives him a puzzled look. It's getting easier to doubt the telepathy thing all the time.

"Come on," says Connie, and skis away, right past the mental block and down the ski trail toward Abe's place. Maybe she didn't take enough of those shrooms.

The trail is in perfect condition. Connie's moving along nicely for a beginner, but it's hard for Abe to rein himself in behind her. After a while he settles into a plodding pace that gives him plenty of time to think. He knows now why Connie didn't see the mental block. It's because she doesn't know about Sky.

The inside of Abe's head feels a bit like his back does around bedtime, ever since the accident. All summer he and Sky were a population of two, so involved in each other that everybody else in the world, even his own family, seemed distant. Discovering that he can feel the same way about Connie, and practically at first sight, has left him dazed. That's how he sees himself now, like somebody wandering around in a daze. His mind keeps racing back and forth between the two women, picturing himself with one, and then the other. Both prospects are so perfect, so . . . so crucial, he's devastated by their incompatibility. The perfect rightness of him and Sky can't possibly coexist with the perfect rightness of him and Connie. A song the old man used to sing to himself on the trapline comes to his lips, and he sings as he skis.

"*Did you ever have to make up your mind?*"

"What?" Connie says, stopping and lifting her hood away from one ear to hear what he's saying. Abe has to toe in suddenly and plant his poles to avoid hitting her. He gets a twinge in his back, but the shrooms make it feel like a pain somebody else is having, something he's aware of, but only from the outside. "What did you say?" Connie says, clearly oblivious to the fact that Abe has just performed a brilliant feat, and saved them from a nasty crash. He has to think. What was he saying, anyway?

"Oh, I was just singing."

She laughs. "What song?"

"Oh." Abe thinks it might be better not to say. "It was... um."

"What, you don't remember?"

"Um, it'll come to me in a minute."

"You're fucked up," she says, and skis away.

Abe's mouth is so dry he can hardly get it open.

The cabin's not too cold at all; you can barely even see your breath. It's only about six hours since Abe left to ski over to Rowan's place, and there's still a pretty decent fire in the airtight. He flips open the chimney damper and spins the draught with the toe of his boot, then lifts the kettle out of the way and steps on the pedal to open the lid. He tosses in a few sticks of split wood, and sets the kettle back down on top of the lid. Almost immediately it starts to sing. He hums about three notes of "Did You Ever Have to Make Up Your Mind," realizes what he's doing, and twists it around into "Put Another Log on the Fire." Connie gives him a look, but he's pretty sure it's just for whistling hokey cowboy songs. One of the things Abe has observed about women is that very few of them seem to appreciate Waylon and Willie. Jesus, he tells himself, don't be a dickhead, will you? You're singing this song that's about a guy who's just crowing about having two chicks on a string, and that's the total opposite of what you're going through. And try explaining that. And then you try to cover up and you sing the most what-do-you-call-it song there is. Chauvinist. Abe needs a drink of water, bad. The bucket's just a couple of steps away. He turns toward it, and the anticipation of a drink is like the ecstatic moment before a sneeze. He pauses to enjoy for half a second the bliss of expectation, savouring for that instant his parched mouth, the better to enjoy the cool relief of water.

It's at this moment that Connie makes her move. She puts her hand out and rests her fingertips on his face, spread out so that the baby finger is actually on his neck, and she gives him about a second and a half to get used to that, and then gently draws him closer, and kisses him. He closes his eyes, and the patterns of light behind his eyelids respond to the changing pressure of Connie's lips. Her kiss moistens the very outer part of his mouth—lips and a tiny rim of gum, but millimetres away the dry zone begins. He tries to communicate to Connie that he just needs a dipper of water and then he'll be happy to kiss her all day, or at least until the tea's made, but she's really getting into this kissing thing and he doesn't know how to interrupt. He starts inching toward the water bucket, still attached to Connie at the lips, drinking in every blessed bit of moisture her tongue can spare, until finally, one step from the bucket, he breaks away, tears off the lid, plunges in the scoop, and drinks the whole four cups at one go. Connie laughs so hard she has to hold onto the cabin wall to stand up. Abe starts to laugh, too.

"You're a riot, Abe," Connie says. It takes him by surprise, the same words Sky uses, exactly. Of course, it's only four words. Or five, depending on how you look at it. It's not that much of a coincidence. Really. A lot of people say *You're a riot*. It's some TV thing or something. And anyway, this is a very bad time to be thinking about Sky. Although he is now, and can't get stopped. Something changes in the room and Abe has that weird feeling again, like they're reading each other's minds. Shit, he hopes not. The kettle's boiling and he moves to make tea, while Connie sits down. When he brings the teapot and mugs, she's sitting on the bed, staring at the wall in absolute wonder. Abe sets the things down on the bed, sits down himself, and stares. It just looks like log walls and moss chinking at first, but then, after he's been staring for a minute or so, the grain in the logs begins to show, and then to swim around, and then to make fantastic patterns. Connie reaches out with her hand and makes a stirring motion, and the pattern of the grain swirls away from her hand like stirred water. Soon they're both manipulating the patterns with their hands, making them spiral off across the room and bounce off the far walls. They laugh until their jaws ache, their bellies hurt, and they're too weak to sit up properly. They fall to the bed hugging each other in laughter, and have to struggle for enough self-control to move the tea onto the floor before melting into the mattress in a puddle of giggles.

There's no one moment when the giggling gives way to undressing each other; the two seem to blend like coloured oil flowing into water, until you can't tell oil from water, laughing from undressing, clothing from skin. They kiss and kiss, the delightful rubber-lipped comedy of kissing on mushrooms making them laugh and kiss and laugh again. Abe has never felt like this in his life, in his dreams, in his craziest fantasies. His awareness of every tiny nuance of Connie's body and his own is so intense that he feels like one big hard-on, throbbing from his temples to his toes.

Abe blushes. Connie shakes back her hair, and the motion draws attention to the necklace that hangs almost between her breasts. Abe wonders briefly how he missed it before. Bear claws and beads. At one time he wouldn't have known one hippie necklace from another, but now he does. He knows the real fur trade whitehearts from the modern ones, which Venetian styles are rarest, the different ways of arranging the patterns on a string. He knows this necklace. Sky made it.

"Where'd you get this?" he asks, reaching out and taking it in his hand.

Connie falters. "I, bought it from this girl."

"Sky."

"Yeah. You know her."

"She's my—was my—"

"Oh." She digests this for a minute. "Is it *is* or *was*?"

"Um."

"Oh."

"No, it—it's was."

"Does she know that?"

"Uh, kind of. We kind of left it—up in the air. You know? Where'd you meet her?"

"In Dawson." There's something strange, furtive, about the way she says this. It's almost as if it was her, and not Abe, getting caught at something.

"Dawson?" he says.

"In the lineup for the ferry. She was selling stuff, you know? But then I, er, saw her again. In Whitehorse. Because I didn't have enough money. In Dawson."

What the heck is wrong with her? She's stammering like a guilty kid. With every gesture, every missed word, every facial expression, she seems to be telling a story. But the story can't be true. With the mushrooms wearing off, he sees that what felt like mind reading was really nothing more than body language, reading the signals, sensing what's in the air the way everybody does all the time, except the drug made him more aware that he was doing it. Without the drug, the same thing happens, except it's more subtle. That's how he knows—but it can't be true. He can't believe what seems to be written on Connie's face, not without the confirmation of words.

"Did you...?"

She doesn't quite shrug.

"You and Sky?"

"Look," Connie says. "It was—it wasn't like, you know—we didn't exactly..."

"Jesus," says Abe. "Holy shit."

The first time Connie saw the bush, the real bush, far from the highway, it felt enormous. She felt like a little kid left all alone in the biggest building in the whole world. Or she would have felt that way, if it hadn't been for Rowan in the stern seat of the canoe, sitting back there as comfortable as if she was in her own living room. Who would have guessed that less than ten weeks later, Connie would be skiing five miles all by herself, in the middle of nowhere? She is a bit nervous—everybody says that wolves will never attack you, although she's noticed they almost all say "never attack a man," which is not really as reassuring as it's meant to be, but anyway, what if it's a rabid wolf, or a starving one? What if it's one of those winter bears?

The clean precision of the ski trail is immensely comforting, like a double slice of civilization right through the wilderness, with all the power of the magic path through the marsh behind her parents' house in Markham where the monsters couldn't get you if you stuck to the middle. Maybe she'll tell Rowan about that when she gets there. Keep it light. Yeah, that's it. Breeze in like nothing's going on, make small talk for a bit, and then say, "Got a minute? I need to talk."

What she needs, really, is to sit on Natalie's Persian rug with the steam banging in the radiator and Isabella Street crooning in the background, to drink Lapsang Souchong from cracked Royal Doulton, and Glenlivet from tumblers, and turn her head upside down like a cluttered purse, dump its contents on the floor, pick through and hold up the most interesting bits for inspection. Here's where I stabbed a guy in the butt, and here's this huge incredible moose crumbling, like one of those buildings they blow up from the inside. Here's the untouched wilderness, and here we are touching it, sometimes easy, sometimes rough. This is me falling in love with the cutest guy you have ever seen, bar none, but this over here is me admitting that I sort of had sex with his girlfriend.

"*What short of shex did you short of have, shishter?*"

Failing Nat, tea, and whisky, there is only Rowan, who will

not make jokes, who will disapprove, who will without a single doubt give Connie the right advice, the advice she least wants to hear: don't get involved when you're in the bush; wait and see how you feel about him when you're back in town; find out what the real story is with the other woman. Although she doesn't want to accept any of this obvious good sense, she needs an opportunity to argue with someone about it, to try to convince Rowan, and herself at the same time, that the best thing she can do is go back and sleep with Abe. It worries her that she'll have to admit that she fooled around with Sky that night, but it's unavoidable. Her need for female support outweighs her embarrassment.

Either Connie's wax is worn off, or there's been enough of a temperature change since yesterday that she's got the wrong wax for the conditions. Her skis slip backward when she tries to kick. The only way she can make good progress is to rely on her poles. Her arms are getting tired, and she's not even halfway there yet. She starts to experiment with shifting her weight more over her skis, kicking harder, softer, and finally finds a motion that helps to ease the strain on her arms. It only took about an hour and a quarter yesterday to ski this far, but that was with good wax and Abe along to keep her moving. It could take two hours today. It could take longer. A little bit of fear creeps in when she thinks about this. What if it's more than three hours? She wouldn't have any daylight left to get back on. What if she runs out of steam and has to stop? Nobody's going to come looking, because Rowan doesn't know she's coming, and Abe's not expecting her back for hours.

"Nat, look at me. I'm all alone in the wilderness. And I'm okay. Honest. I swear I'm not being plucky."

"Kid, Lou Abner says—*you've got spunk.*"

"Shut up, Nat. You don't know me now. I'm different. Tougher. You'll see."

"*I hate spunk.*"

It's not like Abe thinks, or probably thinks, between her and Sky. She'd never deny there was something—there was definitely something. But if Sky had been a man, Connie would have said nothing really happened, they didn't actually do anything. The night after Connie bought the necklace, she dropped in to visit Sky, while Rowan was getting together with relatives in Whitehorse. They drank a bottle of wine, got high, and ended up petting. The word sounds silly, but that's just what it was like: like high school, only it was quite a bit nicer than fending off some teenage boy at the drive-in. That was the thing she couldn't deny to Abe. It wasn't so much a matter of what she had done with Sky, which bordered on innocent, almost, but of how it felt. Somewhere among those kisses and caresses, something washed away from Connie. She traded something in for a couple of hours of cuddling and one small but satisfying orgasm: something about her right to judge other people for running around the Yukon in bandanas and buckskins, acting as if it was the Summer of Love, ten years too late: something about reserve, and self-control.

The low sun comes around a bend on the river and for a second slips behind Connie's shades. She blinks it away; white light flashes under her eyelids. She's been skiing with her head down, thinking, and she's covered much more ground than she expected. Just up around this bend is the place where Rowan shot the moose. After that it's no distance at all to the cabin. For a second, she thinks she hears an engine, but dismisses the idea. And then, gradually, the sound asserts itself. Somewhere up ahead, on the lake by the sound of it, there's a snowmobile, faint but getting closer. Curious, Connie tries to speed up, but her skis slip backwards. Doesn't matter, anyway, if somebody's in for a visit, they'll still be around when she gets there. The sound disappears, obscured by the point in front of the cabin, she guesses. She can barely hear the dogs from here, although even from the faint sounds it's obvious that they're going bananas. Starved for company, just like the humans, she thinks. The dogs go suddenly silent. Connie can picture Rowan at the brow of the hill, holding a hand up for silence, looking over to see who's coming. For a second she can hear the snowmobile, just faintly, and then it stops. Whoever it is must have found the dog trail from the lake up to the cabin. There's no sound for a few minutes, and then, out of the silence, there's a gunshot.

Connie freezes for a second, and then the dogs begin to scream, an urgency in their caterwauling she's never heard before, it goes on and on, and then the snowmobile starts up, and drives away.

Gunshot Wounds

Abe sets the last of the breakfast dishes in the rack, shakes the suds off his hands, and turns to put his boots on, to take the washwater out to the slop tree. He wonders what he's going to do with himself all day. He considers the options: get some wood in, set out a snare line for rabbits, shoot a grouse for supper, go ice-fishing, sit around the shack and read a book: today he's too antsy for any of them. Mom would say he's on Cloud 9. He feels like there should be a huge attack of guilt or remorse or something coming on, and he's been mentally baring his chest at it, anxious to feel the first blow and know how bad the assault is going to be, but nothing happens. He's been preparing his excuse, which amounts to little more than the fact that she did it first, "she" referring to Connie or to Sky, depending on which area of guilt he's getting ready to fend off. In the end, all he feels is the same walking-in-clouds kind of excitement he felt about Sky until—until when? That's the question he can't answer; he's not sure if it ever stopped. Maybe he still feels the same way. He thinks he does. Hey, maybe this is Free Love. That's what it is, he decides. Free Love. It's one of those hippie things. It's probably the main thing about being a hippie. He reaches behind him and feels his hair. It's over his collar about three inches. Maybe he'll start wearing a bandana. This is going to be great. He wants to yell and kick his heels.

His bush packs are cold when he slips his feet into them. It's been cold in the cabin this morning, must be cooling off outside; he puts on his coat. When he opens the door a curl of fog comes in, and he thinks about Connie: it must be thirty below out there, can she cope with that? She's dressed all right if she keeps moving; it's not that long a trip on skis.

She left while he was still lying in bed: handed him a cup of coffee, kissed him on the cheek, and said, "I'll be back this afternoon." Then she seemed to think about that for a second, and said, "Okay?" Yeah, it's okay. It's miles better than okay. Except, with the temperature dropping, she'd better get to Rowan's and stay put. And what if she has some kind of trouble out there? He doesn't know what kind of trouble he's thinking of, on a straight, well-broken ski trail with no branches to get off on, no chance of fresh snow in this cold. Overflow? That would be a pain in the ass, but it's not that far; she knows enough by now to knock the slush off her skis and keep going. Anyway, there won't be overflow on that stretch. Frozen feet? She's wearing Rowan's spare ski boots, with three pairs of socks to make them fit.

Still.

Maybe it's just that he's too excited to do things he'd do on an ordinary day. For whatever reason, he decides to follow Connie and make sure she's all right. His ski boots are just cheap things, no good after about fifteen below, so he decides to walk. He goes to the rack by the stove where he keeps his liners and takes down the duffels. Stuffing them into his moccasins, he wonders if he'll be able to catch up to Connie out on the trail, wonders if she'll be glad to see him. Maybe she'll take offense, like he didn't trust her to make it on her own, either because she's a woman, or because she's from Toronto; he's not sure which one would piss her off more. But with her on skis and him walking, it's more likely he'll get to Rowan's and she'll already be there. He wonders if she'll have told Rowan what happened last night. Probably won't have to. He doesn't know why he wants her to know, she's probably going to roll her eyes and tell them they're nuts, ask him what happened to "the girlfriend," be offended that Connie's moving over to his place for a while. Still, he's dying to tell someone, and Rowan's the only candidate.

God, this is slow. Goddamn goddamn wax. Sore shoulders stiffening, thighs stiffening. Come on, girl, get going. River mouth, come on, you're at the river mouth, it's just over there. The dogs are still barking. Rowan, Rowan, tell them. Tell them to shut up. What's the matter?

She tries not to think about it, but it's there, inescapable: the snowmobile, the gunshot, the dogs still barking. Her mind goes to the obvious reality, touches it, burns itself, shrinks back, goes to it again. *Oh God no, he didn't, he can't have, she can't be.* Push, stride, push, stride, her mind battering at the inside of her head, round and round, *he can't have, it can't be, he did, it is, the dogs the dogs, screaming. Shut up, shut up, I'm coming as fast as I can.*

She'll never get there and she'll never get there and she'll never get there, and then she's there. At the bottom of the stairs. The dogs' tone changes, they've seen her, they're barking hello, but crazy with it, like: *hello, hello, get up here, quick quick quick.* She drops the poles, snaps open the bindings, kicks the skis off, leaves them scattered on the ice, runs up the stairs. Blood, blood, *no, no,* a drag-trail of blood from the middle of the trail to the cabin door. The door wide open. A few feet from the door, where he's been kept tied in a effort to socialize him, Virgil is in a state of crazed confusion. He leaps toward Connie as she approaches, and then bolts away when she gets close.

She blinks in the sudden dark. Rowan sits propped against the far wall, panting. Blood in thin streaks across the floor. Connie runs over and kneels beside her, takes her head in her hands. "Rowan," she says. Rowan raises a feeble arm and tries to point. Connie looks, but there's nothing there. Rowan tries again: a blue metal box on the wall, with a red cross on the front. She must have been trying to get to it. Connie gets up and takes it down, kneels, sets it on the floor, and opens it. Rowan waves at it as if she's trying to point again. Then she points vaguely to her left breast, to a bloody hole, and makes a weak snipping gesture with her fingers. Connie looks in the box and finds the scissors.

"It's okay," she says as she cuts away the bloody shirt. "It's okay, Rowan." There's a dark hole in Rowan's chest, about a hand's breadth above her left breast. The blood around the wound is so dark red it's almost black, but none is coming out. Now that she's exposed the hole, Connie has no idea what to do. Rowan again tries to point into the first aid box. There's a bottle of something green in there, with no label. Connie opens it and sniffs. It smells like Dettol. Rowan nods. Connie tears open the seal on a cotton pad and pours the liquid onto it. As gently as she can, she swabs around the wound. Rowan takes a shallow gasp and stiffens. When the skin around the wound is cleaned, she leans to the right, and sets her elbow on the floor, and laboriously turns her shoulder until her back is toward Connie.

Oh my God, oh Christ, blood, oozing out, puddling on the surface of the saturated shirt, jagged, ugly, bleeding, bleeding, what can I do, stop the bleeding, oh God, what do you do? She looks in the first aid box for bandages. Nothing seems big enough, until she rummages and comes up with a package marked Triangular Bandage. She tears open the cellophane wrapper with her teeth and spits it away, and then holds it gently over the wound. The blood keeps seeping out. *What do I do? What?* She tries pressing harder. Rowan flinches, but the flow of blood seems to stop. *Now what?* She can't let go or it'll start again. She looks around at the amount of blood in the cabin. She remembers hearing somewhere that the body has an extra pint, that's why you can donate blood, it has one to spare, and it makes a new one after a while. How much is there spread on the doorstep, the floor, the wall where Rowan's been sitting? It's smeared around so much it looks like gallons, but maybe it's not so much. While she's trying to think, Rowan starts to shiver.

What now? Is this a convulsion, death throes? A silent voice in her head yells at her. NOT DEAD, NOT DEAD. *He missed her heart, shot her in the shoulder. People never die from a shoulder wound. Look at all the movies.* She looks back in the first aid box and sees a broad roll of Elastoplast. She puts the disinfectant bottle between her knees and opens it with her free hand and then tips some more onto the swab. She lifts the bandage aside and tries to wash the wound, but as soon as she does, the blood starts to flow again. She ends up stuffing the bandage up against the wound, and holding it in place while she tries to tape it on with the Elastoplast. Her first attempt doesn't stick on one side, but it holds everything in place long enough for her to do a second strip, using two hands this time. Rowan's shivering more now; Connie decides to get her onto the bed. But how? Even if she could grab her by the armpits, which is impossible with the wound, Rowan must outweigh her by thirty or forty pounds. Still, they say you can do things when you have to, that your mind can make your body do things it's not really capable of. *Abe, Abe, come to me now, please. Please.*

"Rowan," Connie says, gently into her ear. "I'm going to try and get you up on the bed. Can you help me?"

By a hideously painful combination of crawling and dragging, they make it across the floor and onto the bed. Rowan opens her mouth as if to speak, and Connie wants to make her stop, because that's what people do before they die, isn't it? Pull all their strength together to get one last word in. But Rowan doesn't speak. Her eyes are open, but she doesn't seem to see anything. Her breathing seems to be getting shallower. Connie's head is so light it feels like she's floating above the whole scene, thinking,

You can't, you can't, I can't, it can't be. She stretches out on the bed beside Rowan, brushing a lock of hair out of her eyes.

"It's okay, sister," she says. "It's okay."

Lying there listening to Rowan's rasping, shallow breath, she opens a button on her shirt and reaches in to hold the necklace: a talisman from the old bear who chose her own time to die. *Help me,* she thinks. *Help me.*

Abe's about a mile from home when he hears the gunshot, very faint. Sounds like a thirty calibre, probably Rowan's .303. His mind runs over the possibilities. A sled dog? Not likely, that's not Rowan's style. There's a big pack of wolves around, but they wouldn't come marching up in the open in the daytime. Wolves come at night, and in the morning you find your dog's head chewed off at the neck. It's the wrong time of year for a bear and he knows she wasn't interested in shooting another moose. Porcupine, muskrat, everything else he can think of she'd have used a .22 and he'd never have heard it from this far. She could be sighting in the gun, getting ready for something, but that takes more than one shot. He strains his ears to hear more. He's not certain, but there could be a faint whining sound. A Ski-Doo?

There's no reason to be worried about hearing a single gunshot in the bush, or a Ski-Doo if that was one, but something nags at the back of his mind. Something about guns. And then it comes to him. That guy, the one they're hiding out from. He shot his old lady and disappeared. Abe starts to run, but his feet punch through the ski trail and he can't keep it up. He switches to the fastest walk he can do, wishing he'd worn the skis after all.

When he finally bursts through the door of the cabin, they're both lying on the bed. There's blood all over the place. He thinks for a second they've both been shot, but then he sees that Connie's crying, and brushing at Rowan's forehead as if there were flies on it.

"Abe. She's shot," she says.

"Where?"

She rolls off the bed out of the way and Abe leans over to look. Rowan's lying on her side, her breathing fast and shallow, her complexion white. He pauses, closes his eyes for a second to collect himself, remember the drill: check the breathing, then the pulse, stop any bleeding, look for signs of shock. He listens for gurgling, but there's none, so it missed the lung. "How did she get onto the bed?" he asks.

"She kind of crawled. I helped her."

"She use her legs?"

Connie nods. Good. No spinal injury, then. He takes her pulse. It's fast, but not too fast. Shock, but not critical, he thinks. Not yet, anyway. Her shirt is cut away from the wound, so it's not tight around her neck, but her pants and belt are still done up. He unbuckles the belt and unzips the pants and then gets to his knees on the bed and turns her toward him, carefully placing her in the recovery position, belly down, face to the side. That's when he sees the exit wound: blood seeping out of a big lumpy mess of a bandage.

When the wound is properly dressed, the bleeding stops. But her life signs are low, she's already lost a lot of blood; she should be in a hospital. There's no radio; SBX has never worked well from here, something to do with the lay of the land. No way to get her out except on a dogsled. He forces himself to be calm, leans over and speaks in Rowan's ear. "Rowan? Rowan, can you hear me?" She opens her eyes. Good. "You're going to be okay, Rowan."

That's what you're supposed to say.

"What are we going to do?"

Yeah, Abe thinks, that's the question, all right. What do you do when there's only bad choices? Rowan's been passing between drowsiness and stupor all night. That's what they call the stages in the St. John book—*stupor. Casualty can be aroused with difficulty and is aware of painful stimuli such as a pinprick, but is not aware of being spoken to*. The next stage after that is *coma*. They've been taking turns sleeping and watching her, wetting her lips with a cloth. He's never had to deal with anything like this before, but in his St. John Ambulance training the rule was clear for patients who slip in and out of states of consciousness: get them to a doctor right away. Her bleeding has stopped, but he doesn't know for how long. He suspects if they tried to haul her out of here on a dogsled it would start again. Also, it feels like a cold snap coming on. It could be forty below by tomorrow.

"How long would it take to get to the highway with the dogs?" he asks.

Connie looks blank. "Two days? I think Rowan said two days. I don't know."

"Okay, let's think about it. How long did it take to go around the lake trail, with two of you in the sled?"

"Um—"

"If you went out after breakfast, when did you get back? In time for lunch?"

"Oh yeah, quicker than that."

"Two hours, maybe?"

"Something like that, I don't know."

"Okay, let's call it two hours. And that's the trail that goes all the way around this lake, and up to those two little sloughs. Say about eighteen miles. So nine miles an hour. Figure they slow down after a while, call it—what?—seven average? Less a couple for rests, feeding, whatever. So five miles an hour. It's about forty miles. Think they could make it in eight hours?"

Connie looks like she's been asked to calculate the distance to the sun. After a moment she puts her hands over her face. "I don't know. It doesn't sound like enough." After a long pause she takes her hands away and says, "I remember she said they do about thirty miles on a good day."

"So forty in an emergency, they've got to be able to do that. It's almost full moon, you could just keep going."

"*Me?*"

"Connie, I've never drove a dog team in my life."

"Well, but, I've never—"

"Listen, Connie, I don't know if she can make it if we don't get her to the hospital. Seriously. You weigh less than me. You know how to drive the team. The dogs know you." He pauses. "You're probably stronger than I am."

"But—"

He can see in Connie's face that there are so many questions she doesn't know which one to ask.

"What do I do when I get to the highway?"

"Isn't Rowan's truck there?"

"I—yeah, but—"

"What?"

"I've never driven a truck."

"It's the same as a car."

"No, it's a standard. I can't drive a standard. What if I can't get it started? And the dogs, I can't even lift them into the boxes. And Rowan? What do I do with Rowan?"

Abe struggles with this. Could he get the dogs to go? Then what? Leave Connie in here by herself? He can't lift Rowan, either. If she drives the dogs, he can walk along after her. If the dogs really only average seven miles an hour, he won't be that far behind. The old man could walk to the highway in around ten hours on a broken trail, if he took it into his head. Abe's back will slow him down, so maybe he'll take fourteen, sixteen, who knows? But he'll be behind, so he'll catch up if there's any trouble. If Connie makes it to the highway, if she can't get the truck started, the White Pass drivers will stop for an emergency.

"I just don't know what else to do," he says. "I don't think she's going to make it if we don't get her out."

Connie puts her hands over her face again. This time she doesn't take them away to speak. "Okay, when do we start?"

"It's just about daylight," he says. "Better start getting ready."

Forty Below

A cloud of ice fog billows into the Edgewater. The door slaps shut behind a bulky figure in a green parka, the hood snorkelled up tight around the face. He pulls his hands out of a pair of black fur-backed mitts and lets them dangle on their braided cord while he unzips the parka and shakes the hood back to look around the room.

"Hey, Pigpen," someone calls. "Get your truck started?"

"Na," he says, pulling his coat off as he goes over to sit down. "It ain't worth it. I hiked 'er."

"Mine started," says Backhoe Mike. Mike's the kind of guy who'll tiger-torch his truck for an hour at forty below just to drive two miles to the bar and brag how it fired right up, no problem. "Fired right up," he says. "No fuckin' prob. Abe's old lady catch up with you?"

"Thanks, Candy," says Pigpen as the waitress puts two glasses of draught in front of him. He hands over a two-dollar bill.

"That's good," he says, waving away his change. "Nope," he says to Backhoe. "Fuck does she want?"

"Beats the fuck outa me. Come in here couple hours ago says where's Pigpen."

"What'd you tell her?"

"Said you'd be along."

"She comin' back?"

"Yeah, hey, Candy, what'd the fox say?"

"Who?"

"Hippie chick there, Abe's old lady."

"Oh, Sky. She was going to do her laundry and then come back."

"And she's lookin' for me?" says Pigpen, talking to Candy, as if he doesn't trust Backhoe to get the story right. "She say what for?"

"I don't know, Pigpen," says Candy. "Hard to imagine."

"Maybe I'd better stick around and check this one out."

"Fuck were you goin' anyways?"

"Got a point there. Better bring us a jug, Candy."

Not like this, Jesus Christ, not like this, not frozen, not in the middle of a white, burning white, lake, not inside a bowl of white lake and blue sky not pierced pierced pierced by the sun, not on a dogsled with a dead woman. NOT DEAD NOT DEAD: she's not dead yet, we're not dead yet.

Jesus, Connie, pull yourself together. Take stock. That's what Rowan says. You have to stop and take stock. Start with the difficulties.

Okay, difficulties. One. Overflow. We know about overflow. Last week. On Ashcan Lake. What did Rowan say?

"*Shit.*

"*What is it?*

"*Look up ahead.*

"*Oh my God. It's wide open.*

"*It's okay, it's just overflow. It's not deep. Pull the robe up around you. Go ahead now.*

"Ahead?"

The lead dogs stood ankle-deep in slush, on the edge of a pool of black, slush-filled water; what could she mean, go ahead? With the caribou robe pulled around her, the siderails up past her armpits, Connie sat wedged down into the sled as helpless as a baby in a basket.

"Rowan, what are you doing?"

"Get up, Kitty. Attagirl. Relax, eh? It's on top of the ice. We'll get through 'er. Virgil, get up now."

Back in the cabin, alive, hands wrapped around her blue enamel coffee mug, Rowan explained.

"Weight of the snow pushes the ice down on top of the water. Water finds a hole—or makes one, I don't know—comes up and sits there. Lot of the time it'll be under the snow, you won't see it till you're in it. Snow insulates it, see. Forty friggin' below, you'll still get overflow. Trick is just to keep rolling. Dogs'll always make it through. One thing, if you had booties on 'em going through it, you for sure have to get them off soon as you get out. They get ice in there, they're going to get real sore feet."

How long does this patch stretch? Connie has no way of knowing. She's only encountered it that one other time; it ran for about a hundred yards and then stopped. *Thank Christ for that,* was all Rowan said. It's like a sharp pain, the wish that she'd paid more attention, asked more questions. How bad could it be? Could the whole lake be overflowed? Could they die here?

"What, are you nuts?" Pigpen says. "It's forty fuckin' below out there."

"The cold front ends below Carmacks," Sky says. "They said on the radio it's minus seventeen this morning."

"Yeah, how long's that gonna last?" says Backhoe. "Get a cold snap here, you can bet your ass they're gonna get it in Carmacks, too."

"But I'm not going to Carmacks."

"Look, if it's cold here, and it's cold in Carmacks, it's cold in Shitcan fuckin' Lake."

"But it ends below Carmacks."

"Seventeen below, eh?" says Pigpen. That's when Sky knows she's got him. She doesn't say anything. Best just to wait. He fills his glass from the jug and takes a drink like he's thinking it over. "Outa my fuckin' mind," he says, and pauses. "Ah, fuck it anyways. Le 'er buck, eh?" He looks at his watch. "Be a couple hours' drive. Pick you up tomorrow about eight."

"If your truck starts," says Backhoe.

"She'll start," says Pigpen. "You ever ride a snow-go?" Sky shakes her head. "Wear lots of clothes."

"That's a new one," says Backhoe.

"Fuck off, asshole."

Headache. White-hot headache. Connie knows exactly where her shades are, on the kitchen window ledge, back in the cabin. Pain sits behind her eyes, just controllable if she doesn't open them or move her head. But somehow the dogs can tell when she closes her eyes. Every time she tries it, they slow down, and then stop. She squats down on the runners and leans her head against the driving bow, so it's close to Rowan's head sticking up out of the sled-bag. She holds her mittened hand over her forehead so that the long hairs of the wolf-fur trim hangs over her eyes.

"Wake up, Rowan, wake up," she says, over and over. "Wake up."

Abe made the mittens. Moosehide gauntlets, wolf-fur backs and cuffs, duffel liners. Imagine a guy who can do that. All winter they've kept her hands warm, in any weather. Her fingers are numb now. How cold is it, anyway? Thirty below, at least, which is difficulty number three. The dog booties she'll soon have to pull off are held on with hockey tape. Her own feet will freeze, standing in the slush, before she pulls them open with these numb stubs of fingers. Her only choice is to plough forward through the overflow, and then stop and deal with everything. Oh, God, how far does it go? The snow-covered trail looks innocent enough, but so did the puddle they're standing in now before the dogs walked out in it and broke through the snow to the water underneath.

"Get up," she says. Nothing happens. "Get up," she says, sharp this time. Virgil lunges to escape from her voice, and the sled budges; the gang-line droops, and the rest of the team steps into the slack. "Get up," she says, while they're still moving. This time Virgil bolts and throws his weight at the line. Tricked into motion, the team steps forward. "Get up," she barks, once more, and they put their backs into it. The sled rolls along, not quickly, but not so slow that it's in danger of stopping.

Dry socks and liners in the pack. Fifty yards of overflow, a hundred, two hundred, she runs behind the sled, thankful for the burning in her feet that means they're not frozen yet, on the edge of panic the whole time because if the dogs stop—

Jesus, no, don't let them stop.

The kid at the Mini Mark doesn't want to pump Pigpen's gas unless he turns his truck off.

"Turn 'er off, she'll be in your way all fuckin' day, bud," Pigpen tells him, unscrewing the gas cap.

Sky's hurrying in to get some juice for the road. Out of the corner of her eye she can see that the kid doesn't know how to deal with this big, brash guy, who just goes ahead and pumps his own gas, grinning at him the whole time. When she comes back the kid's finishing the fill-up, stamping his feet against the cold. Pigpen's up on the back of the truck, and he's got the filler cap off the snowmobile.

"Jerry cans too," he tells the kid. When it's all done the pump reads thirty-eight dollars. Pigpen's reaching for his wallet, but Sky stops him and pulls out two twenty-dollar bills she's been saving loose in her parka pocket, and hands them to the kid.

"Keep the change," she says.

It takes a few minutes to get back onto the highway through the commuter traffic from Crestview and Porter Creek, every truck and car pumping out a stream of white smoke, like its own personal little puff of ice fog. On the highway they whiz by, making up some time; when they get downtown they're in a narrow stretch of valley between the clay cliffs and the riverbank, and the ice fog is a solid block they have to crawl through. Even in the dark it was a shock this morning to drive up Two Mile Hill and pop out of the fog, to suddenly regain visual contact with the world, with snow and stars, and street lights that are more than just a faint glow in the fog.

The last street light is at Rainbow Road, the entrance into Crestview. Beyond that, so far as Sky knows, it's darkness and stars all the way to Carmacks. Just after they turn right onto the Mayo Road, officially leaving Whitehorse, Pigpen lights up a joint and passes it over. Sky shakes her head. He takes several short puffs and holds them in while he speaks.

"So what's the big rush?"

Sky knows without the slightest doubt that she should go to Abe right now. She doesn't know why, nor how she knows, but she knows not to question this feeling. What she doesn't know is how to explain this to Pigpen. She tries to look as nonchalant as possible.

"He needs me to come now."

"What's he got, a single side-band in there?"

"No, I haven't spoken to him. I just know, you know?"

"Sure," says Pigpen. Sky sneaks a glance to see if he's mocking or humouring her. He catches the glance and responds as if she'd spoken. "No, I know what you mean. Seriously. You get a feeling. One time I was on this highway crew—right in the middle of a shift, eh?—and I get this feeling like I've gotta go home. Didn't even wait for coffee or nothin'. Drove straight through. Turns out old Spook had gotten into a porky—face full a fuckin' quills, eh?—and nobody could get near him to get them out. Took a chunk outa the guy I had lookin' after him. When I showed up they were just headin' out to shoot him. Just shows to go ya, eh?"

"Did they fire you?"

"Na. Went back the next day, they hardly said nothin'."

When they catch the first distant glimpse of Lake Laberge, there's a hint of dawn on the horizon, a tinge of pink on the mountains. It's so beautiful it doesn't look real. Sky's staring out the window, drinking it up, when Pigpen speaks. "You know Rowan?"

She turns toward him. "Rowan?"

"Chick's trapline we're headed for."

"I don't know."

"Big gal, total bushwoman. Dyke-o-rama."

"Is that the woman Connie's been with?"

"Yeah, that's her, you know them, eh? Although Rowan says they ain't exactly with, if you know what I mean. Says she don't go for the girls, that one. Just buds, eh? Or so she says."

"Oh?" says Sky. "Anyway, what about Rowan?"

"Nothin'. Just we'll probably see them two before we see Abe. Talked to his brother last night, says the shack he's in's out past her place."

A couple of things click together for Sky. "Rowan's the one who bought the trapline?"

"Yeah. Guess Abe never figured on her showin' up this year. Somehow him and Frank had the idea she don't use the place, I don't know where that came from. Don't know how it went over, Rowan findin' Abe on her trapline."

"Does she know him?"

"Not that I know of. Or she didn't. Does by now, I guess. Likely won't be any big problem. Rowan's good people. We'll stop in and say hello. She's good buds of mine."

It's so cute that Pigpen's showing off about having a lesbian friend. Sky had to suppress a smile when he said that about Connie. She remembers Connie, sweetly: that half-flirting, half-mocking look in her eyes, her hard edges melting away, her t-shirt tanline from spending a summer in camp. Her kisses, with the faint taste of lowbush cranberry. She feels a shiver, first in her belly, and then her neck, and wonders if it's really Abe who's pulling her toward the bush, after all.

Connie's found some weight, something steady inside herself she doesn't recognize, to lay on top of her panic to keep it from surging up. This morning on Ashcan Lake she wanted to drag the brake to slow the team down to a walking pace, not to pull away from Abe, not to be responsible for this journey alone. But Rowan lay bundled semi-conscious in the sled and there was nothing she could do but go. *Come on, sister, no time for panic now.* She tightened her grip on the driving bow of the sled to keep from screaming—*I can't do this alone*—and kept looking back over her shoulder until she couldn't see him anymore. The scream is still there, submerged and threatening, like overflow beneath the snow, but whatever it is that's keeping it down is holding steady.

Rowan's breathing is very shallow. The dogs are standing on an uphill trail, just off the end of a lake, and Connie's pulling frozen booties from their feet and dropping them on the trail. She hates to litter, but this is an emergency; she's not putting twenty-odd frozen, slush-filled booties in the sled with Rowan. Maybe someone will come along and pick them up. Her fingers are so numb she can hardly unwrap the hockey tape from the booties. Her head is pounding. When she reaches the lead dogs, the trail is in shade, and the relief nearly brings her to her knees. She's dying to scoop up a handful of the cold snow and rub it in her aching eyes, but snow at this temperature doesn't cool, it burns. Abe told her that when he was putting the thermos in the sled. Don't eat thirty-below snow, stop and have tea. She pushes her mitt down and her parka sleeve up to look at her watch. One-thirty, she's been on the trail since eight. Five and a half hours. Have they been making good time? She thinks so, or she thought so, up until they hit the overflow. It took them over an hour to get down this last lake. She tries to remember from the canoe trip how far along the trail she is, but everything's so different. She thinks this might be about fifteen miles. That would mean she'd be on the trail for another—but her head hurts too much, and she can't think. It's too hard to think. Till after dark, anyway.

Nat, I need tea, whisky, steam heat. A transit pass. I need help.

She thinks about the old bear, coming out of her den in the middle of winter, coming into town to die, to find a man to shoot her, put an end to the misery, the hunger and cold. Who did the bear call to, in her mind, in the depths of her misery? Who ever helps a bear in all its life, except its mother? Do bears in distress bleat for their lost mothers, comfort themselves with imagined snufflings and nuzzlings? Does a bear who chooses to die know what it means to be dead? Does Connie?

She has to knock the slush from around the runners and under the basket of the sled. Checking inside, she finds that a tiny bit of water has found its way through the canvas tarp, but none has made it through the caribou hide. That's when she comes across the bag of fish and decides to give the dogs a snack. She's carrying two small fish for each of them; it's all there was room for on the sled. She hopes she's a third of the way through the journey. They can have the other one when she thinks she might be two thirds. When she comes with the first armful of fish, several of the dogs try to turn back toward her, yanking at their neck-lines. Kitty pulls out hard in lead in an effort to keep the others in line. Connie remembers then that Rowan told her always to feed the leader first, and work her way back. She has to go out in the deep snow, off the trail, to avoid getting knocked down by the team dogs lunging at her as she goes by with the fish. She feels herself start to sweat inside her layers and layers of heavy clothing, and discovers a new danger to fear: getting a chill from damp underwear. She slows her movements right down and tries not to be afraid of the dogs diving toward her, held back only by Kitty's determination. She reaches Kitty.

"Good dog," she says, and gives her a fish. She tosses out four fish and goes back to the sled for two more for the wheel-dogs, Homer and Virgil. The only sounds from the rest of the team are crunching and soft growling, but the two unfed ones are having a fit. As she passes, Homer catches her in the chest with his nose, like a solid punch. She threatens him with an upraised hand and he cowers back, and then lunges again, just as Virgil tries to jump away. They tangle in each other's lines, one of them growls. Instantly, they dive at each other. In seconds they have reached a level of ferocity beyond anything Connie has ever seen in her life. She shrinks back, terrified.

"*Hom*er, *Vir*gil," she screams, but nothing changes. The dogs drive at each other with frenzied force, snarling, hideous, and utterly threatening. Some of the other dogs are starting to growl at each other; all up the line it's tense. For a moment it looks like the entire team is going to break into a brawl, and then, as suddenly as it started, the fight stops. Both the dogs snap into place as if someone had yanked them round with a string, and the whole team stands looking over their shoulders at the sled, silent and transfixed. Connie follows their gaze and sees that Rowan's eyes are open, and she's staring straight back at the dogs. "Rowan," she says, but there's no response. The eyes go blank, and then close. After that, there's no more fuss out of the dogs. She tosses out the last two fish, and goes to the back of the sled to wait for them to finish.

Her headache has reached the point where it's the only thing she can give any attention to for more than a few seconds at a time. She takes the thermos out of the sled and pours a cup of tea. Drinking it, she has that feeling again as though the slight relief is too much to bear. She puts her head down on the driving bow and starts to cry. There's a tiny movement inside the sledbag. Slow and feeble, Rowan's right hand, in a silver fox mitten, comes up and touches her on the side of the head, half on her parka hood, and half on her face.

Blue sky, white lake. The sun working its way in a low circle just above the mountains. Abe didn't realize when he set out how much this was going to hurt. He's carrying what he can't do without: his bedroll and some jerky and tea bags, his billy can, some matches, a dry pair of socks. He should have dry liners, but there were none at Rowan's that would have fit him. The pack weighs next to nothing, really, but after ten miles it's killing him. That's just life now: he carries anything, it's going to hurt. Thing is just to walk, and keep walking, one moccasin in front of the other, parka hood pulled out at the front, as much to keep the sun out of his eyes as for warmth.

As soon as he left Rowan's main trail, the snow turned punchy. One snowmobile going in and out and the dog team going over it once aren't enough traffic to make a solid trail, although in this cold, the snow's set up to the point that it almost takes Abe's weight. With each step he sinks in just a couple of inches, not enough to slow him down noticeably, but each step gives him a small pulse of pain in his back. Still, he's making good time. The old man called this Top Lake. It's only about a third of the way out, but it's the high point in the trail, so the going is usually quicker after this. It's mostly bush trail now, except for a couple of sloughs and the pothole lake they never did give a name to, because it's the place Mom's first husband died. The trail runs through a willow swamp down there, where the rabbit paths are often tracked up by wolves. It's not a place Abe would normally travel without a gun. He's heard that stuff everybody says about wolves never attacking a human being, but he doesn't believe it. The old man knew wolves.

"Never underestimate a wolf, lad, he'll never underestimate you. Or overestimate you, either. Wolves know the weak from the strong. That's how they survive."

He put Rowan's .303 in the sled, thinking he'd be catching up to them once they slowed down. Connie figured the dogs would be down to a walking pace after fifteen, twenty miles, but neither of them calculated just how fast they'd go right at the start.

Connie disappeared off the end of Ashcan Lake before Abe was a quarter of the way down. The whole time Connie was turning around to look at him. She started to drag the brake at one point, and then shrugged at him and let go. He wanted to yell after her to slow down, not to go out there alone. How much does she really know about the bush? He knows she can build a fire now, but she only really caught on to it in the last couple of weeks. Can she do it with cold fingers? Will she remember how to work that gun? He ran through it for her before he put it in the sled, but he wonders how much attention she was really paying. But that shrug said it all; going slow enough for Abe to keep up could cost Rowan her life.

It wasn't until the sled disappeared that Abe realized how much he'd been counting on being able to keep it in sight. Being alone in the bush never used to bother him; he made this trip by himself for the first time when he was fifteen. But things were different then; he was strong. He could carry everything he needed.

As long as he was drinking, he could laugh at pain, disability. And then, when he was mostly lying around with Sky, getting great massages and having tons of sex, his back didn't bother him much. When he came in the bush last fall he was rested up okay, so he managed to get his meat and his wood in, although he realizes now he'd never have made it on his own. The whole idea was crazy. He's so used to letting people like Frank think for him, he never looks at anything for long enough to make the right decision; he just goes with what somebody suggests. Lately he's been feeling it a lot when he hauls his water up from the creek, splits his kindling, when he swings his legs up onto the bed at night. Normally, he wouldn't have considered taking on a hike like this.

He thinks about Connie, and what might be going on out there with her, but all he can do about that is worry, which makes the pain worse, for some reason. He finds himself thinking about walking with his father. What it meant to him as a kid, say nine years old, that his father gave him a hero's name like Abel Walker, someone who is able to walk, no matter where, no matter what. A real bushman. Someone who can look after himself, never dependent on anyone. What a joke. What would the old man think of him now, living on his pension at twenty-one, can't even make it in the bush without help? What would he think of him tearing up the Sally Ann?

The thing about the old man was he could do anything, except put a foot wrong. Every step he took was the right one, everything he did was perfect. When other men's furs were rejected, his fetched top dollar. His log cabins were built tight and the roofs never leaked, his fishnets were always full, and so were his meat cache and his root cellar. Every knife he owned was sharp enough to shave with, and his garden grew as if it was in southern California. Abe tells people that's why everybody left him: Mom, Frank, finally Abe himself, although he never really chose to leave; Mom yanked him out of there to go to school. But it makes a better story if he tells the guys in the Edge how nobody could handle living with his old man, that each of them left, one by one, because it was too much trouble to try to keep up. "*Oh man, he was a tough old bugger. Walk sixty miles for a bag of tobacco. His only bad habit. And you had to keep up, eh? Living in the bush is fuck all. Living with my old man—that was tough.*"

Of course he knows he's not really talking about the old man. It's just part of the way you talk when you're with a bunch of guys, a kind of inside-out bragging that everybody does, where you go on about what a hard traveller some guy was when everyone knows you kept up to him, or how hard something is when they all know you're good at it. He first caught on to this in Faro. That was the first time he'd ever been in one of those all-guy situations, where you need to speak a whole different language, not just the words, but the kind of things you're supposed to say, a lot of them things you were never supposed to say anywhere else. Some of them are pretty gross—things about women, blow-job jokes, mostly aimed at the guys you're with, dumb racial jokes, usually not about the guys you're with, although they can be. Just childish shit. That's what people think of when they think about men together, but it's not that simple. A bar table is a circle where you tell your best stories. You have to tell them well, or the guys will shut you up *"Get to the fuckin' point, Jesus Christ."* He figures he's pretty good, he can always make them laugh. After he got out of the hospital, shooting the breeze was one of the first pleasures he discovered. That's how he got started into the bars, just a few laughs in the afternoon, sitting in the cosy darkness of the Capital, swapping stories, half hearing the guys at the table next to you telling their own stories, the same as yours: the time three moose came all at once and you didn't know which one to shoot, the truck that took two days to get out of the mud. Sockeye this big. Then it was the Edge in the mornings, the KK on Friday nights, with its log tables they sand once a year so people can carve a new bunch of names and slogans into them, hippie chicks dancing with no guys. Saturdays at the Sandman watching wrestling on the TV, fights breaking out in the corners. The Whitehorse Inn Saturday night, the music so loud the barmaids and the customers have to communicate with hand signals.

One Saturday night at the Inn he saw two hippie girls grab a guy who was trying to keep in the background, down at the end of one of the long tables, as far from the pounding speakers as he could get. They dragged him up on the dance floor, made him dance a couple of times with both of them together, and then marched him out the door, one on each arm, both of them goosing him and kissing his cheeks as they went. Once in the Capital, a guy puked on the floor, and the barmaid came with a mop and cleaned it up. "Jesus," the guy who had puked said, "I don't know if I want to drink in a place that doesn't throw you out for that." At the Kopper King he watched a girl leaning against the bouncer, her hands up against his massive chest, making sure he got a good look down her halter top while her boyfriend packed two curved-back wooden chairs out the other door. Half the hippie cabins in the Yukon seem to have those chairs.

Coming into the bush to dry out was a bit of a joke—what

the hell, if it makes them happy, he figured. But really, he does one stupid thing when he's on a toot, and it's like he's the number-one drunk of all time. He knows so many guys who get drunk and out of hand four or five times a week, and they're not going for treatment. Look at Backhoe Mike, he's an asshole when he drinks, but he's never had any trouble getting a job, keeping it, making his payments. He likes to party, but he keeps it together, except once in a while when he gets shitfaced. Big Jack's been in jail a couple of times for stuff he did when he was drunk, he's still the best mechanic in town. Pigpen doesn't get too rowdy, but that's just because he can drink all day and never feel a thing. Abe can take it or leave it alone; the drying-out thing was just to get the judge off his back. Oh sure, he was dying for a beer that first few weeks, but who wouldn't be, working all day with a face full of blackflies? Naturally he was thirsty. There's been times in the cabin, too, when he couldn't quite make himself believe that he wouldn't taste another drop of Jack Daniels till after break-up. He'd have this feeling like there had to be a bottle, somewhere, even though he knew there was no possibility. It was kind of freaky, he'd start to get panicky about it, imagine himself going shack-wacky, tearing the place apart for a bottle he knew wasn't there. People do weirder things than that when they're bushed. There's that story about the two partners in the gold rush who cut everything in half one winter—cabin, sled, boat, the works.

Abe could use a drink right about now. Just a couple snorts of whisky to ease the pain in his back a little, although when he imagines it, it's more like one long, sweet, burning column of liquor, searing down his throat, hitting his stomach and then his blood, and that good, warm feeling coming up. He can taste the phantom of it in his mouth like a word on the tip of his tongue, teasing him so acutely he feels like shouting out loud. He's still walking with his head down, protecting his eyes behind the fur trim on his parka, when something in his peripheral vision, a glimpse of dark against the white, makes him look up; the trail ahead is a black pool of water, full of suspended slush. *Connie.*

She must have gotten soaked going through this. Oh shit, she must have gotten wet. Rowan's probably dry, inside those caribou robes, but if Connie got her feet wet— He lifts his hood away from one ear and turns to listen. Nobody around. It's about sixty, seventy feet to shore.

Shit, I hope she stopped and changed her socks.

He decides to back up a bit, hoping to avoid the overflow. After backtracking about forty feet or so, he takes a first cautious step. His moccasins are snow-sealed to the point of looking like oilskin, although they're actually made from smoked moosehide; he could put his foot in water and come away dry. If he gets it out again quick enough. But as soon as he steps off the trail, he's in snow up to his nuts. To take a step he has to lift his boot high up and come down hard enough to break through the crust and into the deep powder. It takes a good fifteen minutes of this to cover about a hundred feet. The shore seems never to get nearer until suddenly it's close, and the snow is a little less deep. On the windswept hillside that rises up from the lake, there's almost no snow at all. He staggers out and falls, leaning against a scraggly pine tree, trying to control the throbbing in his back. After a few minutes he moves on. By the time he's back to the trail, he figures he's lost half an hour, and he needs a rest. There's a bunch of frozen booties lying around. He checks them; they're filled with ice.

The sun has gone behind the mountains, much to his relief, but the temperature's starting to drop. It's probably around three-thirty, he figures. Pretty soon he'll be walking in the dark. He feels like flopping down on the trail and sleeping. Even when he reminds himself he'd never wake up, it still feels like a great idea. He shifts the weight of the pack, takes a deep breath—*You'll live up to your name today, lad*—and keeps walking.

"That what you got for clothes?"

"This is warm," Sky says, pulling her army coat tight around her.

"Not warm enough," says Pigpen.

"I've worn this at forty below."

"Not on a Ski-Doo, you haven't. Try these. They're too small for me."

Out of a huge duffel bag on the back of the truck, he offers her a caribou-hide coat and pants. "From the Delta," he says. "Guy's auntie I know made 'em when I was working up in Tuk. Cost me an arm and a leg. I told him size large. Should of said: that's Polack large, not Eskimo large." He grins and holds out the coat. Sky shudders. She knows she has to get used to it, but the thought of wearing another creature's skin, it makes her own skin crawl. "Hey," Pigpen says, "it's that or turn back, I ain't takin' you out there in that thing, no overpants or nothin'. Fuckin' freeze out there." The coat and pants are heavy, and make her walk with her arms out to the side like someone in a gorilla suit. Pigpen checks her mitts and boots, both of which pass inspection. "All right," he says. "Let's get at 'er. You ever ride one of these?"

"No. Is it anything like a bike?"

"Not really. Why, you a biker?"

"Total."

"No sweat then, you'll figure 'er out."

Black shadows and golden moonlight in streaks across the trail. Numb: toes, fingers, brain, all numb, Connie stops the team, hooks onto a tree, and goes into the sled to look for the fish bag. The dogs have slowed down to a walk, looking over their shoulders and dipping their butts toward the trail. All day her mind has been dashing around inside her head as if it just woke up in a cage. Finally exhausted now, it does nothing but record and report: toes numb but still wriggling, dry socks, spots in front of the eyes, pain dull, headache under control. No reaction from Rowan when she lifts the corner of the robe and takes the fish out of the sled. She drags the bag up the trail, a single frozen fish in her hand. Homer and Virgil jump up as she passes, and she slaps their noses, hard, with the fish. They cower back, whining, and the next pair are more cautious. They hold back at first, but as she passes, one of them tries to grab the fish. She bonks him on the top of the muzzle, and he yelps. The next pair of dogs shies away from her, the nearer one shoving his partner off the trail, and she threatens them with the fish. It's only then that she realizes she's growling, low in her throat, like Kitty. She tries to tell Nat, but she can't form the words in her mind.

Back at the sled, she leans on the driving bow and listens to the sound of bones crunching. She leans closer to Rowan and hears the faint rasp of her breathing. She touches the back of the slumped head. *This is all I can do, sister.*

When the trail's good, riding on the back of a snowmobile is kind of like riding on the back of a bike; you lean into the corners and hang on tight. But when the trail's rough, it feels like riding a jackhammer. The first few miles were on the flat of a riverbank, and Pigpen kept the battered Elan wound right out—it felt like about forty miles an hour. After that they started to climb, and now every bend or hump in the trail is a pocket of soft snow that throws the machine half on its side. Pigpen is up on one knee now, getting his weight high so he can heave it into the corners, fighting the machine all the way. Sky hangs onto the rack behind and leans out as far as she can, putting all her weight on the inside foot. Behind, she can feel the skimmer whipping around like a cork on a string, pulling on the back end of the machine. She's concentrating on keeping her balance and doesn't see right away why Pigpen suddenly veers off the trail and dumps the machine, nose down and leaning hard to the left, down the hill.

Climbing off on the high side, taking care not to tip the machine any further, it takes her a minute to notice the other snowmobile, stopped in the middle of the trail. Pigpen scrambles up onto the trail, and stands brushing snow from his clothes and looking at the abandoned machine. He takes off the gas cap and peers in, shakes the jerry can that's bungied down to the rack, shakes his head. He pulls the scarf down from his mouth to speak.

"Outa gas. Fuckin' burn up the fuel humpin' over this shit."

Sky comes up beside him and looks at the machine. They're going to have to get it out of the way, the sidehill drops off too sharply beside it to make it around.

"Look at this," Pigpen says, chuckling, and points to the keyswitch. It's hanging out, and the wires at the back have been pulled out and spliced together.

"Hot," Sky says.

"Hey, let's not jump to conclusions," he grins. "Coulda lost the key." He walks down the trail a few steps, looking down, turns, and walks back up. He checks the ground behind the Ski-Doo. "What the fuck?" he says.

"What?" Sky asks, but then sees for herself. There's a single set of tracks leaving the machine, heading back into the bush. "Maybe he went back for help," she suggests. Pigpen considers for a moment, shakes his head again.

"Guess so," he says. "Long ways back. Funny we never seen a truck."

"Oh, yeah. How did he get out here?"

"One jerry can, he never came all that far. Somebody must have dropped him off at the road there. But where the fuck's he goin'? It's fuckin' miles back."

"Maybe there's a cabin in between somewhere."

"Yeah, I don't know. Frank said there was fuck all till you get to Rowan's place."

"Maybe it's new."

"Well, whatever the fuck. Gimme a hand to get this piece a shit off the trail."

Even in the patchy moonlight coming through the trees, Abe thought, you wouldn't have to be Daniel Boone to read Connie's tracks and know exactly what's going on. Every fifty feet there's another sled-sized hole in the deep snow off the side of the trail. Some of the trees on the corners have chunks of bark missing, branches freshly broken off. She must be exhausted, totally unable to manoeuvre the heavy sled. By the look of the tracks, the dogs were poking along pretty slowly most of the time. They might be tired out, too. He finds something sticking up out of the snow; it's a frozen felt boot liner, must have fallen from the sled when she tipped it. He hopes she changed them in time. What was he thinking about, letting her go by herself like that? He should have—

What? Done what differently? Where did I make my mistake? When did it get to be too late to go back? Take responsibility for yourself, the old man would say. If you're in this situation, you walked into it one step at a time. How did he keep believing that? Didn't he ever feel life yanking his strings?

Abe was in intensive care when his father died. They didn't tell him until a couple of weeks later.

"His heart give out," Frank told him.

"The bush got him," Mom said.

"Frank said he had a heart attack."

Mom made a gesture with her hand that said she couldn't talk about her husband, the life he put her through for his beloved bush, the double abandonment of separation and death. It said, leave me alone, I can't take anymore.

He's almost at the crest of the hill when he sees the dog turd on the trail. It's only about half frozen. He starts to walk faster, putting everything he's got into climbing the last hill before the trail drops away to the pothole. The last few yards are steep and he almost falls forward on his hands and knees before he crests it. There's a bald patch on top of the hill and he can see above the trees to the far side of the lake below. His eye catches a movement through the bush and by the length of it he knows it's the dog team. He starts down the hill.

So many lives. Which one did I live? Home-schooling in the trailer, the loader roaring in the background, the smell of fresh-baked bread. Was that me? Dad's old pack dogs, short-legged and broad-backed, waddling up Nogold Pass, ptarmigan flushing in a scurry of wings. The old Cooey .22, the male's red eye patch framed in the vee of the sights. Pop! Was I there? Or did Mom keep me home that trip, to finish my geography? Did I have a sister, Michelle? Did she grow up to be a hairstylist? Or did Mom and Dad have an argument that night, sleep back to back, shoulders hunched like barricades? A million moments, a billion possibilities. Did I take this path, or that one? And then, and then, and then? The thing that wants to be, that won't fade into the perfect, featureless light, the thing that craves the highs and lows, the contrasts, what is it? Does it deserve to win? It's a battered, beaten thing, a lonely thing, a thing that never learned to deal with the world. A thing that would be at peace forever if it went to where the unwavering light beckons. It wouldn't have to think. It wouldn't have to work at loving, at being loved.

No, no, I was okay. I was doing something, I was going—somewhere. Where? Who with?

Cold. It's cold, cold at this end. Hard, so hard to hold on, not to slip away. Down toward the welcoming light. Darkness at this end, darkness and pain. Distress like ice fog, a cold, bleak veil. Fighting, why am I fighting? Something pulling, demanding—hold on, stay, don't go. Down the easy trail. Toward the warm, insistent light. A pulse of need, above and behind, something, someone, demanding, needy. Stay, it says. Help me. Who? What? Colder at one spot, struggle toward the cold. Push up toward it.

Rowan comes up to the surface to discover that the cold fresh place, the place she's been grasping toward, the centre of waking consciousness, is her face; her eyes and nose, poking out into the cold air. She feels herself breathe, tastes the sharpness, feels her eyes opening, remembers life. *Right, it was like this. So much sensation. So tiring.* Above and behind her, Connie's crying. Shaking with sobs. She remembers now: Connie, alone on the trail, trying to go somewhere—where? Somewhere important. Rowan can't remember. She tries to move, to speak, but there's nothing, no response from her arms, her mouth. She doesn't seem to be attached to them anymore. *Connie, it's all right. It's all right.* If she could just get Connie's attention, look in her eyes, let her know: it's all right, she doesn't have to fight fight fight, there's a warm light, a safe place. If she could just tell Connie about the place. Then she could let go. She remembers she did this, just a little while ago. The arm, the hand, could communicate, could tell Connie, it's all right, it's okay. There has to be some connection to her arm, it used to belong to her, exclusively to her, only she could lift it, grip with its strong hand, work its fingers. It's her arm, she's got to be able to find it. She searches everywhere, the world, the universe. It's such a small place.

When she finds the arm, it hurts. It hurts so much to be here, fighting, trying, knowing that there's a peaceful place, so close. It moves. In agony, in exultation, in love, it moves. When her mitten fur tickles Connie's nose, she stops crying.

"Rowan? Oh Rowan, thank God."

No, no, don't. This is just to say—this is—don't need me. Let me go.

The sled picks up momentum on the hill, and the dogs run to keep ahead of it. It chases them around a couple of hairpin bends, and on the second one, Connie flies off. "Rowan!" she screams. The sled tumbles the last thirty feet to the lake, and lands on its side. Rowan lolls out, flopping face down on the trail with only her feet still caught up in the sled. Connie falls down twice, running to her. "Rowan," she says, pulling, pushing, "Rowan, come on, get up."

"She ain't goin' no place, sweetheart."

Dale's coming out of the trees, not twenty feet away. He's walking on snowshoes, limping badly, and carrying a gun. He's almost at the sled when he stops and points the gun at Connie. "Bang bang you're dead," he says. "How do you like that?"

Connie stops shaking Rowan and stares at him.

"What was on that fuckin' knife?" he says.

The switchblade, he thinks you poisoned him with the switchblade. Did somebody say that? Gary, Gary said it.

"Nothing, there was nothing."

"Like flying fuck there was nothing. I been cut with knives before, sweetheart, I never had fuck all like this. You poisoned me. You poisoned my ass and you poisoned my fuckin' brain. Didn't you? You made me shoot Andra. You've got some kind of fuckin'—some fuckin'—brain poison or something. Don't you? *Don't you?* Thought you got away with it, didn't you? Well, we got our own fuckin' justice around here."

He raises the gun to his eye, and pulls the trigger. Everything in Connie's body lets go. The gun clicks. The whole scene swims around for a second, and then she collapses. Dale laughs, pushes the clip into place, and chambers a shell. He shoulders the gun and points it at Connie, slumped over Rowan.

"Goodbye," he says.

As the Elan whines across the lake, Sky burrows into Pigpen's back. Even so, the icy wind claws at her cheeks. The lake is windswept into patches of black ice and thin streaks of snow, the trail neither visible nor necessary, so Pigpen takes the shortest route, right across the middle. The ice that holds the speeding snowmobile doesn't look any different from the ice that gives way underneath it. It ploughs nose down into a patch of slush, and throws both its passengers onto the ice. Sky hears Pigpen make a horrible crunching noise as he lands. Her own fall is broken by the caribou clothes. Even so, she feels a solid thump through the hood, and a stunning pain in her head. She stands, looking around, trying to put it all together. Pigpen, the snowmobile, something else going on, further away down the lake. She staggers, and puts her arms out for balance.

Connie is icy cold. Not the cruel, numbing cold that assaults the body from every side, but a clear, pure chill of fear that starts deep in her guts and spreads outward. She's about to die. Dale has already shot two women; he won't hesitate to shoot her, too. *Non dubitare,* she thinks uselessly, and for a moment she smells her musty Grade 10 Latin class: not to hesitate. He does hesitate, of course, but only to enjoy her terror. If her bowels let go he'll smell it and smile. But they won't, because she's not that kind of scared anymore. She's scared cold, scared numb. She's waiting for the end. For some reason, her final thought is of the bear-claw necklace under her shirt, the slight scratch of the claws against her bare skin. The old sow who chose her own way to die. And this was her choice: gunned down in the snow. And then, of Rowan: did Rowan have a choice? Could she have told Dale where to find Connie, and saved herself? Better if she had, because now they're both dead. Any moment. Dale grins at her from behind the rifle, and moves his eye down toward the sight. And then, for an instant, his attention wavers, returns, wavers again. She follows his glance toward the middle of the lake. What she sees is unbelievable, but in this last moment of her life, she doesn't think to question it. There's a bear, standing on its back legs. Its arms are out to the side. It looks like it's dancing. The necklace burns against her skin. Choose your time, it says. Choose how you'll die. And then she sees, or realizes: the dogs are poised, tense. Looking back. Kitty with her ears pricked, waiting for a word. Dale only a few feet from the line, still gaping at the impossible dancing bear. And without knowing she's about to speak, without pausing to consider how it's going to work, she calls.

"Kitty, gee come."

Kitty moves like a spring, leaps around, and bursts back toward the sled, the team dogs hurling themselves behind her. Before Dale can react, he's caught in the lines and yanked off his feet. The rifle booms, the lethal shot flung harmlessly into the air, just at the moment that Virgil and Homer tangle up with Dale's tumbling figure. At the shock of the gunshot, Virgil tries to leap away, pulling Homer with him. Homer snarls and snaps at Virgil, and Virgil turns and pounces. Whether in confusion or sudden clarity, Connie will never know, the dog leaps, fangs bared, not on his brother, but on the man clawing and cursing in the tangle of lines and dogs. White down puffs up from Dale's parka as Virgil tears through the fabric and goes for his throat. For a second all Connie feels is relief, and then she's horrified. Dale is screaming. Connie leaps over the sled, and grabs Virgil by the neck-line.

Abe's coming around the last bend in the trail when the gun goes off. In less than a second he takes in the scene in front of him. A few seconds more and he's floundering chest-deep in the snow, just out of reach of the struggling group. Dale reaches for the gun, but he's too tangled in the lines to pick it up. In fury he turns to Connie.

"You're dead," he says. "You're fuckin' dead." The dog struggles snarling toward Dale. Connie holds his neck-line with both hands, her feet planted hard on the trail, her body rocking forward each time the dog lunges.

"Fuckin' bitch. You're next."

It's on the word *next* that the change comes over Connie. Abe sees her glance toward Rowan, a heap on the snow. She looks at him for a second, and their eyes meet, and he sees the decision pass over her face. She shows him the decision in her eyes, not asking, but allowing time for acknowledgement. Yes, his eyes say back. I know. Do it. And then she releases the dog. For the rest of his life he'll wonder, did they do the right thing. As Dale screams and thrashes, Abe stares in shock. Dale tries to grab Virgil by the loose skin of his neck, but the dog drives on him with terrible force and tears first at his protecting arm, then his face, and then his throat. By the time Abe struggles through the deep snow towards them, Dale has stopped screaming and begun to twitch. Abe kicks Virgil, hard, in the ribs, over and over until he stops and stands snarling at Dale, still dangling limp in the lines. Homer snarls in response, and for a moment it looks as if both dogs will leap on the bloody mess, as if the whole team might leap, a wild, murderous pack, and tear Dale to shreds. Abe fumbles under his parka for his knife, yanks it out and starts cutting lines until Dale is freed, and slumps to the snow. At the same time, Connie shouts, "Kitty, line 'em out." The lead dog struggles to pull the rest of the team straight, and Virgil and Homer are dragged clear of the body.

"Abe," Connie says, *oh Jesus,* "is he—"

"It's okay, Connie," he says. "It's okay." But what's okay? He crouches beside Dale and puts two fingers to the bloody throat. Nothing. What about Rowan? He checks.

"Abe," Connie says. "Is she—?" For some reason she has that bear-claw necklace pulled out of her coat, and is clutching it like a rosary. Abe doesn't answer the question. He looks across the lake at the approaching figure, all dressed in furs, staggering across the lake toward them. The creature's gait looks strangely familiar. He recognizes the voice at almost the exact moment that he starts to make out the words.

"Pigpen," it says. "He's hurt."

Sleep

Sleep, sleep.

Connie needs to sleep. Real sleep, fully immersed, not this drifting in and out of the shallow end, not these weird snatches of dreams and half-awake fantasies that she can hardly tell one from the other. Halloween witches, magic bears, white white light, blood. A dog gone mad, a woman gone mad, mad, everything upside down, blood-soaked, insane. Who's dead? Who's alive? Who killed Dale?

Who killed Dale?

Where did Sky come from? Out of the lake. Out of a dream. Like magic.

I'm an entertainer. A comedienne, dahling.

Nat, no. No, it's not like that. No cloaks, no wands.

Was there a bear? A black bear on the lake?

Is Rowan—?

Dogs, blood.

Rowan, Rowan.

It's not a bear, it's—
The necklace.
Sky? Was Sky—? Was Nat—?
Or she needs to wake up, so she can think. No, sleep. Sleep. But first, there's something she needs to remember. Rowan. Rowan's hand. A tiny—the tiniest—motion of the fingers. To touch the necklace. The bear's claws brushing her face. Where it hung down from Connie's neck. When she leaned over, her top buttons still open from when she had reached for the necklace herself, when she thought it was the last thing she would ever do. In the bitter cold. Where she'll wear a patch like flaming sunburn for weeks, a tiny puckered scar for the rest of her life. Leaned down close. To say Rowan, Rowan. Please.
Did she?
Is she? How many wounded? How many dead? How did they carry them all? Who drove?
The truck. Propped up in the cab, hot air blowing, blowing. Mmm.
Pigpen's truck.
Pigpen?
Actually, it's Mike.
Mike. Wake up.
Rowan, wake up, wake up.
Connie, wake up.
Dale.
No.

The nurses all know Abe. They bring him coffee, they stop to chat. *Rowan's got a chance,* they say, and later, *She's pulling through. But we can't do it all here.*

Abe's asleep in a chair when the Mounties come. Mr. Walker? A few questions. They won't let him see Rowan before they move her. Vancouver for at least a month, they say. She's through the worst. Pigpen's still unconscious. They won't let him see Connie before they speak to her. *Just a few questions.* They take a statement.

What did happen? Does Abe really know? He works his way backward through it. *How did the dog come to attack Mr. Stoltz?* He just—did. *What's your connection to Miss Sky Blue?*

The cops act like there's something fishy going on. Abe goes through the story for them the best he can. He doesn't know why Dale shot Rowan and then left. He can only guess. *Okay, why don't you tell us your guess?* He guesses Rowan wouldn't tell him where Connie was. *Why did he leave, then? Why not wait around for her?* Rowan must have made something up to get rid of him. *Why would he turn back when he ran out of gas, then, instead of keeping on going to the highway?* How the hell should Abe know? Maybe he heard a dog bark, figured out there was someone behind him. Maybe all of a sudden it dawned on him he'd only shot one woman. Maybe he was out of his fucking tree. *Mr. Walker, had you been drinking? What? What were you doing at Ashcan Lake? What was your relationship to—what was your relationship to—what was your—* You want to tell us about your problems with alcohol and violence? Fuck off. And then the question that scares him most, the one that brings the situation home, suddenly.

Where can we find you for the next few days?

He looks up from a three-month-old *Maclean's* and she's there.

"Sky."

Sky baled out of the truck when they got to town last night, refused to go to the hospital. Insisted she was fine, she just needed to go home and sleep.

Abe's on his feet. "You okay?"

She feels like nothing in his arms, a mirage.

"Yeah. Yeah. You?"

"I'm okay. My back's fucked. Situation normal."

"You heard about Rowan?"

"Yeah." He stands back and holds up both hands to show her two pairs of crossed fingers.

"Connie's awake."

"How's she doing?"

"They say her eyes are going to hurt for a couple days. Got some blisters on her feet, a little sun- and windburn. Come on, they're gonna let us in now."

Connie's lying in bed with her eyes bandaged. The skin on her face is red and puckered like it's been left in the water too long. When Sky touches her finger, she smiles, and then grimaces because her lips crack. Abe goes to the other side of the bed and takes her hand.

"How you doing?"

Connie leans towards Abe.

"My fucking head is killing me," she says. "But they give me these weird drugs. They don't take the pain away, but you don't mind it so much."

"I know the kind," Abe says.

She squeezes his hand. She's not as weak as she looks.

"Help me sit up."

Sky lifts and Abe pushes the pillows up.

"I'm supposed to get out of here tomorrow," she says. "They're going to take these things off in the morning and see how I'm doing."

Sky leans over and kisses Connie on the cheek. "You want us to go and let you sleep?"

Connie touches her face, smiles, winces, and lets her hand drop. "Stick around for a minute," she says.

"Connie," Sky says. "Rowan's going to make it."

Connie starts to cry then.

Abe is lost in this situation. Just the fact of a woman crying can undo him all by itself without all the complicated background in the air around here. Connie hasn't said anything but her face below the bandages has been full of questions. So far, they've given her one answer. Although Sky was exaggerating the optimism a bit as far as Rowan goes. She's got a good chance, the nurse said. Or was it, *a pretty good chance?*

As for Sky, she's got that Virgin Mary look of hers on that

always makes Abe feel like she knows something he doesn't. So far, he's never been wrong about that.

"They flew her to Vancouver, but she was pretty much out of the woods when they put her on the plane."

"Oh God," Connie says. "I never—I thought she was—"

"Oh *no,* babe," Sky says. "You thought—?"

"At the lake ... she ..."

"Oh *no,* you poor *thing.* No, her vital signs were pretty low, but she was in there. You got her out alive. She's going to make it. They're going to have to give you a medal or something." There's a pause. "I guess you didn't hear about Andra?"

"Andra?"

Abe's eyes ask if this is the right moment. Sky's face says might as well get it all out in one go.

"She didn't make it, Connie."

"Oh my God." Connie takes a deep breath. "Dale?"

There's about three seconds of silence in the room.

"Shit," Connie says.

"They put the dog down," Abe says.

Sky glances over and shushes him with her eyes.

"Virgil?" Connie looks like she might cry again.

"I'm sorry," Abe says. "I had to tell them which one. They were going to shoot them all."

"Are the rest of them okay? Where are they?"

"In my brother's backyard in Porter Creek. Causing a neighbourhood feud."

Connie nearly laughs at that, winces again, and then looks rueful. "That's too bad about Virgil."

"Yeah," Abe says. "It's too bad about a lot of things."

"Cops talk to you yet?"

"Oh yeah."

Connie picks up on something in his voice. "What?"

"I guess I'm some kind of suspect."

"That is so stupid."

"I ever tell you about the time I trashed the soup kitchen?"

"Yeah, right."

"He's not kidding," Sky says.

"I was shitfaced," says Abe. "That's why I had to go on some kind of program. To dry out, like. I wasn't drinking that bad, it was just that …" He thinks better of going into a long explanation about the clay cliffs, and getting the guys to fix his house. "Anyways, they wanted to know what I was doing in there, if I'd been drinking, how well I knew you, whether I knew Dale, the works."

"Jesus Christ. But yeah, they asked me a lot of questions about you, too. I was just too damn groggy to get what they were on about. What do they think you had to do with it?"

"Beats me."

"Did you say anything about Virgil?"

"Virgil? What was there to say?"

"You didn't tell them what happened?"

"I said you tried to pull him off and you couldn't hold him."

"That's what I told them, too."

Connie's starting to cry again, tears of relief, he thinks, although her expression's hard to read with the bandages on.

Sky's looking from Abe to Connie and back again. "Well, isn't that what happened?"

Connie reaches out her hand toward Abe, and he takes it in his.

"So?" Sky says.

Connie doesn't speak, so Abe says, "Basically."

"Basically?"

"That's basically what happened."

It's like at that moment, a little space opens up between Abe and Sky. What's being left unsaid now will never be said, and all three of them recognize it. Abe doesn't know what to tell her. It all happened so fast. Connie probably couldn't have held the dog if she'd wanted to and anyway, how could he explain? But leaving the question unanswered makes a divide in the room, Abe and Connie on one side of it, and Sky on the other.

Connie's crying again. After a while she reaches for a tissue from the half-sized box on the steel night table, wipes the snot from her face, and asks, "Did anybody go with Rowan?"

"Her mom," Sky says.

"Oh, that's so good."

"I'm going to go and see her."

Connie's just as surprised as Abe. She seems to forget about the headache for a second. "Wh—when?"

"Tomorrow. There's a bus out first thing in the morning."

"But—?"

Sky's holy virgin smile deepens. She glances up at Abe. "I'm going to travel for a while. I'll go and see Rowan, make sure she's okay, then I've got to go on down to Montana. Pretty sure my mom's going to be at a gathering there next month."

Abe says, "Didn't the cops …"

"Yeah," Sky says. "Don't leave town. They're so melodramatic. I don't know anything they can't learn from someone else. Just don't mention where I went, okay?"

"Sure," says Abe.

Sky remembers it the way she remembers the first time she got drunk on cheap wine—through a cloud, in snatches. All the bodies, the wounded. Rowan barely breathing, her pulse so weak. Pigpen breathing loudly, but unconscious. Connie snowblind, babbling, but still standing. Sky herself barely coherent. It was Abe who got it all figured out. Starting with Rowan, rolling her back into the sled as gently as possible. Sky next, perched in the front of the basket, trying not to sit back and squash Rowan, not to lean forward and put extra weight on the nose of the sled. Connie on the runners, hanging on. Abe's soft coaching. *Come on, Connie. Just a little farther. It's better than we thought. There's a truck at the highway waiting. We're all still alive. We're alive, Connie. Come on, hang on. Okay, Sky? You handle this?*

The snowmobile had nosed into a pocket in the ice and

stopped dead. Pigpen landed in front of it, knocked his head pretty hard. The cowling was smashed up but the motor wasn't damaged. Abe got it started and drove it over to the sled. He tied a line from the back of the snowmobile to the main tug-line, right behind Kitty's line. Then, holding Pigpen in front of him, he took off slowly, holding it all together. All together.

When they reached the highway, Abe loaded them all into the truck. Sky was still too much in a daze to be any help. He lifted the dogs into the back of the truck, where they immediately curled up with their noses under their tails and slept. He shoved them all out toward the edges and made a bed in the middle with all the sleeping bags and the caribou robes from the sled, and laid Pigpen and Sky in there together. *Keep your head under there, okay? And his too. I don't want you to freeze yourselves at this stage.* Surrounded by the sleeping dogs, snuggled up to Pigpen's back, Sky felt the vibration of the truck under her, and slept warm and safe.

Rowan's in a quiet place.

There's nothing in here but her. She can get out any time she likes. She could stay in here forever. But something's seeping in. Some thought. Connie.

Connie. I should have told you. Dale always knew where to find me. I knew he could show up any time. I just thought he'd calm down before it ever happened. But I watched. Every day, I listened. I slept with the gun beside my bed. Told you it was for the wolves. I never thought he'd come, but just in case. . . . I should have told you. What if you'd showed up when he was there?

Thing was, when he did show, he wasn't raving like I expected. He was totally calm. He wasn't off the deep end in any way that you could tell. He wasn't crazy, there weren't any chemicals screwed up in his brain. He was cold, hard, angry. That was all.

Don't fuck with me, Rowan. I'll shoot you dead. I'm not fucking around this time.

I tried to tell him you were never there. He kicked me in the crotch. I told him you left, went back to the city. He shoved the gun barrel in my chest, shoved me against the wall.

Nobody's been on that trail this year.

I told him you went out before the snow. He pulled the trigger. Oh fuck, Connie. I can't even tell you. It's like—it's not like anything. But he knew what he was doing. He didn't mean to kill me, not straight out. He leaned in close. His breath was sweet, like sage grass.

Want to tell me now?

I could still talk. Or rasp, I think you call it. I told him you were gone. He threw the gun down, grabbed me by my feet, and dragged me into the cabin. The first aid box was hanging on the back wall, big red cross on it so you couldn't miss it. He dragged me across the floor and dumped me under the box.

Bullet missed your heart. You're not bleeding that bad. I could save your life, right now. Where is she?

I told him you went out before the snow. After that he believed me.

Well, I'll be fucked.

He thought he'd fooled me. He laughed at me.

I guess that means nobody's coming to save you then, don't it? That don't matter, you were gonna die anyway.

I knew then that he was the one fooled.

Think I'm fuckin' stupid, don't you? I know all about you. I know you hid her from me. I seen you at the airport. I seen you go to the cops. She fuckin' poisoned me, you know. I'll get her. Like I got you.

Then he laughed, and then he walked out. But I knew something he didn't know. Besides where you were. I knew I was going to live. I knew right then I had the power to choose. I don't know where I got it, or if everybody has it, but I had it right then. I could have died before you got there. I could have died when you loaded me on that sled and the blood started to ooze again. I could have died on the dogsled a hundred times from the cold, from that same numbing cold you were feeling, that burns you on the outside and numbs you right through, except you had all your blood, and you were moving around. I nearly died, nearly chose to let go. But it was always my choice. He would have had to put that bullet right into my heart to kill me, it was going to have to be a clear killing shot, because I was too strong to die from blood loss or exposure or anything short of massive destruction of vital organs, unless I chose it.

One time when I was a kid, my dad took me prospecting. One day we climbed up on a high ridge to get a look around. There was an alpine meadow we hadn't seen from below, and we circled around and got above it to look down in and see if there were sheep in it. We didn't have a rifle along to take a sheep with—just the .22 for ptarmigan and rabbits to eat along the way—but my dad always liked to have a look, 'cause you never know when you'll run into a really hot hunting spot. He was never one to carry a gun just for bear protection. Said it was too much of a pain to lug around a big enough gun to save yourself from a bear, made more sense just to watch where you were going and keep out of their way. We had to go really wide to find a passable trail around the meadow and up onto the ridge. When we were high enough to look down in, we were far enough away that we needed to use binoculars. There was one of those loud, gusty high-country winds blowing. It obscured what must have been an almighty racket, because below us, in the most beautiful meadow full of blue and yellow flowers you ever saw, a wolverine was busy putting the run on a grizzly bear. I mean, a full-grown boar grizzly that did not want to give way. But this wolverine was all over him like hives. To look at those two animals, you'd have said no way will the wolverine survive. He's tiny compared to the bear. Well, I tell you, he didn't look so big, but he had to have been packed in there pretty tight, because there was more of him than there was of that bear. Scared the shit out of me when I realized he was driving the grizzly in our direction, but as soon as the bear got on the sidehill, out of the meadow, the wolverine left him alone. Bear was about a hundred feet below us, but he never even noticed us. He just started motoring along that sidehill without looking back.

See, I nearly gave it up there, on the lake, at the end. I was so tired. And then I heard the gunshot. From way down inside myself, I heard the gunshot. It was like I was at the bottom of a well, except the well didn't really have a bottom, and I was ready to drift away into it, down and down until I was gone, and then from the bottom of the well I heard a gun. And I got this feeling that there was something about that gunshot that I should care about, but I couldn't care enough to come up. Just enough not to go any further down the well. And then, I felt something. A physical thing, a touch. I hadn't been conscious of a touch, of any sense of touch at all, for so long—touch couldn't penetrate that deep. But it was there. I even knew what it was. It was that bear-claw necklace. Tickling my cheek.

Don't talk to me about magic. That's a load of crap. It was you, Connie. It was the touch of a friend.

A friend.

Thing is, the bit inside me, the bit that was still alive, was real small. But it was packed in tight, like the fight in that wolverine. It was all there.

I been needing a friend, Connie. You were getting to be someone I could talk to. Especially since freeze-up. Since Abe started coming around. Once you quit playing me like a trout on a hook. After that I knew one of these days you were going to come home all full of news, like you'd slept with Abe, or he wanted you to and you weren't sure, or you were moving out and into the squirrel shack, or whatever it was going to be. And it was going to feel so good. So best-girlfriends-ish and uncomplicated. Just to sit there in the shack, with supper on the wood stove, and the world on the outside, and talk about your new boyfriend.

And then on the lake, I'd just about decided to let go, to choose this time, when I felt the necklace brush against my cheek, and I knew I was going to live. And I knew you were, too. That's when I started to climb back up. Nobody noticed until the next day, when they decided to fly me out. But I'm here. I'm going to be all the way up soon. My mom's beside my bed. She held my hand today, and I held it back. I know she felt it. Soon, soon.

Break-up

Connie wiggles the point of the shovel under a mushy gob of black dog turd and flicks it into the open dog-food bag, already half-full of shit, straw, and chunks of snow. As she drags the bag to the next dog's pawed-down circle, a flash of movement to her left tells her Homer's about to catch her full-force on the shoulder with his front paws. She swings the shovel handle round and taps him on the nose. He yelps and backs off, but he's still wearing that I'd-love-to-knock-you-down-and-lick-your-face grin, so she knows there's no hard feelings.

Two days till Rowan gets home. Nobody guessed when they flew her out she'd be gone so long. Abe says she'll need to rest up for weeks after she gets back. Connie feels like she's on hold until she finds out what Rowan's plans are. If Rowan comes home and announces she's taking her dogs and going in the bush, and to hell with the doctors, Connie will need to decide what to do with herself. If she arrives home weak and tired and wants to lie in bed for six weeks and be nurtured, then Connie can put off the decision about where her own life is going for that much longer.

It's a miracle Rowan's alive at all. She was shot in the exact same spot as Andra, above the heart and to the left. It's like Dale wanted to hedge, to be able to say he didn't really mean for them to die. Or like something else in him, some tiny spark of rationality, said, don't do this. Poor Andra didn't have Rowan's strength. But who does? If they'd both survived, it would have been two miracles.

She shovels the last turd and then closes the bag and drags it to the garbage box. Her disgust threshold is about a mile high since she's been taking care of the dogs by herself. She's also lost all fear of huskies, despite having woken up twice a night for the first six weeks with the image of Virgil worrying the bloodied rag doll that used to be Dale. In the daylight, she makes no connection between that recurring nightmare, now thankfully past, and this tail-wagging, attention-demanding bunch of teddy bears.

Sometimes Connie wakes up crying. She cries for Rowan, and for Andra, and sometimes she cries for Virgil. She can't get over the fact that he got shot for saving her life. She said that to Abe a while ago. Abe shrugged.

"I know, it's the shits, but what can you do, eh? He killed a guy."

"If he was a cop, he'd get a fucking medal."

"It's too bad. But, I mean, what do you expect, a fair trial?"

That was Connie's cue. She could have opened the subject. What about us, she could have said. *What about what happened to us, what we did?*

She was glad Gale agreed to look after Mike's dogs, as well as Mike, down at her place in Carcross—huskies are one thing, but pit bulls are another. When Pigpen flipped his snowmobile out on the lake, his head found the only completely bare patch of ice around. He was out for over a week. Gale was the only person he recognized when he first came to. Every time Connie's seen him since then, she finds he's filled in more of the gaps. He denies there was ever anything wrong with him.

"Oh hell no, I'm fine. I had my bell rung worse than that before."

He will admit that he doesn't remember anything that

happened between gassing up at the Kopper King and cracking his head. Another thing that hasn't come back is any memory of his nickname.

"Pigpen? No way, Jose. Must be thinking of someone else. Called me that, I'd have kicked their ass."

He swears he's always been known as either plain Mike, or Hurricane. For some reason, Gale rolls her eyes and wriggles when he says that. Gale doesn't seem to mind that Mike's a bit off-kilter. They drop by every week or so to see how Connie's doing, and Gale always looks like the cat that got the cream. It was her idea for Connie to stay at Mike's place and look after Rowan's dogs. That way, Gale can look after Mike. Last time they were by, they brought another guy to help load the Harley into the back of the truck. When the bike was loaded and tied down, Gale stood back and stared for a minute, and then she closed her eyes, and her head rolled back and she sighed like someone was stroking her neck. Connie figures she can probably stay at this place as long she needs to.

There's less than half of a jerry can of water in the porch, so she carries that inside and dumps it into the big stockpot on the wood stove, remembering just before she touches the handle to take off the dog-yard gloves and throw them on the shelf and then wipe her hands on her work coat. With one jerry can in each hand, she goes out the door and turns down the steep trail to the creek. The path lies in the shade of some thick spruce trees, so it's thawing slowly. Today it's half in snow and half in frozen mud, slick enough to be treacherous footing. The railway ties dug into the bank for stairs are worn round and glazed with ice. The willows along the bank are beginning to swell with buds. Connie brushes them and sniffs the air, but there's nothing to smell. Things haven't woken up enough yet.

The creek is frozen to the middle, where it's begun to break up. Every day the open spots are wider. Connie stamps on the ice to test it, takes one step and then stamps again. She watched from the shore while Rowan did this on Ashcan Lake during freeze-up.

The idea is to stand sideways and stretch your legs, stamping the ice as far away from yourself as possible in the hope that the patch that breaks out under your forward foot will be small, and in particular won't include the ice under your rear foot, which bears your weight. It seems insane, but it worked when Rowan did it, a half-moon section sloughing off and leaving her standing on the newly created edge, where she calmly dipped her bucket and walked back.

The water's barely deep enough to immerse the buckets, but Connie can't look at the black water racing past, disappearing under the ice and churning up in another hole a little farther down, without imagining being swept away. She tells herself it's impossible, you'd never fit under the ice unless you stretched perfectly flat with your arms and feet straight out, but the terror that wakes in her at the sight of the disappearing water refuses to respond to logic. Anyway, she doesn't want to go in even if it's only up to her knees, so she tests the ice with more and more caution as she nears the hole, stamping hard four or five times before taking the final step to the water's edge, where she crouches to lower in the first bucket, thinking of the May afternoon at Squatters' Row when Dawn taught her to do this without freezing her hands.

Climbing back up to the cabin with two full five-gallon jugs, a hundred pounds of water, she feels tough and strong. She feels renewed, like somebody else walking around in her old skin, slightly damaged by wear and weather. If she could look on herself today with the eyes of last year, what would she see?

"Nobody's watching, you know. Just relax and go through the steps. If you fuck it up, try again. Nobody's going to know. Long as you don't chop your damn foot off. Here, give me that axe. Like this, straight down the middle. Keep your eye fixed on the spot you want to hit."

Rowan was wrong, somebody was watching. Somebody was recording every moment, and now she plays it back over and over, trying to get it straight. *What did I miss in that first look around? How did I get it so wrong?*

One fall day while they were out picking cranberries on the

ridge behind Ashcan Lake, Rowan was trying to show her a black bear mother and cub in their own berry patch on the high slope across the bay. Connie swept and swept the hillside with the binoculars, but couldn't make out a thing.

"*Slow down there, sister,*" Rowan said, laughing. She guided Connie's gaze to the general area.

"*Now take your time and go over that patch and you'll see the mom, and then you should be able to pick out the little guy.*" Then, after Connie found them, first the sow's comic fat behind, and then the cub, like a medium-sized black dog, snuffling around on the ground "*See, once in a while, it's worth it to slow down and take a good long look.*" Her tone said she was talking about more than bears.

Connie laughed at her. "What's that, some kind of Sourdough wisdom? You sound like Poor Richard's Almanac."

"Never heard of that one, is it out of Toronto?"

Rowan reads books that teach her how to fix her transmission, or build mortarless stone walls. She doesn't understand why anyone would waste their time reading a made-up book. Beneath Connie's awe at Rowan's strength and self-sufficiency, there's always been a bemused indulgence, a tendency to shrug off her little pronouncements of bush wisdom. Given the passage of time to absorb it all, she realizes she'd never have recovered from that day with all its horrors, that day when she gave herself up for dead, if it hadn't been for the strength she had learned in Rowan, strength she didn't discover until it was called for. She has no doubt that without this discovery, that bloody day would have undone her mind. Connie went into the bush such a greenhorn that she relied on Rowan for her survival every day. It made it hard not to idolize her at least a little, and then, in an effort to bring her down to a human level, to ridicule her slightly, to laugh to herself about Rowan's hillbilly wisdom. Yet so much of what she inwardly mocked turned out to mean her survival, not just on the trail, but afterwards, when her mind couldn't stop straying toward blood and horror, and sometimes the only peace she could find was in the memory of a canoe slicing the ripples on Ashcan Lake, the hypnotizing effect of the sun rippling on the water, Rowan's voice behind her.

"It's incredible, eh? It just keeps on making itself, you know what I mean? But it does it so slow nobody's ever around long enough to notice when it's made itself into something new."

"Wonder what it's working on next?"

"Same thing. Only different."

That was the first time Connie ever experienced the sensation that she was standing—or, in that case, sitting—at the centre of the universe. All her life she had felt like a barely relevant satellite in a world that revolved around other people. It was as if a childhood in a prosperous suburb had prepared her for nothing but life on the outskirts. Trent was not her place, Toronto was not hers, neither was Whitehorse nor Dawson, camp nor the bush. The feeling was fleeting then, a product of euphoria, but right here and now, at Mike's cabin on this dirt road off the Alaska in April of 1979, it seems to be real. Connie can close her eyes and feel it, everything spread out at her feet, one view of the universe that only she can ever see. This is the accumulation, to date, of a life's experience—finally to be at home in her own footprints. In the course of a year, Connie has learned how real brutality can be. She's come to expect that her life may be punctuated at random intervals by shock and horror. She also knows that if the worst happens, she can adapt. She can become who she needs to be. That's what you do. That's the thing she's learned. She surprises herself every day with who she's becoming.

Along with her new-found reserves of strength, she's surprised at how well she's able to cope with cabin life, and with taking care of the dogs. She can lift a log into the crossed poles of the sawhorse and buck it up with the Swede saw. She can split the wood, light the fire, haul the water, clean the lamp glasses, and trim the wicks. She can mix the dog food, shovel the shit, untangle the dog chains, and replace worn-out snaps. She knows enough to throw a handful of wood ashes in the outhouse hole to keep the stink down, and to knock on the stovepipe with the poker every couple of days so the creosote doesn't build up on the inside. She remembers to dump the slop bucket before it overflows into the sink cabinet.

It helps that Abe and his brother Frank come around once a week in Frank's truck and bring supplies, cut a few days' worth of wood with the chainsaw, and take away the garbage and the dogshit. It also helps that Frank brings his kids along to toddle around the place in mud-caked gumboots, their faces smeared with peanut butter and forgotten tears, getting into the tools Mike left behind and having to be chased away from the dog-lot. They ignore Frank until he picks them up and moves them, and as soon as he's out of reach they go right back to what they were doing. Maddy, four years old, is a miniature grown-up. Billy's two. He makes unintelligible sounds that Maddy claims to understand. Frank and Abe both find this hilarious.

"What's Billy saying, Maddy?"
"He wants to play with the puppies."
"Well, he can't."
"Daddy says you can't."
"Now what's he saying?"
"He says you're a big poo."
"Mad Walker, you're making that up."

Frank treats his children with what Connie can only think of as careless love, letting them do almost anything that won't get them seriously injured, and a few things that might. Every time they come to visit they lift her spirits twice, first when they arrive, and again when they go.

The days, which receded to about three hours of cold hard light in December and then crept back painfully slowly until March, are all of a sudden long and golden. Connie knows that this is not how it works, that the change has been gradual, six minutes a day since winter solstice, but she could have sworn that one week it was eighteen-hour nights and the next she was waking up and going to bed in full sunlight. Her daily chores take about an hour and a half. To fill the rest of the long daylight hours, she's taken to going for walks. When she first came to live here, Mike's snowmobile trails were well packed for walking, but she had very little strength, and less tolerance for sunlight. She'd walk maybe half a mile and then turn back, already starting to develop a headache. Amazed to learn how few cloudy days there are in mid-winter in the Yukon, she spent most of her time in the cabin, reading books on the couch by the window while the light lasted, and then in the armchair by the stove, with the hanging oil lamp lit. She tried walking in the moonlight one night, a month ago, before spring came flowing in like a tide, but her frost-nipped fingers and toes, though they looked and felt healed, began to ache in the night's bitter cold, driving her back to the cabin where the heat from the wood stove brought on spasms of agony that started deep in her thawing bones and brought tears to her eyes before they peaked and ended.

For two months after Christmas, the weather was hard-edged and brittle. The dogs moved in white veils of their own breath as they ate, crapped, and hustled back into their straw-lined beds. March nights were cold, but the long days glowed with an intense sunshine that made the afternoons feel warm. After the equinox, the sun declared victory. Day after dazzling bright day, the temperature has broken records. There's talk the mountain ash tree in front of the post office could bloom any day, bursting with white flowers a good month early. The local radio's gone from breast-beating about the record-breaking cold winter to rhapsodizing over the record-breaking warm spring. They're offering a prize, so far unclaimed, for whoever finds the first crocus.

The low, intense sun slants in the windows and makes the cabin a little pocket of summer. Outdoors, it's like three seasons at once, with summer sun beaming down and winter's snow and ice retreating toward the hollows and shaded patches, while the roads wallow in spring puddles and mud. It's less than two weeks since the melt began, starting around the trunks of the trees. Every day since then the patches of bare ground have grown as the snow shrank back. For a few days when it warmed up, Connie was out hiking the trails, still frozen and solid underfoot, and then suddenly one morning it had all turned soft, and her boots were sticking in wet and sloppy snow. Until it melted away, she had nowhere to walk but down the driveway and along the shoulder of the Alaska Highway, feeling exposed and infamous every time a car went past. *Hey, isn't that the chick who ...*

For the past week the trails have been dry enough for well-greased hiking boots, and she's been walking farther each day. Keeping in mind a warning from Abe about grumpy spring bears, she tries to stick to open country, and keeps a good watch all around. She's cautious, but she's not afraid. Rowan said something about this, when they were paddling home from the moose hunt, a million years ago.

"Fear isn't going to do you any good. Everything you're scared of is faster than you are, and has way keener senses. It's not like a moose—moose function great when they're scared—it's when they're aggressive they fuck up and get shot. But we're predators, eh? Respond better with a cool head."

She remembers being churned up by sixteen separate emotions in the wake of the moose hunt, tired and straddling a line between irrational joy and depressed guilt, and wondering if all this was a put-on, a show for the Cheechako chick, like pulling her leg about bears, or telling her the one about the Sourdough. *Do I look like such a tourist?* She came close to saying it out loud. Now she realizes it wasn't a pose, it was a lesson. And if it sounded awkward, it's because Rowan's not used to having to explain things to people. Connie thinks of the first time they met, on the mine road, how Rowan and Dago hardly needed to speak to understand each other. And again with Abe, on the moose hunt. Even between her and Ida, there was lots that didn't need to be said. These are the people Rowan's used to dealing with, people who share a language, a set of gestures and facial expressions, a history. Maybe that's why the bushwoman-wisewoman act sounded a false note, because the nature of fear is the kind of thing Rowan wouldn't normally have to talk about. Everybody else already knows this stuff, the way they know the difference between a tie rod and an oil pan. Connie laugh, when she thinks of this, because it's something else she now knows. She got Rowan to show her last summer, when they towed Dago's truck into camp.

"Oil pan, that oily-looking unit under the motor, with the big ding in it. Big pain in the ass, eh, 'cause he's got to lift the motor to get at it. Tie rod up there at the front, black metal rod, see it? It's part of the linkage for the steering."

Rowan's not going to know Connie when she sees her, so strong and capable on her own. She feels like a whole different animal now. *The cat that walks alone.* She laughs at herself. *Corny.* But she does have this feeling of profound change. She feels like someone Rowan's never met.

And what about Rowan? She'll have changed, too. She lost part of a foot to frostbite in spite of the caribou blankets, and her shoulder and chest were badly damaged by the bullet wound. She's had skin grafts, bits of her have been replaced with metal. She's still got problems breathing. They say she's skinny and weak, but she's getting better all the time. Rowan will be fine, eventually. Or, if not fine, okay. It could have been a lot worse. Connie tries not to think too much about Andra, although she wishes she'd had time to know her better.

Andra was cremated in Vancouver. They brought her ashes home and held a memorial service in the Anglican church in Whitehorse. It was forty-eight below. They were going to spread the ashes on the mountain behind the family claims. Connie didn't learn until the funeral that Andra grew up in a placer mining family a lot like Rowan's, except they only summered in the Yukon, packing up and heading for better weather every year as soon as the creek started to freeze. Her parents are retired and living in Kelowna, but her brother and his family are still on the creeks, and one of her sisters lives in Whitehorse. Her father, a tall, bent man of seventy or so, sat in the front pew and drooped.

He looked as though his forehead would rest on the floor by the end of the day. Beside him, his wife's expression was cold and closed. She had no desire to know her daughter's friends, to delve into the world that took her child's life, or to share her grief with these dishevelled strangers.

The sister from down south was a plump, perfectly coiffed woman who scowled all around the crowded church, condemning every bearded face and frizzy head of hair, every olive-drab greatcoat and fifth-hand fur. It was a face that saw nothing but hippies and bums, a bunch of drug addicts who thought they knew the bush because they'd spent the summer in a wall tent at Long Lake, and the winter in a cabin in Sleepy Hollow.

Outside the church a washed-out hippie type—he might have been one of the guys Connie saw sitting on a curb singing at the airport last summer—appeared out of the ice fog. "*Hey, you're that chick, man. You were there.*" The guy was drunk. His moustache hung so thick over his lips it seemed to be a factor in his slurred speech. "*You were with her, man.*" Connie didn't respond. He patted her shoulder. "*You're good people.*" Then he raised a grey woollen fist and said, with funereal seriousness, "*Rock on, man.*"

Connie drops the buckets inside the cabin door, and then steps back outside to stretch. The thermometer says it's forty-five degrees, but in the direct sun it feels like a summer day. She takes off her coat and lets the heat get through her t-shirt and soak into her back. She turns and lets it flow over her face, her breasts and belly. It's the first caress she's felt in months, since the day—she still finds it hard to give the day a name—the day of the nightmares. She's felt too fragile to touch since then, other than to be held sometimes.

Sky held her at the bus station. "*Don't cry, baby. You'll be fine.*"

Sky held Abe at the bus station. "*You'll be fine, too,*" she said. As the bus drove off, Abe held Connie, Connie held Abe, and they stood in the bitter cold and waved and waved.

Sky asked Connie to look after a couple of things for her when she went away. One of the things was her stereo. She never did say what the other one was. As it turned out, Sky had to wait until the Mounties were finished questioning everybody before she could leave. At first it looked like the investigation might take some time, that the cops might make trouble. The two uniforms, a man and a woman, who took their original statements asked a lot of questions about Abe. That was the first time Connie heard about him busting up the soup kitchen. The woman asked her if he'd been drinking while he was in the bush. She made a lot of notes on her pad.

Connie talked to them about stabbing Dale. She didn't have the energy to hold back, except she didn't mention the switchblade, saying it was a hunting knife Dale had lying around. And, seeing no way that the situation could be improved by the cops talking to Gary, she said she was hitchhiking that day, and the guy who picked her up insisted on dropping in at Dale and Andra's place. She didn't remember his name, or what kind of car he was driving. They took more notes. The woman asked Connie if she'd ever been in trouble with the law.

A few days later, Abe, Connie, and Sky all had to go in for another interview. This time they split them up and questioned them for a couple of hours. They asked Connie what Mike was doing in there, whether Abe had acted violently or made any threats, what had taken place on the night she stabbed Mr. Stoltz in the buttock. She could see it bothered them that there were so many violent people at the scene, and plenty of violence to account for, and yet all the blame fell on a dead man and a dead dog. It was clear that they found it too tidy, but everybody told the same story and there wasn't any evidence to suggest they were lying. About a week later Abe came by to tell Connie the cops had phoned. The case was to all intents and purposes closed.

At the Greyhound station, Connie leaned against Abe and cried, not for Sky leaving, or for Rowan lying at death's door in some Vancouver hospital room, or for Dale or for Andra or for Pigpen, the dead and the wounded. She cried for herself, for the guilt she's going to carry around, maybe all her life. Maybe she couldn't have held on to Virgil, but she could have tried. If she'd tried to hold him and failed, she wouldn't have this feeling that her life—she herself—had been changed forever. She cried out of relief, because she knew then she'd got away with it—*it* being another thing she shrinks from naming—and out of despair because she'd never get away *from* it. She cried because Abe knew, Abe alone in the world, and she hadn't said a word to him. She still hasn't, and neither has he. It's something that will have to be opened up and examined before she can confront a lot of other important questions. Such as, did she pick Abe up on the rebound? Was he the other thing Sky wanted her to look after, indefinitely? Was he Sky's to dispose of? And if Connie has picked him up on the rebound, or if he's at least available for the picking, does she want him? Is it a wise idea? Does she plan to tie herself to the Yukon for life, or to try to untie Abe? It would do him good to get out of the North, discover a broader range of possibilities, but does she want to take responsibility for dislodging him?

No, that's not the question. The question is, does she want to spend her life looking in the eyes that shared her darkest moment, the one—she's sure there'll never be another—when she allowed herself to be taken over by pure barbarism? It's a horrible thing they did together, they didn't speak, but they agreed. Even if it was only with their eyes, they conspired to the most terrible vengeance imaginable, to allow a man to be killed by a beast. Connie has examined again and again the moment when she let go of the dog's collar. She's relived it every day. She forgives herself for what she did at that moment, stressed beyond the limits of her endurance, at the extremity of every violent human emotion, fear, vengeance, rage. She doesn't excuse what she did, but she confesses it, owns it, and finally she absolves herself. If grace escapes her, it's because of the moment before that one, when her eyes met Abe's. When hers said, *should I?* When his said, *Yes.* If there's to be any absolution for that moment, they're going to have to find it together. What comes after that is anyone's guess.

The sun strokes her like a lover. That's something Jason could never accept. For Connie, the sun is like a third partner in love. She'd lie in the yellow square that washed Jason's bed in the middle of the afternoon and the sun would nuzzle her and she'd moan, and he'd be annoyed that she could be more audibly aroused by that inanimate touch than by his. She tried to make him see the game, play along, but he was jealous about it. He pouted. Abe's older than Jason was then, and he doesn't seem to pout, but he's more innocent, too. Now that he's out of the bush, Connie's amazed at how boyish he seems, but maybe boyish is what she needs, at least for now, malleable enough to learn to make a threesome with the sun without getting jealous. Her nipples tingle in the heat. She won't know if she wants to attach herself to Abe and the short, painful history they share until she tries it. She does know that today for the first time she doesn't feel fragile.

The dogs have begun to notice her. A few speak in quiet huffs, and then somebody barks, and somebody else answers. Kitty leaps up and growls around protectively, wondering what she's missed. Connie puts her finger to her lips. "Sh," she says. "Kitty, shush," and the dogs lie back down, or turn and nose at their empty dishes.

Hey, Rowan, did you see that?

We'll make a bushwoman out of you yet, sister.

She picks up her jacket, steps back into the cabin, picks up one of the jerry cans, and sets it down on the counter beside the sink. She takes her water bottle down from the shelf and fills it at the bucket's plastic tap, drops it in her oversized jacket pocket, and turns to go. There's a trail that leads high up on the ridge behind the house. Abe says if you were to hike along that ridge far enough, you'd come out looking over the Yukon River, just below the bridge at Marsh Lake. He says if she's lucky, there'll be trumpeter swans on their way north to the breeding grounds. He says that scientists can't figure out why the birds wear themselves out travelling all that way to the Arctic to nest when there's so many more prosperous places along the way. Connie doesn't care why. She plans to hike this ridge every day until she sees them. She hears they're majestic. Up to her knees in mud and dogshit, still struggling with doubt and remorse, nothing could be more attractive at this moment, more rampant with hope, than the image of a flock of pure white swans lifting off from an open patch of black water, soaring over the decaying ice to form a long ragged vee in the sky, and then wheeling north toward the mating grounds in pointless, perfect, majesty.

Acknowledgements

This book was written with financial assistance from the Advanced Artist Award program through the support of Lotteries Yukon. The work was completed at the Sage Hill Writing Experience, with the help of the Cultural Industries Training Trust Fund and the Jack Hodgins Scholarship.

"Klondike Highway" was first published as a work in *Out of Service,* April 2001. A shorter version of "Drum" first appeared onstage at Longest Night 2000, and was later published in *Urban Coyote,* 2001.